REALITY BITES

NICK LENNON-BARRETT

To Yvonne
Happy reading
(and laughing!)
Nick

FUNNY BOOK
PRESS

For my husband Tom,
the world's greatest undiscovered Reality TV star!

PROLOGUE

Stiffy's Bar, New Year's Eve

Daniel ended the call and looked out over the cemetery at the reflection of the neon sign emblazoned across one of the more elaborate tombstones. *Stiffy's*. He turned back towards the club with a smile. Joke never got old.

He'd wished his grandmother a Happy New Year, albeit an hour early. Daniel never understood why the first thing people do to welcome in a New Year, besides the obligatory kiss and grope with their new *friend,* is to disappear into a corner to make a call to their dearest, ignoring the nearest. He only had his grandmother left, so just the one call to make. She'd again wished him a happy twentieth birthday; it was a strange feeling no longer being a teenager.

Daniel re-entered the club with a smile and nod to the bouncer, who'd told him not to worry about getting a stamp to come back in, for which Daniel was grateful. No matter how hard he scrubbed, it always took almost a week to remove, and having *Stiffy's* on the back of his hand was always a tad awkward when he was serving the city types their pint of bitter. Still, it wouldn't be forever. He was halfway through his degree, although after experiencing the worst year of his life, he still couldn't think about what he'd do after graduating.

The club was heaving with people jostling and thrusting to the din of music booming so loudly that each song sounded the same. The white t-shirt look appeared to be one of those fads which would never die out, and it looked like the gay boy beard was going to be another lifer, especially now the heteros had caught on.

A man approached and tried to engage in conversation. Unfortunately, Daniel couldn't understand what was being grunted in his ear. Could be anything from "What's the time?" to "Wanna fuck?" Daniel simply smiled and continued to push his way through the throbbing bodies, acknowledging friends and acquaintances on the way – it had been a busy couple of years in London. Although, wasn't that what his youth was supposed to be about? Daniel never understood teenagers who wanted to meet *the one* as soon as possible. His thirties and beyond would be the time for all the melodrama of domesticity.

Significantly poorer after buying a round of drinks, he was making his way back to his friends when he saw the man who would change his life forever. The stranger was wearing a bulky coat and muttering to himself. Daniel thought nothing of it as lots of weird and wonderful people frequented here, until he caught the word *sodomite*; was it 1885?

The man seemed in a world of his own, with a determined look on his face, although his eyes betrayed him. Daniel would never forget those eyes. The sadness and despair within them was the last thing Daniel saw before everything went black.

CHAPTER ONE

Nine years and one day later

Daniel waited for his name to be called. He still wasn't sure he was doing the right thing or, to put it another way, he was doing the right thing but he didn't think he was executing it in the best way. Now he was older, he realised how fickle people really were; the only way to raise awareness about an important issue would be to make a tit of himself on TV.

It had been nine difficult years and very few people still remembered what had happened that night. Perhaps that was unfairly harsh: they simply chose not to talk about it but, by doing so, they were accepting what had happened. Daniel was here to change all that.

The producers had no idea who he was. He had gained his place on merit and deliberately omitted the juice for later. If he'd been honest, he was in no doubt that he would still be here, but not on his terms, and he wanted to keep it that way for now.

"And our first neighbour in the single men's apartment is

Daniel North," bellowed the voice of Zelda BonBon; the hyperactive TV presenter who came across like a Duracell Bunny with an amphetamine addiction.

This wasn't too far from reality. Zelda was a diet-pill addict, which meant she was permanently wired. There were rumours she hadn't slept during the two months of the entire first series. *Complex Neighbours* was a complete *Big Brother* rip-off, although the man behind a new wave of Reality TV shows, Felix Moldoon, claimed this was a completely different format and had won his court case to prove just that. There were some obvious format changes but, in a nutshell, a bunch of strangers would live together and, after nine weeks of *executions*, as they were called on this show, someone would walk out one million pounds richer. There would still be the fame-hungry wannabes, although there would also be the master manipulators only in it for the money. Daniel considered himself to be in neither of those categories, although as part of his *journey* Daniel knew he would be edited into one of those groups.

He walked out to a cheering crowd. Why they were cheering for him when they didn't know him was a mystery. Still, it could be worse.

"Welcome to *Complex Neighbours*, Daniel. How are you feeling?"

Zelda was bouncing around so much that she either desperately needed the toilet or had OD'd on her diet pills again.

"I can't wait to get in there, Zelda, and meet my new neighbours."

Daniel knew how to play the game after watching these types of shows since childhood. He had to get on side with the baying mob which surrounded him, holding up banners asking to be impregnated and similar social niceties.

"Well ladies, take a look at him will you?" bellowed Zelda

into the microphone, which wasn't necessary. She had one of those voices which carry beyond the horizon.

She paraded him to the crowd, who were screaming, whooping and whistling. It was all such a blur that he didn't really notice anyone in the crowd, although he knew there would be nobody there for him. His grandmother supported him, although she wanted to remain off radar during the entire experience. She knew his reason for doing this and would keep quiet out of respect for his wishes.

"Sorry ladies, he's not for you. I know, I know. Such a shame as he is well fit ain't he?" squealed Zelda to a gaggle of twelve-year-old girls dressed like they were walking the lane, hunting for trade.

"Think you'll find a fella in there, Danny?" she beamed.

So, in a few seconds and before he had even entered the complex, he had been outed and called Danny, which he hated. However, he couldn't help but like Zelda. She was just such a happy person. Daniel did wonder if it was only an outward confidence and that, perhaps at night, she sat alone crying into her Chardonnay contemplating popping open a vein.

More whoops from the crowd as Daniel climbed the stairs. He just wanted to get in there now and meet the people he would be living with for the next two months – if he lasted the distance. One last look and wave to the crowd as he reached the complex door and that was it: he was in.

The place was immense, six apartments in one complex. There would be two couples, two families and two groups of strangers – one of single men and the other of single women. That was all he knew about his fellow neighbours so far. Daniel was the first to arrive. The corridors to the different apartments they would live in were blocked off until everyone had entered the complex. The communal area comprised a huge open-plan living space with fully kitted out modern kitchen and an enormous dining table. The décor was very white and clean looking – that wouldn't last long based on previous series. The furniture was all bright and vivid colours. Neon pink and lime green dining chairs automatically caught the eye, although contrasted against the pristine white walls they worked.

Later in the evening there would be sixteen people in this space, all sussing each other out to see who would be a new friend and who would be their biggest rival for that million-pound prize. Everyone entered on the first night. There would be no newbies or replacements. There would be the inevitable twists and turns, but only one would get all the money.

All he could do was sit back with a drink and wait for the others to arrive one by one and very, very, slowly, taking into account the thousands of commercial breaks in between which the actual programme would be sandwiched.

After about ten minutes, the door opened to a cheer, so he stood ready to meet his first neighbour. He watched as she descended the staircase. She had very light colouring. He suspected she was of West Indian heritage. She wasn't slight and was close to six-foot tall, but she glided with grace and elegance. Daniel instantly adored her.

"Hi, I'm Stephanie, Stephanie Chapman."

She kissed each of Daniel's cheeks and, shockingly, her lips actually touched his skin. There was no air kissing phony shit with this one.

"I'm Daniel, Daniel North!"

"Cheeky fucker."

She had the most beautiful blue eyes, full of expression and warmth.

"Are those contacts?"

"Cheeky fucker."

"Do you say anything else?"

"Where's the booze?"

He gestured towards the vast array of beverage options on the table.

"What you drinking?" she asked, glancing at the glass in his hand.

"Water."

"Do you love Jesus or something?"

"Nah – Jesus no like the gay boys."

"Thought you were."

"What gave me away?"

"Erm – everything, dear."

He laughed; something he hadn't done for a long time.

"So why the water? Have you got a dose or something?"

"Cheeky fucker."

She roared with laughter. It was a wonderful laugh; loud, boisterous and yet still dignified. He had no idea how those three elements could come together but here they were in six foot of diva.

"I'll get stuck in later, when everyone has arrived."

"Oh, you're one of those."

"What?"

"A nice person."

"Erm, no dear. How can I judge and make assumptions about everyone when I'm inebriated?"

"I knew I liked you, but perhaps just sip some champagne or everyone will think you're a pretentious twat."

The door opened again and the cheers were the loudest so far. Daniel distinctly heard, "I love you," from the crowd.

"Milking it much?" said Stephanie.

The guy was still waving to his adoring fans. After a gentle nudge from the security guard, he turned and walked to the top of the stairs. There stood the most beautiful man Daniel had ever seen.

Adrian Labouchere introduced himself to Daniel with a

knuckle-cracking handshake, before introducing himself to Stephanie who was acting like an irritating giggling schoolgirl – or was that Daniel?

Stephanie rushed to get the new arrival a drink, which gave Daniel the opportunity to suss him out without obviously staring. He was a big fella, probably at least six foot four, with tanned olive skin, definitely not out of a bottle or from the electric beach so he had either just been abroad or it was his natural skin tone, probably the latter – bastard!

He had the black hair, blue eyes thing going on and was dressed in jeans with a tight grey t-shirt and suit jacket which showed off a physique which implied that he spent three hours a day at the gym. Daniel suspected that half of that gym time would be spent trying to find the right lighting so he could take photos for his thousands of Instagram followers which would be a combination of teenage fan girls, yummy stay-at-home mummies and thirsty gays.

Adrian was very well spoken and gave off the impression of being positively charming to Stephanie. Some people were just gifted with everything.

"Work out much?" he asked Daniel, looking him up and down.

"Not really. I'm lucky I don't put on weight."

"Ah, one of these skinny fat types, then."

"What?"

"Well, you look good with your clothes on, but not with them off."

It was accurate, but still...

"Won't last forever, you know. How old are you?"

"Twenty-nine, and you?"

"Twenty-one. What do you do for a living?"

"I'm an outreach worker."

"What groups do you work with – junkies?"

"No, lesbian and gay youth."

"Rather you than me, mate, backs against the wall and all that, although I wouldn't mind trying to turn a few dykes, show them what they're missing out on," laughed Adrian whilst grabbing his crotch – yes, he actually grabbed his crotch.

Thankfully the conversation came to a halt as another woman entered, much to Stephanie's dismay as she had clearly been enjoying having all the male attention. Hopefully her opinion of Adrian would change once Daniel told her what he'd said.

The new arrival was dressed like a whore, no other way to describe it. Her skirt could be better described as a belt and she was basically wearing a bra – in January. She must have been freezing. She was also a bottle blonde and was wearing so much fake tan she looked like an Oompa Loompa, with false eyelashes, nails and heavy makeup. Daniel suspected she was probably pushing towards forty. Adrian, clearly oblivious to the age gap, made a beeline to greet her.

"Fucking hell, you're well fit," she remarked in a strong Birmingham accent.

"Not so bad yourself love," replied Adrian who leaned in for a kiss and then squeezed her arse, causing her to squeal with delight.

Her name was Claire; Stephanie looked like she had been slapped in the face. Daniel doubted they were about to become besties – this was going to be an interesting night.

The next to arrive was another man – well, boy would be a better description. Good looking, he wore glasses, but he had the whole Clark Kent thing going on which was good on him. Another six footer, but a blond this time. His name was Callum and he had a lovely Irish accent. What was it about that accent? They could be talking about killing you in the most violent way imaginable and you'd still be getting moist over that voice.

This one was a puzzler as he did some jock type hand-shake fist bump crap with Adrian and asked for a beer. He then politely introduced himself to Stephanie who was still reeling from Claire's arrival so came across as a bit rude; he then went bright red when Claire introduced herself by groping him. However, when he introduced himself to Daniel it was a firm, but not knuckle-breaking handshake that lingered for a fraction of a second too long, as did the intense eye contact. Yep – definitely a question mark.

The final singleton to enter was blatantly a lesbian. The casting team had clearly worked through a pre-defined check-list and were capitalising on gay marriage being legal again and the subsequent switch in public opinion. Her name was Helen and she was tall for a woman, but next to Stephanie she looked like a midget. Adrian barely acknowledged her presence, with Claire following suit – was this because she was a bit butch, or because she was German? Or perhaps they were just rude twats. She had tattoos on her hands and neck, so god knows where else and was dressed like a docker. These producers really did no favours to the cause with the *representation* they put on TV.

Daniel chatted to Helen as nobody else was. Stephanie had her back to Claire and was talking to Callum. Claire was focussed on Adrian and given how handsy they both were already they would no doubt be screwing before the last person arrived, probably in front of everyone. Claire evidently had no morals and Adrian would assume everyone would want to witness it. Perhaps these were sweeping assumptions about people Daniel had known for less than an hour, although he tended to be a good judge of character. Helen was shy and nervous, very different to what her image suggested; so three out of five were potential human beings. Not a bad start.

Now all the singletons were in, the rest would be the

groups who had pre-existing relationships outside the complex. In the last series there had been a mother, daughter and boyfriend, except the guy was boyfriend to both of them. It was very fucked up and the public had quickly executed them in the second week. The daughter had been hounded by the press after her exit and had sadly taken her own life. There had been none of the backlash and outrage which would have been the case once upon a time. Online conspiracy theorists had surmised that this was an example of just how powerful Felix Moldoon and his media empire were in making it all go away very quickly. Although there could be some credibility to that theory, Daniel knew the reality was that there had been a gradual switch in public attitudes over the past few years; the once lambasted snowflakes had turned into uncaring and entitled blocks of ice.

Next into the complex was the first couple, Frank and Judy, who were both at least seventy years old. No one this old had featured on the show before, as they didn't naturally appeal to the target demographic. She was wearing a bling top with the word 'fabulous' in gold lettering and had bright red lipstick on. Her husband was wearing a wig, a really bad one; they seemed lovely, though, on first impression. Adrian and Claire were still too wrapped up in each other to even acknowledge them.

Another couple eventually joined them. The man was about eight-foot tall and immediately got Adrian's attention and there were more fist bumps and requests for beer.

"Hey, I'm Mike," he said, gripping Daniel's hand, but in a way that wasn't typical for the meathead persona he had just demonstrated with Adrian. "This is my wife, Jamila," he said, introducing his wife who was wearing a saree and looked very beautiful apart from an unfortunate hooked nose.

"Pleased to meet you," she said with a slight Mancunian accent.

She air-kissed Daniel's cheek and then happily took a glass of champagne from Stephanie's proffered hand.

"I'm an accountant, what do you do?" Mike asked Daniel. His wife was chatting to Stephanie.

"I'm an outreach worker for lesbian and gay youth," Daniel replied, his tone more accusatory than he would have liked.

"That's brilliant. My best mate's son is gay and he got a really hard time at school. He had no confidence but he joined one of those support groups and he's doing really well. His grades have improved and everything. Let me shake your hand again."

Somewhere there was a book with the wrong cover on it.

It was clear there been yet another commercial break as it had been some time since Mike and Jamila had arrived, and there was still no sign of the family groups. Stephanie had gravitated back towards Daniel so he told her what Adrian had said.

"Knew he was too good to be true, you can't have it all can you. Looks and personality. Still, I suppose you don't fuck a personality."

"Stephanie Chapman!"

They both laughed.

"What's funny?" asked Helen, who was being largely ignored by everyone else.

Daniel told her what Adrian had said.

"You is gay then?" she asked.

"Yes," Daniel replied, a bit bewildered.

"I never meet gay person before. Good for you."

Somewhere in the distance, Daniel heard the sound of a library exploding.

.   .   .

The final two groups eventually arrived, both sibling groups; three sisters and three brothers. The sisters were incredibly hyperactive and irritating, so Daniel helped himself to his fourth glass of champagne. The three brothers were a mixed bunch, one was very good looking, one looked like a geek and the other had a top knot and a tattoo on his neck which said 'RIP Nan,' so Daniel kept his distance in order to retain politeness.

So here they all were, the fifteen people that Daniel would be living with for up to two months, although in just three weeks there would only be three apartments left. He hoped his group, the single women and Mike and Jamila, would be the ones competing at the end of the show. He had never been let down by snap judgements and had made his assessment after three hours – these launch shows were long.

There was an announcement over the loudspeaker that it was time to see their new digs. They were informed that the corridor to the apartments was open. Adrian led the way, probably to claim the biggest bed for himself. As long as there were enough to go around, Daniel didn't care.

Their apartment was a two-bedroomed, one bathroom with a small open-plan living space and kitchen. It was nothing like the main communal one in the centre of the complex. Still, it would provide an opportunity to break away from the main group at times. The complex was designed to provide ample opportunity for alliances to form and enjoy secret plotting and bitching sessions.

"I call the main room, don't want to be sleeping with a pillow over my arse all night do I?" laughed Adrian.

Daniel decided not to bite and turned to Callum. "Do you mind sharing?"

"Not at all," he smiled, causing Daniel to blush.

"Oh you're not an arse bandit as well are you?" sneered Adrian.

"No, I'm what you call sexually fluid."

"What the fuck does that mean?"

"Look it up, you homophobic prick."

Daniel swelled with pride.

"I just don't want to hear you two at it like rabbits. That's not homophobic, it's just good manners." He turned and walked out of the apartment.

CHAPTER TWO

Felix Moldoon removed his dark glasses and puffed on his vape, whilst watching the screens which showed every corner of the complex. Adrian was the *chosen one* this series and Felix would ensure it happened, just as he had determined every winner on all his shows from the start. No need to try to rig the public vote; the regulators were a ball-ache at the best of times. It was all about the edit – the public were like puppets and they would dance to his storyline.

"I reckon that Jamila will be a bit of a snake. Still can't get over her audition tape."

"You're not wrong. She'll be gold," replied Felix to Desiree.

Desiree was Felix's number two and would deal with the day-to-day running of the show. When he interviewed her and asked if she had a surname, she had said no – she was like Cher, without the surgery. She ran the place like clockwork and could change the complete narrative of the show in an instant should Felix request it, which he did – often.

Felix knew it was a gamble to put a show like this on in the winter. All those pretty people wouldn't be cavorting half-naked outside like they did in the summer series so social media would not have the usual plethora of emojis; the drooling face and aubergine being the most popular. However, he had spoken to the maintenance guys and they assured him they could fix the heating should ratings start to slip.

"I reckon that Daniel's one to watch. There's something about him," piped up one of the producers.

Felix eyeballed her. "Did you not read the storyboard?"

"Yes sir, I just wouldn't rule him out of doing well, especially when his story comes out."

"But his story won't come out, will it? He didn't disclose it in his auditions so he obviously wants to keep it secret."

"Won't that be his press release when he's executed, sir?"

"Are you completely retarded?"

"No, sir." The young producer was becoming tearful.

"You look vaguely familiar, so this isn't your first series is it?"

"No, sir, I was here last series."

"Then you should know by now how this show works."

"You always said we should put forward our viewpoints."

"Excuse me?"

"You said it to me on my first day."

"Took your fucking time to speak up, didn't you?"

"Can you not swear at me please?"

There was a collective intake of breath from the nearby crew who had stopped what they were doing.

"Get back to work the rest of you."

There were a few inaudible mutters as the crew went back to their work, leaving Felix and Desiree with the producer who was clearly not that relevant to the running of show as she'd worked for him for at least six months and he still had no idea what her name was. The fact she had lasted for more than one series meant there must be something about her which had enabled her survival. He could almost feel Desiree wishing she could speak to him telepathically, begging him not to fire her. Felix decided to give her one more chance to redeem herself.

"Do you want to rephrase your question?"

"No, I don't think it is appropriate to use that language in the workplace. I don't feel that this is a psychologically safe space."

"It's not. Get the fuck out of my studio."

She ran out crying.

Desiree sighed. "That's six people you've fired in one night, Felix. A new record."

———

Complex Neighbours Three: Live Launch First Reactions

DaveBodyBuilder: Great launch night for the new series and looking forward to seeing how different things are for the winter. Any favourites emerging already for anyone?

Sandra304: Loving Adrian, that is one beautiful man. I think Stephanie will be lots of fun as well. Those sisters are annoying. Callum and Daniel are fit as well. Claire seems like a right old slag, but every series has one. Jamila and Mike seem like they could be interesting. Helen, the brothers and the old couple are well boring. Hopefully they will go first!!!

CNFanboy: Adrian might be beautiful, but he comes across as a prick. Daniel is the obvious front runner, but doubt he'll win #Gandy

Sandra304: What's #Gandy?

CNFanboy: Gay eye candy! Agree the sisters are irritating.

Sandra304: Oh – haha. Why don't you think he will win?

CNFanboy: The early favourites never do. Be great if a normal gay guy could win and not some screaming queen. One of the brothers is really fit, so he'll probably get votes.

Sandra304: They are boring though, although not as boring as that old couple. Those t-shirts are ridiculous!!!

CNFanboy: Have you seen the screenshot of Claire's Tinder profile, where she describes herself as "Simple, cheap and yummy!"

Sandra304: OMG Cringe!!!

DaveBodyBuilder: Tinder – where hope goes to die!

CNFanboy: OMG I'm dead!

––––––

Felix entered the boardroom ready for the morning briefing and the room fell silent. Having that level of power over people was an intoxicating aphrodisiac. He noticed some new faces; Desiree must have worked fast to replace the people he'd fired the night before.

"Right, Desiree give me the numbers."

"Overnight ratings have come in at seven million. We had nine out of the top ten trends on Twitter and we were…"

"Did we get number one?" he interrupted, putting his hand up to stop her talking.

"For viewing figures, yes. On Twitter, no…that was Happy New Year."

"Fine, carry on," he gestured with his hand.

Desiree prattled on with her figures, but Felix wasn't really listening. He'd noticed one of the new staff was a bit older than the usual type. She didn't have the wannabe pop star look about her. She was a brunette and wore glasses. He loved the geek look and would be sure to find out her motivations and career ambitions, as well as what was hiding under that tight sweater.

Felix noticed everyone was looking in his direction, so Desiree must have finished her rambling and they were now all expecting him to speak.

"Seven million is a solid start. Our highest launch yet. It's great we won the slot. However, ratings will now slip as they do after launch so we need to keep momentum going. We have the first Complex Guvnor contest tomorrow, but I want it edited and ready to be broadcast that evening, so we can avoid spoilers leaking. We'll need to start it by noon, so we have time to edit it for broadcast. How wasted were they last night?"

"It was a late one, so they may take it easy tonight."

"I doubt it, especially the young ones. Well, I'm not worried with this challenge. The young lads should be able to handle it. We don't want any of the eye candy going first do we?"

"A few of the new team would appreciate a brief overview of the format," piped up Desiree.

"For the task?"

"For the show."

"Haven't they seen it?"

"We've had to cast the net quite wide this time!"

Felix was clear on the message.

"I haven't got time for that, you can do it. I have another meeting to get to."

"Should I introduce you to the new members of the team before you leave?"

"Introduce us after the first execution, if they last that long." He stood up and walked out.

. . .

Felix already had a plan in his head of who should go first and that was the old couple. The initial social media reactions were showing them as the least popular so far, along with the three sisters, so this validated his initial plan for the first execution. Not that he needed validation. Only people who lacked self-confidence sought reassurance – Felix was not one of those people.

It was likely that one of the three single men, or the three brothers would win the first challenge. It was highly physical, so played to the strengths of fit young men. Adrian had been instructed not to do well in the first challenge, but to do well enough to not arouse suspicion. Whoever was the first Guvnor and decided who would face the first public vote always put a target on their back. His homophobic comments had not gone unnoticed and based on some of the online reactions they had been overplayed. Attitudes may have shifted, but after another change of government they were moving back to a more liberal stance. For that reason, the conversation between the three single men in the apartment had not been broadcast.

The online polls did not have him as the favourite to win yet. In fact, he was fifth – after Mike, Daniel, Callum and Stephanie. How could Daniel North already be the second most popular? Felix would have to ensure Adrian's popularity was solid before risking him on a public vote.

Felix arrived back in his opulent office with his expensive art on the walls and real fur rugs. These were a palaver to have imported, but worth the effort. His huge expansive glass desk was centre stage and one wall was full of screens showing what was going on in the complex at that very moment, as well as the studio, so he could keep an eye on his staff at all times.

Desiree swept in with her oversized handbag which

housed her irritating pet Chihuahua. It always stared at Felix with a sense of loathing; the feeling was mutual.

"Felix, what happened to you? You only stayed in the meeting for five minutes. I need your approval on what's going out on tonight's broadcast."

"I'll deal with it later."

"But it needs to go to editing now."

"Fine, what are you focussing on?"

"I'd say Adrian and Claire are emerging as the villains so far."

"Focus on Claire, leave Adrian out of it for now. You know that's not the story we have planned for him."

"I know, but I thought we were going with the villain come good story."

"We are, but I don't want to take the risk this early on; just cut him out of the footage."

"But he's the best-looking guy we've ever had on the show. The amount of memes that have been created of him changing his t-shit after Claire *accidentally* spilled booze over him is phenomenal."

"Fine, but we don't need to hear what's coming out of his mouth, do we? He does a thousand stomach crunches in the morning in his underwear so get some shots of that for tomorrow's show."

"How do you know that?"

"His audition tapes."

"I don't remember..."

"Are you questioning me?"

His tone told her that she needed to shut up. Desiree had been with him a long time and was very good at what she did, so she got away with a lot more than anyone else. Sometimes she needed reminding of her place.

"I want the old people out first. Can we do anything about that?"

"They are actually very funny. Those brothers are boring – maybe get rid of them first."

"Not good to lose the eye candy too early."

"Only one of them is worth looking at, and besides the other men are much better looking."

"Yes but one of them is gay, one of them is a part-time gay, another is married and his wife is in there. The only other is Adrian who I'd like to keep under the radar for now."

"A fair point. The old people will go first."

"Good. I see they stayed up all night drinking with the others, so edit it to look like they weren't there. The viewers will think they're boring and went to bed early."

"Done. Still don't know why you cast them."

"Cannon fodder. Now tell me about the new girl, the one with the glasses."

"No, Felix, she is the only one who actually has a decent amount of experience. I can't keep losing staff."

"Who said anything about losing her? She seems very talented."

"Yes, well exactly. Please don't fire her... or fuck her."

He laughed; Desiree didn't.

Felix's phone rang – it was Mrs P. She was the Group HR Director of the Moldoon Entertainment Media Empire, known as MeMe for short. The only person who could get away with giving him a direct order, she demanded to speak with him urgently. She had been with him from the beginning and knew where all the bodies were buried... literally.

Mrs P was well past retirement age, yet Felix relied on her to handle all personnel matters. Employment rights were just a barrier to him being able to run his many businesses. Her main role was the keep the HR Directors of his many companies in line. He arrived at her office and knocked, waited for a beat of three seconds, and entered.

She was a tiny thing, although there was no frailty about her. She was a formidable woman and held herself with confidence. She had such gravitas that you felt compelled to be quiet in her presence and listen to every word that came out of her mouth. It was something they had in common. Where they differed was that Mrs P had empathy, whatever that was.

"Felix, sit down."

He did as he was told.

"Felix, I know you love to flex your power muscles on opening night, but you need to demonstrate a degree of caution this series. The stakes are much higher, you know that. You can't split your focus. It's bad enough that you ignored my instructions to not have Daniel North in this series, but with Adrian as well, there's too much at stake."

Daniel North had come under Felix's radar when he auditioned for the show in the autumn. He went through the full audition process and it was made exceptionally tough for him, yet no matter what happened he was getting on the show. There was too big a risk in rejecting him.

"You know we couldn't risk him auditioning for one of the other shows. This way, we control him."

"I know that, Felix, but with Adrian as well. Did you have to put them in together?"

"I didn't want Adrian on the show..."

"I know, he wanted to earn the money, rather than just be given it."

"We've had this conversation a dozen times before. Why are you bringing it up again now?"

"One of the producers you fired last night went into a big rant about you having a homophobic agenda with you suppressing Daniel's story and putting in Adrian with his homophobic attitude."

"Adrian isn't a homophobe. It's just an act for the cameras."

"We know that, but she doesn't. She also doesn't know that he's spent six months with a personal trainer so he can look like a Greek god, as well as all the other professionals you've used, to turn him into this character you want him to be. She doesn't know anything, because we've done our job well. How much does Desiree know?"

"Just that Adrian is the chosen one this series, with a redemption arc storyline."

"I'm worried, Felix. Your gung-ho attitude to firing people could bite us in the arse if people start digging around. These are talented producers and researchers."

"I can't not fire anyone. People will think I've gone soft."

She handed Felix a list. He saw ten names on it and didn't recognise any of them so they were clearly new and therefore had limited employment rights. He smiled and thanked her, before getting up to leave. This should keep him going for a couple of weeks.

"Felix."

He turned and saw her walking towards him, beckoning him to lean down. She wanted to talk to him quietly. The walls had ears, although this was the only place, besides his own office, which wasn't bugged.

"Please be careful. You know I can't be here for the whole series."

"I know and I will be." He kissed her on the cheek.

"Felix, if anyone finds out that Adrian is your son, you know you'll be finished."

She was right, nobody could find out. Not even Adrian himself.

CHAPTER THREE

Daniel was now settling into life inside the complex. He found the majority of his fellow neighbours delightful company; the arseholes and irritants seemed to have gravitated towards each other. Unfortunately, the gravitational pull of Adrian and Claire was to the bedroom next door. Callum had made an observation the day before that if someone needed to have sex that loudly, they were either deeply insecure or compensating for a shortcoming. This had caused much laughter, only for them to be told to be quiet by the rutting cats in the next room. This had been in the afternoon and the thought of listening to them all night had persuaded Daniel and Callum to move to the single girls' apartment. Stephanie was sharing the two-bed room with Helen, leaving the boys sharing the king-sized bed.

Callum had made no other comments or suggestions since the first night and sharing a bed had resulted in no wandering hands, although they had only been here two nights. Daniel had put the first night down to the champagne and was pleased that he wouldn't be distracted with trying to avoid any form of romantic relationship. That was not why he was here. Yes, he hoped to make new friends, but nothing more. Had this been the outside world things might have been different, but he wasn't about to do the gay version of Adrian and Claire on national TV and make himself the talking point of his grandmother's bridge club.

Stephanie was brilliant; they were in such sync that it was like they had already been friends for years. Helen was still withdrawn, although you could force a conversation out of her after a few beers. Daniel wanted to make the effort with her – and not just because Stephanie's survival in the competition was reliant on her at this stage. There was something about her which made Daniel feel compelled to support her. The fact that they all had to rely on Adrian and Claire to avoid an early execution was a necessary evil, which Daniel could tolerate... for now.

Everyone had made the assumption that Frank and Judy would go first, although Daniel wasn't so sure. If he won the first Guvnorship he wouldn't be putting them up; Callum was supportive of this approach, so they'd need to convince Adrian. Besides they were actually decent people and a good laugh. They had led such amazingly rich full lives, full of experiences.

The three brothers were the favourites to be put up first as they were definitely a threat in terms of strength. The hot one had shagged two of the sisters already and was working on the third, although she seemed to be having none of it. Meena was the youngest, quiet and mixed race, unlike her two sisters, Sassy and Hope; they were loud, irritating and never shut up. They seemed to be on a mission to offend as many people as possible, although the public would no doubt love them for it. Ever since a change in government had seen equal rights eroded, the public were no longer so easily offended. Although in the past people had become *triggered* far too easily, sensibilities had now swung back about three

decades. It had been a tough five years, but after two ye
the new government and the reinstatement of repe
equality legislation, attitudes were slowly starting to shift
back again. Daniel was hoping they would land on a healthy
balance were people could still take a friendly joke yet knew
when they were going too far and just being a rude twat.

Jamila and Mike were the only other residents who Daniel
couldn't quite get a handle on. Mike was easier, he was just a
bloke's bloke – straight down the line, doesn't give a fuck and
will have your back. He was a very bright guy – being an
accountant that would be assumed, but he actually put across
his point of view in an articulate way. His wife was more of a
puzzle. Jamila came across as lovely and had a sense of
humour, yet her eyes told a different story. When she smiled
it was obviously forced; she clearly had an agenda. They'd
been honest and said their motivations for being in the
complex were for the prize money, although Daniel was
convinced Jamila had other motives.

A claxon sounded over the loudspeaker, followed by an
announcement that the first Guvnorship contest would begin
in thirty minutes. Daniel rolled out of bed. Nobody else was
around. They had probably all gone down for breakfast early
in anticipation of the challenge.

"Brought you some food," remarked Callum as he walked
in, with Stephanie close behind him.

"Thought you'd like a nice bit of sausage," Stephanie said
with a smile.

Callum handed him the plate of sausage sandwiches with
a wink; a friendly wink or a flirty wink? Now was not the time
to consider that conundrum.

"Is everyone else up?" Daniel asked.

"Yes, it's half eleven. You must have needed the sleep,"

said Callum. "Adrian ran a boot-camp class. It was hilarious. Sassy and Hope wanted to try and get in with Adrian so went for it, big time. Claire joined in, as she doesn't want anyone having dibs on her man—"

"Even though Adrian said in front of everyone that they were just fucking and he considers himself single and available," interrupted Stephanie.

Daniel nearly choked on his sausage!

"That was so funny," Callum added. "Anyway, so Adrian whips off his shirt, which gets all the women in a frenzy—"

"Of course he did," mumbled Daniel with his mouth full of food. "Although to be fair if my body was like that I don't think I'd ever wear clothes."

"Same here. So, Mike and me took the class as well, with a couple of the brothers. The geeky one was engrossed in conversation with Helen, though."

"She didn't join in, then?"

"Seriously? No, she's still being very quiet."

"Some people just take longer to come out of their shell," added Stephanie.

"And the closet," Callum mumbled, getting a *shut the fuck up* look from Stephanie.

"Anyway, my point, besides from the whole thing being hilarious as nobody could keep up – I mean I go to the gym, but that guy is a machine – is Jamila. She just sat there watching us, and she would stare at one person for a while and then put her finger to her temple, like she was making a mental note about each person. She was mainly focussing on the men. Stephanie saw most of this as she didn't take part in the class."

Daniel went to speak...

"Don't even think about making some bitchy comment, Daniel North. I think you're right though, there's definitely more to her than she's letting on. I know she wants the money, most of us do, but we all have our own personal motives as well for being here. Maybe we could get a debate going at dinner over why people are really here?"

"No," replied Daniel firmly. "I'm not ready to share that yet."

"Don't you trust us?"

"You two, yes of course, but I'm not ready to share that with the cameras yet either. I have my reasons for being here and you'll just need to trust me."

"Fine, but we better win this contest, or you won't be telling anyone," said Callum.

"What do you mean?"

"We'll be the biggest targets, especially after Adrian and his *look how fit and athletic I am* demo downstairs."

"Not everyone is going to put us up for execution. Stephanie wouldn't, would you?"

"Of course not."

"Look, whoever wins puts up two groups for the public vote," said Callum. "If Frank and Judy win they may not put us up as we've been the friendliest to them."

"Helen wouldn't put us up either. Neither would Claire as she won't want to give up her daily orgasms. I think we'll be fine," said Daniel.

"The three brothers will put us up, so will Jamila and Mike, as we're viewed a physical threat. The only way we can be sure is if me, you or Adrian win this challenge."

"You tell me this now, after wolfing down two sausage sandwiches. I'll probably collapse with a cramp."

"We already know it'll be down to me and Adrian if it's a very physical challenge."

"Cheers... mate!"

"You know what I mean."

"Not really, no."

"Right, boys, let's break this up," Stephanie butted in.

"We can bitch about this later. Let's get down there, we've only got ten minutes before we get started. You better get ready," she indicated to Daniel who was still in his boxers and t-shirt.

Daniel joined the others in the communal living area just as the wall to the task area started to slide back and reveal a climbing wall with water running down it. Zelda was there, dressed in a fire-engine-red dress, with a plunging neckline and full-length split that showed she was wearing a pink thong. She must have been absolutely freezing. Daniel was in a hoodie and still shivering. She had her clipboard and was wearing her sexy school headmistress glasses, which in previous series she would only don for the Guvnorship challenge.

"Can you all come forward please so we can get started?"

Everyone duly obliged. Adrian was wearing clothes for a change – well, a tight white t-shirt. Daniel hoped this was just physical and wouldn't be something dreadful like an endurance challenge. There was a cameraman in the complex focussed on Zelda.

"This is an endurance challenge."

Bollocks!

"Stop the water."

Zelda gave a dramatic flourish, holding her hand in the air. The water stopped gushing down over the climbing wall.

"You will all take your places on the climbing wall. These have been marked out for you at the bottom. You will need a firm grip before I command the water to begin again. Upon my command, the water will pour down on you at a torrential rate. You must not waver. You must be strong. You must hold on. If you fall, you are out. Only the last person standing will choose who faces the first public vote. This is your moment to show us what you are made of. It is in this challenge that you will emerge as either a contender or simple cannon fodder. Only you can take charge of your destiny. Only you can show us how strong you are. Only you can demonstrate that have what it takes to be victorious and win the one-million-pound prize. Now take your places and be counted."

"Did she just announce a challenge like that?" asked Daniel.

"You know Zelda, she has a penchant for the dramatic," said Stephanie.

Daniel smiled and then took his place on the wall. Unfortunately, he was sandwiched between Adrian and Claire, something he wouldn't wish on anyone. Thankfully they would be too busy holding on to the wall to continue their fornications.

"Don't let me down now, Danny Boy. If you have to break a nail then just do it... for the team," Adrian laughed.

"Take your places and control your own destiny," Zelda boomed, before Daniel could offer up a rebuttal. Probably for the best; he needed to focus.

As they all took their places, Judy and Meena slipped straight away into the water below.

"Meena and Judy are eliminated from the contest."

The wall was extremely slippery already, although Daniel had managed to get a decent grip and felt comfortable. He needed to make a call on whether he faced into the wall or stood with his back against it. He noticed everyone, except Sassy and Hope, had their backs to the wall. Assuming this wasn't a group joke, Daniel followed suit.

"Right neighbours, there are fourteen of you left in this competition. We will continue until there is only one person standing. In the interest of health and safety we can't run the water constantly..."

Don't sound too disappointed, thought Daniel.

"This first burst will just be for five minutes. Let's see what you're made of. Bring on the water," she bellowed.

The water was freezing and running at speed, battering down on their heads. Daniel heard splashes, so he knew people had already fallen in. He kept his eyes closed and focussed on pressing his back against the wall as hard as he could and not moving or shuffling his feet. Any little movement could cause him to lose his balance and he was determined not to let that happen.

When the water stopped, it took a few seconds for Daniel to get his breath back. He opened his eyes to see who was left in the competition. Both sisters had fallen in, so their entire group was out of the contest. Two of the brothers were out, with just the hot one left. Daniel was disappointed to see Callum had already fallen in, although not as disappointed as Callum; he looked monumentally pissed off, sitting on the sidelines. Adrian, Claire, Mike, Jamila, Stephanie, Helen and surprisingly Frank had all managed to hold on – good for him.

"Just you and me, Danny Boy, doing it for the lads, let's get rid of those brothers shall we."

"Definitely, just one more to take out."

"That's the spirit, Danny Boy. High five."

"Let's leave that for when we win."

"Piece of cake, Danny Boy."

Zelda's voice broke through. "Only nine contestants left, and I must say Adrian, that I approve of your choice of clothing."

His white t-shirt clung to his wet body, showing every bump and groove.

"Thought you would, Zelda."

"Right, this time we will run it for ten minutes and the pressure will be turned up to the next level."

Had they reopened Guantanamo Bay? How could there be another level?

"Bring on the water."

The intensity of the water was horrific. The excruciating battering on top of his head – how was this even legal? He pushed himself against the wall to ease some of the pain from the rushing water, but it was futile. He couldn't hear anything but water and had no idea if anyone had fallen in. Finally, after what felt like ten hours, rather than minutes, the water finally stopped. It took a few seconds for his vision to clear and he desperately needed a piss.

Callum gave him a thumbs up, seemingly cheerier than he was ten minutes earlier. He had been joined by Stephanie who seemed relatively dry so she must have fallen early into the round. Frank was still holding on, although he did not look well. Mike and Jamila were still in contention as was the hot brother. Claire had fallen in much to Daniel's delight, although this didn't bode well for Stephanie's team. They were now reliant on Helen, although she had a defiant look on her face, showing no sign of fatigue.

"Danny Boy?"

He turned his head.

"Danny Boy, we're the strongest team now. Next go, there'll be another couple of teams out. I reckon Frankie Boy has no chance of another round. Look at the brother, he's actually shivering. I think he's been crying?" Adrian laughed.

"Jamila and Mike still have their full team."

"True, but Mike looks a bit rough don't you think?"

He was right. Mike looked dreadful, although Jamila looked like a very determined drowned rat.

"Me and you are strong Danny Boy, here's your chance to show everyone that not all poofs are pussies."

"I'm doing this to win."

"Exactly, like I said, prove you're not a pussy boy."

He wouldn't bite. "If we win, I don't want to nominate the single women."

"I agree mate, the way that Claire sucks my dick, she ain't going nowhere."

A wave of nausea hit Daniel. "I thought you'd moved on to the sisters?"

"No harm in spreading the seed. Bet you've done the same. You gays are all complete slags aren't you?"

Daniel said nothing, just smiled and nodded again. He was starting to get jaw ache and neck strain.

"Right contestants, are you ready for round three?" screamed Zelda excitedly.

A few groans.

"I said, are you ready for round three?"

Everyone shouted louder in the hope this would make it all be over as soon as possible.

"Right, this time we are turning it up to turbo and we'll be running for twenty minutes."

What the actual fuck!

The water was now really beating down and after a few minutes, Daniel lost his footing on his right leg. By trying to balance again, he opened his eyes and they were hit by water which went into his mouth and up his nose at such a rate that he had no choice but to swallow it. He pushed himself back into the wall as hard as could, still on one leg as he had no idea where the other footing was and didn't want to risk falling in. He didn't care about winning now; he just wanted to beat Adrian, which was rather petty given they were on the same team.

"Just four contestants left," bellowed Zelda, after the water finally stopped.

Daniel found his footing and let the circulation return to his leg. Adrian was still standing. He had now removed his t-shirt. Helen was still in the game, although she looked like she was starting to struggle. Jamila looked like she wanted to knock everyone else into the water and do a victory dance.

Adrian was roaring with laughter and clearly enjoying the whole thing. He didn't look like he was going anywhere, either. Daniel was starting to feel funny after swallowing so much water and was doubtful he could do another round, especially if they upped the time and the water pressure again, so he felt he only had one option.

"Adrian, I think this is between you and Jamila."

"What you talking about, Danny Boy, me and you to the end. See who's the bigger man."

"Yeah, well I'm sure there'll be other opportunities over the next few weeks."

"Don't you forfeit, Danny Boy. Don't show them that you're a pussy."

"This is about our team winning."

"You've got a point, Danny Boy, but I assume you're going to wait to be knocked in by the water."

"Of course."

"Cool, Danny Boy. I got this and you can have my back if we have to do a cooking contest or something."

Zelda's voice penetrated. "Let's start the water again and this time it will be super turbo and we are going for thirty minutes."

The water came again and this time, even if Daniel wasn't intending to just drop into the water, he wouldn't have stood a chance. He held on for a good five minutes before making it look like he'd lost his footing and falling into the water which was like a Swedish plunge pool. He made his way out and saw Helen on the sides who'd also fallen in. It was a straight out fight between Adrian and Jamila. There was no way they could lose this.

Callum came over with a towel and started to dry Daniel off, suggesting he get out of his wet clothes, but Daniel was more concerned with what he was seeing on the wall. Adrian was not holding the wall and acting like a showman, flexing his muscles.

"What the fuck is he doing?" Daniel asked.

"He's been doing that every round and not even wavered once. It'll be fine... fuck!"

In that moment of being a show-off prick, Adrian had finally become beholden to gravity and fallen into the water. The torrential downpour stopped in an instant as a winner had been crowned and you could hear Mike cheering and whooping at his wife's victory.

Jamila was the first Complex Guvnor – she had all the power.

CHAPTER FOUR

"Someone is going to fucking pay for this disaster," snapped Felix. "Desiree, I want you in my office in ten minutes with a plan of action to ensure this first execution goes the right way, or I'll slit your Chihuahua's throat."

She scurried off cradling her beloved pooch, which was clearly a substitution for the fact she could not hold on to a man long enough for him to impregnate her. He was fuming. How could this have happened? He ordered the footage to be played back and watched as Jamila came forward to announce her decision.

"Being the first to do this is always difficult," she started with watery eyes. "We have come to a decision. We have to put up who we feel are the strongest players and use this opportunity when it presents itself. We choose the three single men and the three brothers to face the first execution."

. . .

Felix snapped his fingers for the footage to be turned off and left the main studio to return to his office. Adrian had been told to stay under the radar in the early days. Now he was facing execution. Felix would have to find a way to get him back on script, but first he needed to ensure the brothers would be leaving the complex on Saturday night. There could be no more fuck-ups. He pulled out his phone and dialled.

"Lucinda, darling, it's been too long... yes, tomorrow night, the usual place... well, I will certainly make it worth your while," he purred down the phone and then hung up.

Desiree was still comforting her little rat dog when Felix burst into his office.

"What've you got for me?" he growled.

"Three options," she said confidently.

"Good, I don't want you turning piss weak."

"First, which I know what you'll disagree with, is a backup option if the others don't work. We go to press on Daniel's story, get the sympathy vote."

"You're right, hate it, next?"

"We've got a few stories on the brothers. Obviously we need to save the big one for the execution, but there's a few little things on social media which we got hold of before someone took them down. Just lads being lads, but it makes them look like sexist and disilaphobic twats."

"Disilaphobic?"

"It's a new word, what do you think?" she beamed.

"Terrible. Release the stories anyway. Make sure they trickle out, so it's not too obvious it's coming from us. What else? The social media stuff won't be enough. You know the young ones don't give a shit about those types of comments anymore, and they're the main voting bloc."

"Well luckily I saved the best 'til last..."

She handed him a piece of paper. He scanned it and looked back at her with a smile. This was going to be good!

Manipulation for the Masses?

DaveBodyBuilder: New article from Cecil Vonderbeet about the new series of Complex Neighbours is pasted below. Does anyone agree?

Manipulation for the Masses
Cecil Voederbeet

A new series of the ratings juggernaut, Complex Neighbours kicked off on Saturday night. The show 'executes' people every week under the strapline 'we destroy you with one tweet,' with one person walking away one million pounds richer, but at what cost?

The Reality TV craze was finally dying a slow and painfully public death, until this show came along and catapulted to the top of the ratings. The question to ask is why? The answer is simple – a lazy society with no desire to think for itself, coupled with a younger generation who have their own selfish and entitled view on what is right and wrong. They view people as mere entertainment with their emotional wellbeing deemed irrelevant if it gets in the way of shares, likes and fan endorsements.

This barbaric show publicly reveals a dark secret of whichever poor soul is 'executed' each week, tearing apart families and destroying relationships. The man behind this, Felix Moldoon, has no moral scruples as he sleeps soundly on top of his billions of pounds whilst leaving a trail of devastation behind him. All in the name of ratings!

Alas, the true guilty party here is the viewers. They lap up this bloodbath and it is a bloodbath, with a previous contestant having committed suicide following the utter destruction to her life from this TV programme. Yet, with record viewing figures, we are now going be have to endure two series a year of this glorified snuff movie. Who is the true manipulator here? A billionaire media tycoon? Or the viewers who decide each week whose lives will never be the same again?

> **CNFanboy:** What a drama queen – the new series is already shaping up to be the best yet!
> **Sandra304:** Agreed!!!

————

Felix sat back in his desk chair, glanced at the forum again, then clicked it off in irritation. That vile queen, Cecil Vonderbeet, had a personal vendetta against Felix. He was the one journalist who couldn't be bribed or blackmailed... yet. Felix was working on it.

The one thing Cecil had been right about was that *Complex Neighbours* was now in its third series with viewing figures steadily increasing. With eight million viewers for the last series finale, Felix hoped that the winter series, with shit weather and less to do, meant he could break ten million, a figure most soap operas could now only dream about. That was the soap operas which were still on the air. It had been a wonderful day when the British Soap Awards were abolished due to there being limited competition and replaced by the Reality TV Awards. Felix's shows had swept the board every year since their inception. Although the consolidated viewing figures always saw a rise and were a useful indicator of a show's popularity, it was the live viewing figures which still mattered to advertisers. Paying hundreds of thousands of pounds for an advertising slot which viewers could fast forward did not represent value for money.

Felix had ensured that only those he could use for profit within his empire had won previous series. He didn't care what their talent was – if they had any. Talent was a rarity

these days, and, besides, talented people always ⸨
above their limitations. The winner may become a million-
aire, yet they would be locked into a watertight contract
giving Felix complete control over them. Once every last
penny had been milked from their worth, they would be
tossed back into the gutter they had originally crawled out
from. Fame was brutal, but everyone wanted their five
seconds of it. This new surge of Reality TV had ensured that
fifteen minutes of fame was a relic of the distant past.

Felix groaned as he thrust in and out of Lucinda. She let out
her usual high-pitch scream, which sounded like a dog yelping. Although she served a business purpose, Felix enjoyed his
times with Lucinda. He was a busy man with his TV station,
record company, property empire and investments, and so
without the purpose she served, he'd never be able to make
time to satisfy her needs. He'd been satisfying those needs for
two hours, but she had important information and longevity
was her price.

"So, I was expecting your call as soon as I saw the results
for this week's execution. We've had over a million votes in
the first twenty-four hours and it's pretty evenly split. The
three brothers have around fifty-five per cent of the votes so
far, but you know there is always a last-minute surge."

"Yes, that's a little too close for comfort. Thanks
Lucinda."

She passed him a rolled-up fifty-pound note and a glass of
champagne. He bent down and snorted the line of cocaine,
downed the champagne in one and kissed her on the cheek
before bidding her farewell.

He'd met Lucinda many years ago when she worked for
him. She was talented and he had ensured that she worked

through the ranks earning her stripes and he supported her in choosing wise investments. The fact that she still required a good screwing for confidential voting information demonstrated that he had taught her well. People who were successful in business did not rely on just polite reciprocation – the latest favour always had to exceed the former. Lucinda worked for the Electoral Commission. In fact, she ran the place. They adjudicated the voting on *Complex Neighbours*, to show it was above reproach. Felix couldn't rig the vote, and even if he could he wouldn't want to. It was too risky and his reputation could be destroyed in seconds. The public might no longer give a shit if you messed with someone's mental health as long as it was entertaining and they had signed a waiver, but they didn't like people breaking the rules; phone vote rigging was still a big no no. However, Felix could still get an insight into how the voting was going and *persuade* the voting public to make the right decision with some clever editing. Time to get back to the studio and put Desiree's plan into action – there was only a few days of voting left.

It was after midnight and Felix asked the producer manning the screens to take a break and take their time doing it. As soon as he was out of sight, Felix flicked the cameras off in the Confession Booth. He flicked another switch for the loudspeaker into the complex. Felix called Adrian to the Confession Booth and waited for him to arrive. They had a deal and he was fucking it up.

Adrian arrived at the Confession Booth and when Felix was sure he was alone and nobody could see or hear them, he entered.

"Isn't this a bit dangerous?" he asked Felix.

"Desperate times – you know you might get executed in the first week?"

"Don't be fucking ridiculous, I'm going nowhere."

"Who do you think you're talking to?"

"Sorry... sir."

"Don't take the piss. Now listen, at the moment it's neck and neck between both groups. You need to get the public on side. For starters ditch that Claire, she's very unpopular with the public and she's not doing your popularity any favours."

"That might be difficult."

"Why, what have you told her?"

"Oh, she knows nothing about our deal, but I think she's a psychopath. Some of the stuff she's been saying, I reckon she would kick the fuck off if I dumped her now and all it takes is for me to flip my shit with her and I'm gone."

"You're right, the public still don't like men arguing with women, even if they are a fucking nut job. You can pick them, can't you?"

"I was horny."

"Grow up, Adrian. I know you're only twenty-one, but try acting like an adult. This is the opportunity of a lifetime for you. You wanted to win the money on merit and you've got no chance at the moment."

"Well you're the one who made me get all buff. I feel like a show pony."

"Your abs are trending on Twitter."

"Cool!"

"Right, now listen. You need to tone down on the homophobia, it's not being well received."

"I did tell you that, attitudes haven't changed as much as you think. Everyone's just too busy for protests and petitions these days"

"You mean your generation can't be arsed."

"Well life is just a lot busier than when you were young."

Felix was exasperated but wasn't going to explain again to Adrian that he was the last generation who knew that success had to be earned and wasn't something you were automatically entitled to. The next generation after him had tried to succeed with their 'gimme gimme gimme' attitude, but being offended by everything had its limitations when it came to success. However, this new generation were something else – entitled, busy and uncaring. This combination resulted in ruthless ambition. Twenty-five-year-old CEOs were no longer only found in the tech industry. Rather than push against it, Felix had adapted in order to utilise this ambition for his own financial gain. There was a lot to be said about being uncaring; it was very freeing.

"Am I to have an early epiphany?" asked Adrian

"Too soon, we need to save that for later."

"So you want me to apologise to Daniel and play nice then so we don't get executed."

"And you think people will buy that bullshit?"

Adrian shrugged and looked bored; this generation also had no attention span. Felix then explained his plan quickly and the approach Adrian would need to take in order to ensure he survived execution this week. He also made it clear who would be next out of the complex. The next Guvnorship challenge would not play to Adrian's strengths so he would need to *persuade* the other neighbours on who to put up for the second execution.

Adrian nodded, hopefully understanding what he had to do, and left the Confession Booth. Felix had taken a risk involving him in this way. There were many others who could have done it, but he owed Adrian. It was the only thing he regretted, that and... well, now was not the time to get melancholic.

It was two days until the first execution and Felix was watching the raw rushes for the evening broadcast. It was fascinating how quickly the complex had split into alliances and it was clear that Daniel was at the centre of his, with his fellow neighbours looking to him for a steer on what their next move should be. Felix would need to be careful that Daniel didn't get too much screen time. The plan was that he would be despatched in the middle of the show, ensuring he was forgettable and they could solely focus on Adrian's victory.

Desiree walked into Felix's office minus her bag and subsequently the dog. She looked excited about something so Felix ignored the fact that she hadn't knocked. The door may have been wide open but that was not the point; people had no manners anymore. She was holding out a flash drive, some-thing his IT department always had a hissy fit about. Felix wasn't the kind of man who logged onto secure file transfer platforms to punch in an authentication code from an app on his phone which could only be accessed by voice recognition software. A spate of brutal assaults and murders had seen the end of being able to pay for stuff with your thumb or face. You couldn't steal someone's voice box; not yet anyway. Felix was old school in some ways. It wasn't that he couldn't grapple technology, in fact he was very tech savvy; he just didn't think it was the best use of his precious time. The main problem the IT department had was that he kept misplacing the flash drives and although they were encrypted, they were now virtually impossible to buy new and were seen as a vintage product of yester-year. Felix took the flash drive from Desiree and plugged it into his laptop, instructing it to beam the footage to the screens on the wall with a simple flick of his finger.

Jamila made her way towards Claire's apartment, who answered the door, wearing glasses; a very different side to her. Jamila suggested they go to her apartment so they could talk in private as Mike was in the gym with the brothers and wouldn't be back for a while. Claire agreed and followed her, looking down at the group of Daniel, Callum, Stephanie and Helen all huddled together having conspiratorial whispered discussions and oblivious to the fact they'd been seen. Once in the apartment, Jamila spoke.

"Claire, I won't waste time with spin and bullshit. I am proposing an alliance between us."

Claire showed no reaction.

"I'm aware that my decision to put the three single men up for execution was not a popular choice, but I stand by it. They are all strong players, but I now know that I have a big target on my back for whoever is left. I think the three single guys will survive as you've got three lookers there and only one of the brothers didn't get beaten with the ugly stick. You know the public are shallow at this stage with their voting."

Claire nodded her agreement. "Although, Adrian, has done himself no favours with some of the stupid things he has come out with."

"I thought you were sweet on him?"

"He serves a purpose and it keeps me safe until we break into singles."

"Yes, but Adrian might win the next Guvnorship and decide to throw you under the bus."

"I highly doubt it. He thinks I'm a psychopathic bunny boiler."

"And you're not?"

"Of course not, he's the best looking guy in here by a long way and the others are nothing to be sniffed at, but a girl's gotta eat and I like five-star dining."

"So the slapper thing?"

"Gets me screen time and the early headlines. I want to be famous."

"What for?"

"Call it a lost childhood dream. Besides, you blatantly want the money at any cost."

"And you don't?"

"That's just gravy, I want to get to the final. That's all and Adrian can help me with that as he'll go far if he keeps his stupid mouth shut. So, anyway if Mike wins the next Guvnorship who is he putting up?"

"That's up to him," mumbled Jamila.

Felix could see that Jamila had underestimated Claire and was losing control of the conversation.

"Look, let's be honest with each other," said Claire. "If you were going to put us up then fine, be honest. Obviously if you want an alliance then that will need to change, so you were going to put us up next weren't you?"

"Yes, someone from the singles group always wins."

"Right, now we're getting somewhere. You're being honest. So, what's your alternative? I suppose the group who survive the first execution?"

"Yes, and then probably the three sisters."

"I would put Frank and Judy up first."

"Why? They won't last the distance."

"They may not win challenges, but they'll win votes. The longer they're here the more endearing they become to the public. They aren't driven by winning money or fame, they are just in it for the experience. People will love that about them."

"But the sisters are fucking annoying."

"Exactly, and they'll stay annoying. I'd target the old couple first."

"It would be best if the single men went first, but I can't see that happening."

"Probably for the best if the single men stay."

"I know why you want them to stay."

"It's not that. Think about it, when we break into singles the brothers will stick together, but those boys came in with their own agendas. Any alliances will be null and void."

"Is that that same for you, Claire?"

"That's up to you. Now, I've got an idea of what we can do..."

Felix watched as Claire shared her plan with Jamila. This was gold dust. Two women scheming and plotting together was always a ratings draw. The viewers, mostly women and gay men, would love to hate them.

"This is brilliant, Desiree. Let's use this to build up to the execution show."

"I was planning to, but wanted to check with you first. We obviously can edit it to build sympathy for the single men. The problem is the brothers aren't really doing anything so we can't really push a hate vote towards them. We have to use the anti-vote, in that the viewers will want to keep the single men in the complex."

"Agreed."

Desiree smiled, nodded and left the office as Felix reached for his phone.

It was Friday morning and it had been a really stressful week. They had drip fed the press with negative stories about the three brothers and focussed the nightly shows on the single men and the drama and excitement around them.

Felix rolled off Lucinda. He'd given her another good seeing to – from behind this time. She had a lot on, so this way she could still respond to her emails. She had a day of meetings ahead of her. Most men would have a severely bruised ego from such behaviour; this did not apply to Felix whose ego was bomb proof. He also didn't care what Lucinda was feeling, he just needed an update on the voting figures.

"The brothers are now just short of seventy per cent and there has been just over three million votes. As you know that's still not enough to guarantee an execution, but if your single boys keep up what they're doing the result will go your way."

"I don't like leaving things to chance."

"What more can you do at this stage? The execution is tomorrow night."

"We can get half the overall votes during the execution show."

"Well Felix, that is something you'll have to figure out," she said, as she rubbed a flannel between her legs and then pulled her dress over her head.

Felix was amazed at the speed in which she got ready and reapplied her makeup. Within two minutes she was blowing him a kiss and walking out the door. She'd chosen Felix's place this time – well, one of his places. This was his flat in Canary Wharf – the view was spectacular from the thirty-ninth floor. It was his home away from home; his main home was a six-bedroomed detached house near the studio on the outskirts of the city, although he barely spent any time there. This place was his favourite in the UK; even his staff didn't know about this place. He took out his phone and dialled.

"It's me... looks like Adrian will be safe this time around... Yes, I warned him... I know it was a risk but some things can't be left to chance... Yes, I saw the conversation between Jamila and Claire... Of course I approved it being broadcast... No I don't think it was a mistake... I don't want Jamila gone in the next round, she brings in the viewers... She won't win, I'll see to that... Okay, bye... yeah, you too."

That woman could really put him on edge, but he was tense enough and knew he didn't really believe what he had said. Tomorrow night, Adrian and Daniel could both be heading out of the complex and Felix's grand plan would be in tatters.

CHAPTER FIVE

It was Saturday – execution day.

Staying in was not the new going out on a Friday night anymore, that had shifted to Saturday. This was for one of two reasons – the stay in on Friday generation now had families, mortgages and other boring crap so they stayed home every night, or they were those that had no such commitments but were old and needed two days to recover from a hangover. Whichever camp people fell into, Saturday was now the only night for big live-event TV.

Daniel was anxious. Had he blown his chances? It had all kicked off the previous night in a stupid moment of vulnerability, followed by something unexpected and topped up with a heavy dose of rage. He was nursing a hangover from hell, as he'd gotten obliterated with Mike and the three brothers, who were actually a good laugh when you got to know them. Helen had drunk them all under the table – not bad going for a short-haired, tattooed, German heterosexual.

"Wish I'd not had an early night, I missed all the drama," said Stephanie

She was clearly disappointed to have missed Daniel's night

of fucked-up bollocks. There were probably better adjectives but there was a bird tweeting outside that Daniel wanted to strangle with his bare hands whilst smashing every lightbulb in visual range. However, this would involve movement which was an unspeakable prospect at this moment in time. It was clear that whoever had invented Tequila was the spawn of Lucifer.

"Where's Callum?" she asked.

"Dunno," he groaned.

"So what happened between you two? I heard you kissed."

"Ever thought of being a gossip columnist?"

"The money's shit, besides I want to *be* the headlines, not write about them."

"That doesn't make you sound conceited."

"Meow, put your claws away, Daniel North. I've made no secret about my reasons for being on this show."

That was true; she had made that clear on their first night in the complex.

That first night, following his run-in with Adrian, Daniel had made his way over to the single women's apartment. Their apartment was the same layout as Daniel's, although Stephanie had nabbed the single room with the king-sized bed all to herself. He filled her in on what had happened with Adrian.

"What a complete fucking arsehole, and you know he'll still get votes because of how good looking he is."

"Yes, people are shallow. So you wouldn't go there now?"

"Of course not."

"Really?"

"Seriously. I have a few morals left... well, if I did it would just be to tell him how shit he was in bed."

They both laughed.

Daniel picked up one of Stephanie's glitzy tops to admire it.

"Can't help yourself you gays can you? Like magpies with your love of shiny things."

Daniel smiled, loving her banter and put the top down.

"So what was all that about with Callum? Sexually fluid is just a slaggy bisexual isn't it?"

"No, there's more to it than that."

"There always is. You know I filled in one of those diversity questionnaires a few weeks ago and I had a choice of fifteen different sexualities."

"I can believe it. I'm not interested in getting involved with anyone anyway. That's not what I came in here for."

"So why *did* you come on the show?"

"Erm... the money."

"Yeah, alright, well I'm not gonna force you to tell me. I guess you have your reasons."

"I do, and I'll tell you when the time is right. What about you?"

"Well I had this dream last night."

Daniel rolled his eyes.

"What?"

"Sorry, it's a reflex. My grandmother has this friend who constantly talks about her dreams not realising that the only person it is interesting to is herself. It's like baby photos on social media, especially ugly babies and you still have to respond with a heart emoji out of politeness."

"Well at least we know what the title of your autobiography is going to be."

"What?"

"*I Didn't Mean to be a Bitch!*"

Daniel laughed. He had known this woman just a couple of hours and he already adored her. He knew he would be able to speak his mind in front of her and there would be no judgement. Stephanie Chapman was a breath of fresh air and he hoped they'd become close friends. In the spirit of not being a rude twat he asked her what her motivations were for joining the show.

"I'm in it for the fame and fortune, no joke. I want to be a famous pop star and I've got twelve months left. I'll be thirty at the end of the year."

"Me too, when's your birthday?"

"New Year's Eve."

"Oh my god, me too – we were born on the same day. How mad is that?"

"It's destiny, babes. I think this is going to be a very special year for the both of us."

Daniel didn't usually go in for all that destiny shit, but this time he thought she might be on to something.

Daniel was still feeling like death when Judy came over with a glass of something which looked like swamp mucus and thrust it into his hand.

"Drink this, love, it'll sort you out in no time."

"Looks like it came from a pond."

"You're welcome," she replied, laughing as she walked off.

"Thank you," he shouted after her.

There was no need for him to be rude. He looked at the glass of whatever it was again, decided against sniffing it, held his nose and downed the lot in one. It felt like cold, congealed spunk sliding down his throat, and there was a lot. Basically, he had just swallowed the spunk of an elephant.

The taste made him gag, so he quickly chased it down with some water he had to hand. Put a blanket over his face and told Stephanie to wake him up in an hour when he might be in a fit state to regale her with the mortification of the previous night.

. . .

Daniel felt better as the water hit his face. Whatever that drink was, it had worked wonders. He felt fine, just a bit greasy and the shower would soon sort that out. Stephanie had not kept to her word as she had left him asleep on the communal sofa for three hours. There was still no sign of Callum. This might be for the best for the time being.

After getting out of the shower, which he must have been in for about half an hour, he walked into the bedroom he was sharing with Callum to find Stephanie plonked on the bed. Luckily his modesty was covered – this one had no shame and would not be going anywhere until she had all the gory details from the night before.

"Don't worry, I know everything, so you don't need to relive it," she smiled.

"What do you know?"

"You and Callum got it on, Adrian kicked off and you and him had a fight."

"Who told you that?"

"Sassy."

"Sassy is a drama queen."

"Did you and Callum get it on?"

"Kind of..."

"Did Adrian kick off?"

"He might have done..."

"And did you two have a fight?"

"I wouldn't really call it a fight."

"Oh I know that. Adrian would knock seven tonnes of shit out of you."

"Excuse me... not all gay men are wimps you know."

"Oh please, this isn't some gay bashing shit. Adrian is built like a brick shithouse and probably pisses protein shakes instead of urine."

"We just had a heated exchange."

"And?"

"And I'll probably be going home tonight, so there's no more to it."

"Nice try. Sit your arse down here next to Auntie Stephanie."

Daniel explained how the looming execution threat had affected his mood and ability to have fun. He knew he needed to be front and centre to secure votes, but just wanted to retreat and be alone. It was a horrible feeling; bad enough wanting to be by yourself; even worse when it's impossible to achieve. The complex might be vast, but when you wanted to be alone it felt like a prison.

Callum had furnished him with a drink, followed by another and then several more. The new mentality of these shows was to forget tasks which cause the neighbours to live on bread and water. They had been replaced with tasks to keep people completely wasted, lowering inhibitions. A few drinks later, Daniel had started crying – yes, crying. How fucking embarrassing. Callum had been lovely and it had been Daniel who made the first move.

It was just a kiss but things could have progressed. Daniel was completely shit faced and the last person he was thinking of was his grandmother, or his promise to her. The kiss was getting heated when Adrian had walked in.

"Fucking hell lads, lock the door if you're going to be doing that."

"He said that about a little kiss?" Stephanie asked.

"Well, we both had no tops on."

"So more than a kiss, but still it's not like you were blowing him... were you?"

"Don't be ridiculous, I wouldn't do that on TV... hopefully!"

"So what's his problem?"

"You know he's a homophobic prick, we could have just been holding hands and he'd have kicked off."

"So what happened then?"

"Callum told him to fuck off and mind his own business."

"You know, the more I hear, the more I like that boy. You want to snap that one up. He's clearly into you."

"That's not the point right now. Adrian then started to get personal about Callum being sexually fluid, saying he must be riddled as he'll stick it in anything."

"Such a way with words that one. It's a shame given how beautiful he is."

Stephanie stared off into the distance for a moment. Daniel clicked his fingers in front of her face to bring her attention back into the room.

"It all kicked off after he said that as I just jumped up and grabbed Adrian by his shirt collar."

"You did what? You know you can get automatically executed for that?"

"I know, but I was drunk and besides I'm still here. Adrian just pushed me off anyway. I landed on the bed – just a bruised pride."

"What did Callum do?"

"Dunno, I told him to leave me alone."

"Oh babes, you idiot. You've probably blown that now – no pun intended."

"Really? How long you had that one ready?"

"About five minutes."

They gave each other a look and just starting giggling and then laughing more loudly. It felt good to laugh after a disastrous night. Callum had stormed out and told Daniel to let him know when he'd developed some empathy – nice. Adrian had brought Claire back to the apartment and started screwing her really loudly so Daniel had sought out Mike for someone to talk to, as Stephanie was asleep. Mike was with the three brothers playing computer games and eating pizza – they had won a challenge for a takeaway and a choice of either a movie pass or games console. They chose the latter.

It was one of the daily challenges. Usually something simple – well, in comparison to the Guvnorship challenge. This had been about finding a certain key in a box of ten million keys – well, it felt like that. The key opened a box with the prize code in it. The others had decided to sit this one out and just let the guys battle it out, as it would be the last night in the complex for some of them. The geek brother had found the key and won.

Daniel had found Mike with them. His wife was asleep, something she did a lot apparently, like most cold-blooded creatures. Daniel had tried to take him away to talk; the brothers were having none of it and had insisted he join them. It had been a good night once he had obliterated any memory of what had happened earlier. He hadn't been called to the Confession Booth, so was hoping this meant his physical altercation with Adrian had been regarded as minor and that would be the end of it.

Daniel knew that Stephanie was concerned that he could be going home as a result of the first execution. Everyone was busy getting ready for their three minutes of live TV exposure. This involved lots of flesh on display. It was evident that his fellow neighbours did not realise the horror that was Ultra Mega HD TV. The say the camera adds ten pounds, well this new HD adds about ten years. It was January and freezing. The execution chamber was outside so those who had decided to appear scantily dressed would be covered in goose bumps, looking like fresh uncooked chickens. Stephanie had thick black tights, black dress and a black jacket.

"Why are you all wrapped up in black? It's not a real execution you know."

"It's Baltic out there."

"You look amazing," remarked Callum who was waiting on them getting ready.

"As do you," she replied.

This was an understatement. He looked so handsome in a long-sleeved figure-hugging top, a dark pair of chinos and his trademark Clark Kent glasses.

Daniel had made little effort and was just wearing a shirt and jeans. They say gays know how to dress. This was in fact a lie – some know how to dress, this one did not. However, he was anxious enough about the evening so was hoping people would keep their bitchy comments to themselves.

"Fucking hell, are you not dressed yet?" remarked Adrian, walking in.

Evidently, Adrian had not received the memo. It also didn't help that he looked absolutely stunning; fully suited and booted in an outfit tailored to show off his physique. That *you don't fuck a personality* line was probably ringing through Stephanie's head until she was brought back to reality by a comment from Callum.

"You're drooling."

"Adrian, can you give us a few minutes," she snapped.

"We all have to be in the communal area in ten minutes."

"Yes, I know, but you hanging around isn't going to get us moving any quicker."

He walked off mumbling something inaudible, although no doubt offensive.

Daniel stalked off back into the bedroom and chose something else to wear. He didn't have much fashion sense and he knew that. He just dressed for comfort and he was okay with that. He grabbed a different shirt and a darker pair of jeans and finished the look off with white sneakers. He walked out and noticed Callum had left; sensible that girl in getting rid of any company.

"How do I look?"

"You look amazing, babes!"

"You can be honest."

"Erm..."

"Just tell me."

"You look like a nineteen-year-old chemistry student."

Daniel scowled at her and then looked in the full-length mirror and started laughing – she was right.

"Help me, please."

After another quick costume change; Stephanie working wonders with Daniel's limited wardrobe, they joined the others in the communal area who were all milling around the champagne. The three brothers were wearing matching white suits with red ties. Stephanie asked Daniel to pinch her arm – yes, it was real. Sassy and Hope were basically in their underwear making Claire look overdressed in a boob tube and mini skirt. Meena had covered more flesh than her sisters with a simple, yet elegant dress. Helen was doing herself no favours in making people think she was straight by wearing a suit and looking more butch than Mike who had made minimal effort and was wearing jeans and a rock band t-shirt. Jamila was looking immaculate in Indian dress. Frank was also wearing a suit and Judy was wearing another of her bling tops, this time with the word 'Mega' emblazoned on it and what appeared to be a woollen skirt – were they still a thing?

Mike wished all the men good luck, gave the no hard feelings speech, which everyone seemed amenable to, as it was clearly genuine. Jamila was not impressed with this development based on the look on her face. Either that or an invisible fly had shit under her nose. Mike picked up a glass of champagne and passed it to his wife. This provided an opportunity for some frantic whispering, causing Mike to look like a scolded puppy.

The three brothers appeared to have binned off Sassy and Hope, who were unsuccessfully attempting to drape themselves over them. This was no doubt to try and get screen time once the show went live, given the focus would be on those at risk of execution. Daniel was enjoying being on his own for a moment before Stephanie came over to him.

"Nervous?"

He shrugged.

"Come and talk to everyone. Nothing you can do about it. They'll be totting up the votes by now."

He nodded his agreement, downed his champagne and they made their way to the rest of the group just as the claxon sounded.

"It's time guys," screamed Zelda BonBon.

She had appeared from behind the screen, which started to slide back. There stood the execution tubes ready and waiting. She explained that they would shortly be live and she would set up for the first execution. Daniel gave Stephanie's hand a tight squeeze.

"Welcome back to *Complex Neighbours*. We are LIVE in the complex for our first execution which is between the three single men and the three brothers. Gentlemen, you've got sixty seconds to say your goodbyes."

Daniel made his way around the room quickly, saying goodbye to Frank, Judy and Helen. He shook hands with Mike and hugged Claire and the three sisters, making it much more pointed that he'd blanked Jamila. It was a petty thing to do, but fuck it; you had to embrace that inner child sometimes. He was then back at Stephanie's side.

"You okay?" he asked.

"I've just been hugged and kissed by five men in quick succession. I've had worse Saturdays."

"Hopefully this isn't goodbye, Stephanie Chapman, but if it is, then thank you for helping me through this week. I don't have many true friends, but you're now one of them and I'll see you in two months."

He grabbed her into a tight hug, not giving her chance to speak. He could feel her body shudder slightly as she was trying to hold it together for him. He smiled at her one last time and walked towards the execution tubes.

Inside the tube, Daniel was putting on a front; in reality he didn't want to leave. It wasn't that he hadn't had a chance to tell his story yet, as he would still have the platform of the show to do that; it was the friendships he had started to develop here. He didn't have many friends; they were mainly colleagues or casual acquaintances. His grandmother was the most important person in his life and his only family. He'd had close friends in the past, but the memories were too painful and it made him reluctant to get close to anyone. There had been someone special a few years ago, but that had ended badly and was something Daniel deeply regretted; had he allowed himself to follow his true feelings, his life could have been very different now.

The way he had just clicked with Stephanie was something which happened once in a lifetime. It was a rarity and he had seen enough of these shows to know that if he left tonight and she lasted until the end, she would have formed new friendships, stronger for the more time they had spent together in this complex.

He wasn't sure about his friendship with Callum. Being away from the cameras might cause them to deal with the obvious vibe between them, but Daniel would prefer to stay in this environment and let a friendship develop instead. He was ten years younger than Daniel and fairly mature for a teenager, most of the time. Who knew what could happen if they were both staying a hotel tonight away from the cameras; Daniel was still human.

Everything was done by computers now, but Felix Moldoon liked the drama so there was a giant red lever which Zelda would pull to open what could only be described as the gallows beneath the losing group; thankfully there was no hangman's noose, but who knew what the show could evolve to.

"So, the public have been voting all week and after an incredible late surge we've had over five million votes," bellowed Zelda. "The first group to be executed from *Complex Neighbours*, with a vote of eighty-five percent, is...."

CHAPTER SIX

Three Brothers, Three Fathers and One Slutty Mother

DaveBodyBuilder: Article from Cecil Vonderbeet on the execution of the three brothers pasted below:

Execution or Murder?
Cecil Vonderbeet

The first people 'executed' from the latest series of car-crash Reality TV show, Complex Neighbours, are devastated by revelations surrounding their parentage following their departure from the show.

The man who raised them, Silas McDougall, is one of four brothers and each of his siblings has fathered one of his children. Silas took it upon himself to take the law into his own hands by shooting his wife at point-blank range. He then sought revenge on his brothers and is now being held for four murders in a secure psychiatric hospital.

The three brothers from the show, are all in hiding, so unavailable for comment. This latest move by Felix Moldoon begs the question – has he gone too far this time?

Sandra304: OMG!!!

CNFanboy: WTF!!!

———

"So Desiree, do you think I've gone too far this time?" Felix asked, putting the printout to one side.

"Of course not, we had no indication that this was how the father would react. He clearly has some mental problems – I mean that is not normal behaviour, is it?"

"People are strange things. You'd be surprised how something can just cause someone to explode. It only takes a little push."

"That was quite a push you gave, though."

"You knew what the press release was, Desiree, so don't play innocent and shut that dog up."

"He needs the toilet."

"Well I need you to stay here whilst we run through the social media reactions. Get that new producer, the brunette with the glasses, to take him out to do his business. I don't want him shitting in my office, even if it is inside that monstrosity you call a handbag."

"You mean Emma?"

"Oh, is that her name?"

"Felix, I told you she is very experienced, so please leave her to do her job. I need some decent people to be able to do the work and she's a good find. You know it was her who came up with the next Guvnorship challenge."

"It's an excellent idea. You think Daniel will win?"

"He's the favourite, but we know for certain that Mike won't."

"He's an accountant earning six figures a year and he's not even thirty. Hardly what I'd call thick."

"But he don't know showbiz gossip does he? The gays know it all."

"Isn't that a stereotype?"

"No, it's a fact. Now I'll go and give Pepe le Pew to Emma, so she can take him outside."

"She can come here and collect him."

Desiree shook her head and gave one of her looks, before swiftly departing. Felix looked again at the viewing figures. They'd averaged seven and a half million and peaked at just over eight million at the moment the execution happened. Excellent figures for the first week but he wanted more. The voting revenue would also be high, although that was pledged to charity. It was good PR and fish food compared to what the advertising brought in. Depending on who was facing execution this week, he would be able to up the costs of the advertising slots. This was the advantage of running the show on your own TV station. No executives to arse kiss – he made all the decisions.

He had to review the rest of the social media printouts Desiree had left for him, although they often bored him. The same vitriol from braindead viewers who were *outraged* and yet still watched the show avidly. The social media commentary did have one use though, it gave an indicator of who was popular, although you had to look very carefully through all the dross for the more intelligent and constructive comments – a challenge at the best of times.

———

Jamila is a skank

Sandra 304: Can't believe the brothers have gone because of that skank Jamila, she is just a jewlous skank!!!

DaveBodyBuilder: The three brothers were forgettable so probably the best choice, although no idea why that old couple are still there. They bring nothing to the show. Jamila is definitely a sneaky one, but it would be boring if she left too soon

Sandra304: Jamila is a skank. She needs to go now!!!!

DaveBodyBuilder: Do you know any other words besides 'skank', and it's 'jealous' you illiterate moron

Sandra304: I'm a catholic not a moron!!!

—————

Felix Moldoon has blood on his hands

Treehugger23: How can this man not have been arrested? Because of his deplorable actions four people are now dead and countless lives completely destroyed. We should boycott this show and when his ratings plummet along with his advertising revenue he will be forced into taking this trash off our screens. I don't know how anyone can lower themselves to watch this show

DeliciousDebbie1985: Are you for real? This is what these people signed up for, it's not like the show has not been on before. This has nothing to do with the producers and everything to do with their psychotic father. I mean, who goes and shoots people because of an affair?

Treehugger23: You are clearly part of this conspiracy of a whitewash. People have been murdered because of this show. Did you vote for the three brothers?

DeliciousDebbie1985: Yes I did – they are boring as f**k.

Treehugger23: You have blood on your hands as well then

DeliciousDebbie1985: Don't be ridiculous, the three

single men have more to offer the show and have already
got involved in the conflict. They make it entertaining.
The brothers didn't do anything

Treehugger23: One of them is openly homophobic,
another is a trendy bisexual who wants to play games
and the other clearly has a hidden agenda – what about
that is entertaining?

DeliciousDebbie1985: I thought you didn't watch the
show?

DeliciousDebbie1985: Hello???

————

"Can we find this Debbie and give her a job?" Felix asked as
Desiree re-entered the room, minus her little rat dog.

"Thought you'd like her, although it's probably a twelve-
year-old schoolboy."

"And the Jamila is a skank stuff?"

"I just thought that was funny... moron." She laughed
hysterically.

Felix gave his fake laugh, coupled with one of his death
stares and she stopped immediately.

"Based on the social media responses there is obviously
shock at the press release and subsequent murders. The three
brothers are now in hiding, we're looking after them."

"And how much is that costing?"

"Mrs P authorised it."

"Fine, just make sure it doesn't get out of hand. Can we
not get them out of the country?"

"They need to be here for the police investigation."

"Bollocks, why did their father have to go on a fucking
killing spree? I mean the headlines are great for the show, but
all this fallout is a ball ache and we need to get on with the
second week of the competition."

"Leave the ball ache to me. At worst it will run for a week until the next execution."

"That will be the three sisters."

"I thought you wanted Frank and Judy out next?"

"They can go after. I don't want to take the risk of one of the sisters winning the Guvnorship next week and making it to singles. They have to go as a group – you know that."

"So the three single men, three single women and Jamila and Mike to make it to the singles phase?"

"Yes."

"So does the order of elimination matter?"

"Yes, it's about control, Desiree. How long have you worked for me?"

"Well if you want Daniel to be Complex Guvnor then he won't put them up, he made that clear when he was discussing the alliance with the others. I believe they will all follow suit and put the two couples against each other."

"Why wasn't I told about this?"

"Felix, it went out in the main show. You approved it."

He hadn't watched it as he'd been so focussed on ensuring that Adrian wasn't executed in the first week so he had just approved it without looking at it. Still, he could work with this change in the story. He would have to find a way to discredit the old couple in the press so they would lose the vote – that would be a challenge as Jamila was about as popular as a fart in an elevator. They'd have to get started on their strategy straight away.

"We'll do the Complex Guvnor contest tonight – it will go out live."

"What? We can't get ready for a live show by tonight. Besides, we only have a skeleton staff on. It's a Sunday and Zelda will be on a comedown and in no fit state to host."

"Get everyone in, if they value their jobs. It's only a fucking quiz and leave Zelda to me. Just make it happen."

Desiree got up and flung the door open, but she had a passing barb before she left.

"Daniel is now the favourite to win. Adrian is sixth, behind the closeted lesbian."

The door slammed as she left.

At least the plan had worked. Adrian had been told to tone it down from now on, but to not make it look like he'd had a complete character change; the public weren't that stupid and every year there was a conspiracy theory about there being a mole.

Adrian had also started to distance himself from Claire, although now the three brothers were gone, Sassy and Hope would have their eyes on Adrian. Sassy was hungry for column inches and believed being a complete slag would achieve that. She wasn't wrong; it was just the wrong type of column inches. Adrian needed to chummy up with someone but there was only Mike left that was an option. The problem with Mike was that he was married to one of the most unpopular neighbours they had ever had and it was only week one. Felix thought she was wonderful; particularly her chats in the Confession Booth as she would talk out her strategy to eliminate the competition knowing full well that it would be broadcast. She clearly didn't care and believed the public would reward her for her game play when it came to the final. She would be disappointed.

Felix picked up the analysed data which indicated who was leading in the popularity contest. It took an amalgamation of data; social media hashtag trends, video likes and shares, forum discussions, online polling and odds at the bookies. This way you got a more reflective picture. Mike was ahead at the bookies, yet taking all data into account he was second, followed by Stephanie, Callum, Helen and then Adrian. How had that happened? He'd potentially need to talk to Adrian again, but could he take the risk? Mrs P had warned against it, but she was now overseas at Felix's private island and wasn't planning to come back until the show was over, even if she was still interfering from afar. She wanted to be on the island in case Adrian left the show early and needed a sanctuary. Didn't she trust Felix to get the job done? This was what he did. It was how he had built his empire and made billions of pounds. He wasn't just lucky; he made sure things went according to his script.

He looked at the data again and smiled. So, Daniel North was popular – this could only end one way.

CHAPTER SEVEN

Daniel woke up feeling like shit. He looked to the left – he was alone. That was something. As he slowly let his eyes acclimatise to the light, his body shuddered with that feeling you get when your memories slowly start to return – oh fuck.

"Fuck, fuck, fuck," he muttered to himself.

"What?" came a voice from somewhere to his right.

Daniel looked over at the other bed and saw Stephanie slowly lifting her head and then squinting at Daniel, no doubt trying to get him into focus. After a few seconds a big grin appeared on her face.

"I don't want to talk about it," he muttered.

"Oh, I think we will."

Daniel threw the covers over his head – *bollocks!*

It had been a chaotic night. After the execution everyone got completely wasted. Even Jamila had a few drinks; Daniel had said he forgave her, although this was a bluff and solely down to Mike, who was one of those blokes who you just can't help but like. Why was he married to a woman like that? The sisters had a cry when the brothers departed, but were soon over it with Sassy making her moves on Adrian. He willingly obliged, sending Claire a message that that she was last week's news. Claire had also attempted to move on with Callum, although he had politely declined. Well, if you can call *fuck off* polite.

Stephanie spent the first thirty minutes after the brothers were executed in tears. Then she saw herself in the mirror which had resulted in more crying, before Claire; yes, Claire, helped her get sorted. It appeared Claire was delighted Adrian had survived despite his wandering eyes, hands and no doubt other body parts. Adrian celebrated his survival by shedding some clothes – why not, it's only January. It sounded like he'd said, "for my fans," under his breath, although this was vehemently denied.

Daniel found some time to talk to Helen, who was also happy with the result.

"I only speak to one brother. You and Callum I like. You speak to me. Adrian is... what you Brits say? Wanker?"

Daniel nodded and smiled.

"Yes, he is wanker, but two out of three is better than one – right?"

"I completely agree. I saw you chatting with Meena earlier. I've not really spoken to her by herself, what's she like?"

"She is very nice woman. Very different to her sisters and I do not mean colour of her skin. I mean she is quiet and very clever. I enjoy talking to her."

"I'll make a note to only talk to her on her own then."

"Don't say I say anything."

"I won't."

"She is very clever too, she guess that Claire and Jamila are working together."

"An alliance?"

"Yes. They team up to try and get rid of you boys. I think they will be after the sisters next and I do not think you are safe yet. Jamila wants the money and Claire wants to be famous. They will stop at nothing."

Dramatic, yet accurate.

"I hope the sisters do not leave before they are split into single people, so those loud girls can go and Meena can be herself."

"Yes, maybe."

Daniel noticed Helen had a different look about her. He knew that look; perhaps he was mistaken. Helen had been isolated during her time here so far, much by her own doing, so it was good she had connected with someone.

"She is very special person," she muttered as her eyes wandered to where Meena was sitting.

Daniel knew he wasn't mistaken, but decided to keep Helen's crush to himself and not even to tell Stephanie. Particularly because she was the idiot who suggested they do a game of spin the bottle. This was following several Tequila slammers and Jaeger bombs – always the best time to do something like that. Another thing he recalled was that it was Mr Callum Peters who had suggested that they should play this combined with Truth or Dare. When this was suggested, Daniel's body composition was around forty per cent proof, so he thought it was the best idea in the world – the night had deteriorated from that point.

"Dare," said Adrian, who for some reason had opted to lower his vocal pitch by ten decibels. It was surprising he didn't beat his chest – he was still not wearing a t-shirt for some reason.

Stephanie was the one to choose and was scanning the rest of the group. Her eyes locked on Daniel.

He willed his body to communicate his thoughts: *Don't even think about it!*

The message had been received as she continued her scan and landed on poor Mike.

"Right, Adrian. Kiss Mike, with tongues."

Were they teenagers all of a sudden?

Mike just shrugged and moved forward, causing Adrian to back off straight away.

"I'll take a forfeit instead. No offence, Mike."

"Well you know the forfeit is a super shot or you're out of the game," replied Stephanie.

Frank, Jamila and Helen had already departed for bed after refusing the super shot. Judy was having the time of her life and hadn't downed any super shots, quite simply because she'd tongue wrestle anybody. Daniel shuddered when he remembered his last dare. His grandmother would be mortified.

Adrian downed the super shot which was a Long Island Iced Tea, without the coke, sugar syrup or ice. So, a shot of vodka, light rum, tequila, gin and triple sec mixed together and downed in one. Who the hell had come up with that idea? Oh, that would be Callum – the nineteen-year-old with hollow legs, who seemed to be up for anything. Something was telling Daniel to bow out now, yet that male ego refused to be the first man to leave the party. Frank didn't count, as if he'd downed a super shot his heart would've stopped beating.

Adrian returned to the game, although there was now an atmosphere because of Adrian's refusal to participate in the dare, especially as he had happily participated in all other manner of bizarre dares which had come out of the minds of the people in the room. It was now Adrian's turn to spin the bottle and it landed on Meena.

"Truth," she said, a little too quickly. Probably not wanting to tongue wrestle Judy. After a series of stupid childish dares, kissing and groping had become a recurring theme and there was bound to be a further escalation before the end of the night.

"So, Meena why are you a different colour to your sisters? Was your mum shagging about?"

"I just have darker skin tone. We all have the same father."

"Bullshit, you're half Indian or something."

"Mummy says it's a throwback," Sassy interjected.

"A fucking throwback! She's not a dog," laughed Adrian. "Oh, sorry retract that."

"Mate, you're being bang out of order," said Mike, trying to defuse the situation. "It's not your place to question people's private family business."

"Dickhead, in case you haven't noticed, we are playing Truth or Dare."

Swearing always sounded weird coming from such a posh speaking voice, although it was clear that the drink had allowed Adrian's original northern accent to slip through. Adrian must have moved when he was young or been educated at one of those schools which stamped out regional dialects so none of their students graduated sounding common.

Mike shook his head and decided to walk away.

"Fucking pussy," spat Adrian. "I bet you couldn't even take on the arse bandits."

Callum stood up and went straight to Adrian, telling him to shut his mouth. Seeing these three tall men all squaring up to each other was fascinating to watch.

"I feel quite horny watching this," whispered Stephanie in Daniel's ear.

God, he loved this woman. "Think I should go over there, or play to stereotype?"

"Just stay here, babes, I reckon you bruise like a peach."

There were a few more butch exchanges before each alpha male retreated to his corner. Shockingly, Meena and her sisters were adamant on continuing to play, so she spun the bottle – it landed on Daniel.

"Truth or dare?"

"Truth."

"Why are you taking part in this show?"

"For the money," he replied, a little too quickly.

"Okay, nothing to do with you surviving the bombing in that gay bar nine years ago? One of our cousins was killed. I came across your blog."

Daniel noticed everyone looking at him intently. He wasn't ready to talk about it yet; he wanted to be in control of when and how he told his story. He certainly didn't want to talk about it during a mash-up game of spin the bottle and truth or dare, when he had been drinking solidly for four hours. He couldn't deny it either, as this was why he was here, to bring it back into people's minds. He needed to speak, because he had left a really long pause which was getting dangerously close to making the situation even more awkward – if that was possible. He chose to give a holding response, for now.

"You're right. I lost a few friends that night as well. I'm sorry about your cousin though, but maybe now's not the time for us to talk about something so personal?"

Meena nodded her agreement. She looked shamefaced for what she had done. It was clear she had been hurt by an accusation, which had no doubt been muttered behind her back for her entire life. However, she had now been confronted about it directly on national TV. She had then lashed out in retaliation; unfortunately, Daniel had been in the firing line.

The atmosphere felt awkward. Daniel wanted to leave, yet he didn't want to make a big deal out of what had just happened. He had deliberately not looked at Stephanie.

Would she be angry with him for not telling her? He glanced to his right and could see her looking close to tears. He looked around at everyone else; Callum, Mike, Judy and all three sisters had a similar look on their faces. Daniel had been wrong – people hadn't forgotten.

Daniel gave a small smile to everyone and then nodded at Meena before he span the bottle, although he sensed no-one's heart was really in it now.

The bottle landed on Callum.

Could the night get any more awkward?

Callum looked like a startled rabbit in headlights. He had always opted for a dare every time the bottle landed on him. You could see there was part of him that wanted to show solidarity to his fellow neighbours. However, they also needed to move the game on to being fun again and away from this melancholic drama which would be making viewers reach for the gin and a bottle of aspirin. You could literally see the conflict going on behind his eyes.

"Dare!"

Daniel decided at this moment to down his drink. It was some bizarre concoction Claire had put together, which was probably more lethal than the super shot, especially as it was mixed with cherryade to mask its potency. He needed to completely change the mood of the game...

"Do the Full Monty." Fuck – did he just say that out loud?

Daniel reached for a super shot to pass to Callum with an apologetic look on his face. Callum ignored him, stood up and started pulling his clothes off. Claire, Judy, Stephanie and the sisters started clapping and singing stripper music. Adrian decided he needed to use the toilet and Mike just roared with laughter. Callum did his routine – a little too rehearsed, Daniel thought.

Forgetting what he was holding, Daniel downed the drink in his hand – unfortunately his body decided it was not so keen on the super shot, straight after a Claire special and a gazillion tequila shots. Even more unfortunate, was that the super shot decided to regurgitate from Daniel's body in spectacular, uncontrollable, projectile fashion at the exact moment Callum reached his grand finale.

"I can never look at that man again," Daniel groaned.

"Is that because he's bigger than you?"

"What?"

"Did you not see what he was packing?"

"I was too busy throwing up on it."

Stephanie started laughing and then couldn't stop. Daniel couldn't laugh at anything. It was mortification on a new level. When she had calmed down, which took some considerable time, Daniel asked Stephanie to fill in the gaps as he wasn't sure how he got to bed.

"Well, you kept being sick for a while and then passed out."

Great.

"Judy helped me clean up. Callum and Mike carried you upstairs. You threw up on Callum again. He was in the shower for half an hour."

Stephanie had then stayed in the room all night with Daniel in case he got sick again; he had not moved all night, just snored his head off.

"I don't snore."

"Well last night you did, pretty loudly as well."

"How loudly?"

"It sounded like a warthog being rogered by a hippo!"

Daniel stayed in the apartment all day. It was now dark and he was starting to feel a little better. Stephanie had brought food so he hadn't seen Callum, thankfully. Daniel hoped he could save the apologies for the next day when he was fully recovered.

The claxon sounded, meaning there was to be a mandatory task, leaving Daniel's desire for a quiet night alone in tatters. Forget Callum, he would now have to face everyone. He reluctantly joined the rest of the group. There were a couple of friendly digs from Mike about toad in the hole or something, which were probably quite funny, but Daniel's brain still wasn't functioning properly and any form of intellectual witticism was beyond him. Most people were intrigued by what the task could be and seemed less interested in Daniel, which was a blessing.

The screen to the task room slid back and there was Zelda BonBon who looked like Daniel felt – death! She was in a dress which resembled a lampshade. Perhaps she was going for a *Handmaid's Tale* look; instead it looked more like the thing they put on cats and dogs to stop them licking the scar from where their balls once resided. What the hell was Zelda doing here for a daily task?

"Neighbours, we are LIVE for this week's Complex Guvnor Challenge."

There was none of the usual oomph in her opening. Daniel suspected she was either on a major comedown or still wired on some form of opiate.

"The winner of this contest will not be conferring with their fellow neighbours as they will make their decision on who will face execution this week straight away, right here, right now, LIVE."

These live shows had given up with the, "please do not swear," line some time ago and only broadcast after the nine o'clock watershed, for that very reason – was it that time already?

He had made a deal with Stephanie, Helen and Callum

that if any of them won the Guvnorship they would put the two couples up; Frank and Judy would act as ringers. They needed to get rid of Jamila before the complex broke into singles. However, he now felt guilty given Judy had apparently looked after him the night before. He could only hope the challenge didn't play to his strengths and he could avoid being the one to have blood on his hands this week.

"This week's Guvnorship challenge will be a showbiz quiz."

Bollocks!

CHAPTER EIGHT

Felix did his usual late entrance into the morning briefing, causing the obligatory silence from the production crew. Zelda still looked like complete shit. Luckily for her, her monumental cock-up the night before had not been disastrous for the game. Even so, her career was now hanging by a thread and a little charity project Felix had lined up for the summer was likely to now be offered to a more stable pair of hands.

"Right, so we have the two couples up for execution, thanks to Callum winning the Guvnorship challenge and sticking to the deal he had made with the others."

Felix glared at Zelda as he spoke, but she was somewhere else.

"Zelda," he slammed his hands on the table, causing her and everyone to jump.

Unfortunately, as Zelda was not in full use of her nervous system, she slid off the chair under the table.

"Zelda, get the fuck out and if you still want to have a job by the end of the day come and see me after lunch when you've pulled yourself together."

The room was absolutely silent, until a familiar sound came from under the table.

"Is she a-fucking-sleep?"

"I'll get her out and talk to her," Desiree said, moving towards Zelda quickly.

"I need you here for the meeting," barked Felix.

"Emma can cover for me until I get back."

"Fine, but don't be too long." Felix sat down. "Give me the numbers."

Desiree summoned a security guard. He threw Zelda over his shoulder and marched her out the room. There wasn't a flicker from her, just low snoring sounds. There were a few sniggers from the crew. Felix ignored them and nodded for Emma to proceed.

"The live Guvnorship challenge pulled in seven million viewers in the overnights and Get Jamila Out is the number one trend on Twitter in the UK," Emma began.

"Right, I want us to break eight million as an average on the overnights for the second execution, which will be Frank and Judy. Although based on the latest analysis, this is going to have to be the most spectacular comeback of all time."

There was a murmur of agreement from the crew.

"What about the spin the bottle game? I know it didn't go in last night's show because of the live task but it will play up to Mike's likability."

"No, the spin the bottle game was not shown because that is what I instructed."

"But, why? There was so much character development in those few hours and some hilarious scenes."

"Are you questioning my decision?" Felix snapped.

"Yes," Emma replied. "I think it was the wrong decision."

There was a chorus of gasps, like a Mexican wave as what had been said reverberated around the room. This was followed by a lot of nervous twitching and people pressing themselves into the backs of their chairs.

Felix smiled. "Okay, Emma, you have all our attention. How would you play it?"

Emma's face indicated she didn't have the slightest idea of how far over the line she had just stepped; even the deathly silence didn't indicate to her that she could be spending the following month at a food bank.

"I know you want to develop Adrian's character arc, so the stuff with Meena should not be shown, but Frank went to bed early..."

"So did Jamila."

"I'm just getting to that..."

Had she a death wish?

"Frank went to bed earlier than everyone, which plays up to the boring part of his character. Jamila was quite relaxed after a few drinks and it wasn't until she realised she was getting too drunk to keep her guard totally up that she called it a night. There was a lot of typical spin the bottle stuff which will titillate the masses. Judy snogging Daniel will make viewers laugh or vomit, but either way it brings attention on to Judy. Mike was hilarious with some of his dares early on in the game and that's where we should focus. Jamila is never going to redeem herself, she's a money hungry snake and no amount of editing is going to hide that fact, so make Frank and Judy seem boring. Jamila creates conflict which people like and her husband is a great guy."

"What about the later stuff with Daniel?" Felix asked.

"It doesn't feed into the story you have mapped out for Daniel so I'd drop it."

Clever girl.

"But... if Meena recognised him, it's not going to be long before a member of the public connects the dots and blabs all over social media. Once it's out there, we are going to be asked why we suppressed it, especially if Meena mentions it when she's executed."

There were some nods from others in the crew. Felix hoped others weren't going to develop a backbone. It would be tiresome.

"So how do we manage it then?" asked Felix.

"Well, I'm guessing he's going to open up to someone eventually. Probably Stephanie or Callum and it will be soon, so we should just go with that. At least then it's done and we can then put no more focus on it. By the time it comes round to his execution people will be making their voting decisions based on more recent events."

Felix didn't want Daniel's story getting out at all if he could avoid it. Meena would be taken care of when she was executed. Her life would be completely destroyed and she would have no inclination to bring up Daniel's story, and nobody would care – she would be the story.

"Let's just monitor it for now. Cut off spin the bottle before Jamila goes to bed."

"I'd just add one more thing," said Emma.

Felix gave one of his smiles, which resulted in more nervous shuffles nearby.

"The Daniel throwing up on Callum thing is hilarious and helps to explain his behaviour the next day. We can easily edit it so it looks like Jamila is still there and that none of the confrontation in the middle ever happened."

"Fine, do it. Anything else you want to add?"

"No, thank you."

Felix needed to learn more about this one. She reminded him of Desiree when she started out. He wanted to move Desiree into another part of his empire once a safe pair of hands had been found to take over this show for her. He'd get Mrs P to do some digging into Emma's background. It was something he always did with his staff, especially the ones who showed a bit of promise. If he was ever going to trust her, he had to know her vulnerabilities in case she ever stepped out of line.

Later that morning, Felix was sitting in his office waiting for a compos mentis Zelda to arrive. The rest of the morning briefing had run in the usual way. Someone else had decided to take Emma's lead and try to interject when Felix was talking. The difference was that what they said was stupid – they were now unemployed.

Emma had gotten away with it for two reasons: there was something about her that intrigued him, she actually made some intelligent suggestions and Felix wanted to fuck her – okay so that was three things. The last one didn't count though, as Felix had promised Desiree he wouldn't go there.

On the subject of fucking, he needed a catch-up with Lucinda. He had to know what numbers he was playing with in the public vote, although he knew he had one hell of battle on his hands to swing public opinion away from Jamila.

Felix looked over the latest social media commentary and found Debbie and Treehugger were embroiled in another virtual row.

———

More victims to satisfy Felix Modoon's blood lust

Treehugger23: Still can't believe the viewing figures for this show. At the weekend two people's lives are going to be completely destroyed. Jamila and Mike have good jobs and what if they want to have children one day? They'll get bullied in school.

DeliciousDebbie1985: I wouldn't worry about it. Mike

and Jamila are going nowhere. Frank and Judy are the boring ones they'll be out next.

Treehugger23: Don't be ridiculous, they aren't going anywhere. The bookies are saying that Jamila is the least popular neighbour of all time!

DeliciousDebbie1985: It's not about being popular, it's about entertaining people and the old couple are nice and boring. Jamila causes tension – she gets my vote. She won't win at the end, but the public will keep her in for now. I'll definitely be voting against Frank and Judy.

Treehugger23: Well you'll be the only one!

———

Felix looked up as Desiree and a heavily made up Zelda walked into his office.

"I see Debbie is in favour of Frank and Judy being executed next."

"She's not the only one. It's the diehard fans who are keen for that outcome," Desiree replied.

Zelda sat down and Desiree went to leave.

"I'd like you to stay here Desiree, just in case she doesn't hear what I've got to say. And did I actually say you could sit down Zelda?"

Zelda stood up shakily to her feet.

"This is your last warning. I don't give a flying fuck what shit you put up your nose, but when this show is running you stay within your limits. You know we add live shows at the last minute so pull yourself together."

"Sorry, boss," she mumbled pathetically. It was obvious she was having trouble staying vertical.

"I'm going to have to pass on you presenting the celebrity special of *Tone Death* in the summer."

"No please, boss. I'll get my shit together. I promise."

latthew Bonjour is available and he's reliable."

rse, he is, he's boring as fuck," she snapped.

ᴊᴇᴇ, now that's the fire I want to see all the time. Not this pathetic drug-addled mess. Take this," he pushed a card across the desk.

She picked it up, her hands trembling slightly and looked at it. "Is this for rehab or something?"

"Rehab?" he laughed. "Don't be ridiculous. No this is where you can get the good stuff from and then stay within your limits. He is expecting your call. Now piss off and be here on Friday for execution night rehearsal. We should have an idea by then how it's going to go."

Zelda left and Felix motioned for Desiree to sit down.

"I hear Emma held her own today?"

"She got lucky."

Desiree raised an eyebrow. "Well, as long as you don't."

"You know I don't like being told what to do."

"No, you don't. Anyway, I've been doing some research and I think you should look at this."

Desiree passed a folder to Felix. He opened it up and after looking at the *what's the point* page he asked Desiree to leave and said he'd call her when he was ready to discuss it. If anyone passed anything for Felix to read there was always a one-page overview at the front which answered the question *what's the point in me wasting my valuable time reading this?* She had very much answered that question and he was going to need some time to go through all the documents she had compiled before he decided what he would do about it. It looked like the game was getting away from him and he needed to stop that.

Felix puffed on his vape whilst a cigarette burned in the ashtray. He kept switching between the two. It had been a horrendous start to the week. Jamila and Mike had an eighty per cent chance of being executed on Saturday night and he now had to make some drastic decisions in order to swing things in their favour. He'd sown a few seeds with the press, with the exception of Cecil Vonderbeet – that vicious bitch was doing all he could to get Jamila executed. Luckily, he was a lone voice in a saturated world of opinion pieces.

Cecil had a pathological hatred for Jamila and his daily articles were driving a very specific agenda. Felix had asked Mrs P for help again, something he didn't want to do. He couldn't get an update on the voting figures as he'd been doing this regularly after he'd tried so many different ways to swing it the other way. Lucinda was available for an update, but his cock was sore from all the *payments* he'd had to make so far, to just to be told repeatedly that Jamila and Mike would be leaving by an 80/20 vote.

Mrs P called to say she was back in England and would *take care of things*. Felix started to plan out how else things could go if the old couple survived. It was a tricky one. The sisters had to go as a group, it was imperative to their story. No matter what happened, nothing could change that.

He had promised advertisers that he was going to hit ten million by the end of the series and his rates were due to increase as a result of this assumption. He needed a good show with villains and if Adrian was to win, he had to be a villain comes good. Once they went into singles, Claire would not last a public vote – there was not a chance in hell, so he was going to have no tension to drive up the viewing figures. He needed Jamila to get to the final so she could get a spectacular comeuppance when she came third; people would want to watch it.

Someone had suggested turning Daniel into a villain and they were fired for being an idiot. Desiree was ripping her hair out with the continuous staffing issues. As Mrs P was working on the latest execution, her investigation into Emma's background was currently on hold; something Felix would worry about later.

The complex had been quiet for the last couple of days, which had made putting a show together challenging. They had enough unused footage from the previous weekend, which could be woven in to make the show more interesting. Adrian was glued to that walking chlamydia advert again. Felix didn't usually give a toss about who was screwing who on this show as long as it brought in viewers. Adrian had been given a character to play and he was playing it a little too well. Claire was one of the most hated contestants of all time, probably because she was mounting Adrian every hour of the day and night and wailing like a banshee. She was living the fantasy of every pathetic individual who watched this garbage television because it brought joy to their worthless little lives.

CHAPTER NINE

It was execution day.

Daniel couldn't believe that he'd been in the complex for two weeks. He was almost a quarter of the way through the show and if he could survive the next execution he would make it to singles and be able to work with the others to get rid of Adrian. The guy was starting to grate. The causal homophobia was tolerable as that was the way the world was these days; people said what they were thinking and if you were offended by that then it was your problem. The thing that was really starting to get on Daniel's nerves, was Claire. She had wormed her way back into Adrian's bed now he was safe from execution. She was a nymphomaniac and a loud one at that. The sound of her faking her fifteenth orgasm of the day didn't half put you off your lunch.

Daniel had been cordial towards Callum since the whole vomiting debacle and people had moved on, although Mike still thought it was hilarious and liked to bring it up occasionally, particularly if days were slow, which the last few had been. Apart from the daily task which determined whether they were cooking for themselves that night or not, there much going on. It was surprising that they hadn't some additional task or another live show. the last had clearly been a disaster and Daniel was still mildly pissed about it.

The quiz had been going well; it was one of Daniel's strong points and despite feeling like Satan's arsehole from the night before he had quickly eliminated the competition. In the end it had been between him, Mike and Callum. A question came up asking who would be the host of a celebrity version of Felix Moldoon's talent show, *Tone Death*, later this year. Matthew Bonjour was the obvious answer as he had fronted the civilian show from the start and had allegedly signed a three-year-deal, similar to what Zelda had done for *Complex Neighbours*. However, Zelda had eliminated Daniel from the competition and said Mathew Bonjour wasn't going to be the host for much longer. She then refused to give the real answer and said it was a secret and started making loud shushing sounds. Similar to what happens when you creep into your parent's house drunk, accidentally knock something over and then shush at it, with a volume of such enormity that it wakes the entire town.

Despite protesting that he had got the question right, he was out of the competition. Thankfully Callum snatched the victory from Mike. He put the two couples up for execution, so the plan still worked out. Mike had taken it on the chin and expected it after the previous week, although it was clear Jamila felt very differently to her husband.

Unfortunately, Frank and Judy did not take their potential execution well. In fact, Frank got very angry. Callum explained that he expected Jamila and Mike to go and they had only been put up as ringers, as the sisters were certain for the chop when they went up. When Frank questioned that if they were so certain it would go that way then why didn't they put the single women up, Callum didn't handle the pressure very well.

Since that day, Frank and Judy had barely spoken to anyone. They barely ate with anyone else and simply came down into the main complex to compete in tasks and only when they were mandatory. The downside to their sulking, other than making everyone feel like shit for doing it to them, was that their reaction to being put up for the chop would not be well received by the viewing public and could get them executed instead. Jamila would then be really gunning for blood.

"What you thinking about?" asked Stephanie as she plonked herself down next to him.

"Who's gonna go tonight."

"With any luck it'll be Jamila and then hopefully Frank will stop the cold shoulder treatment. Judy seems okay, although you have to talk to her on her own. She said Frank was scared."

"Scared of what, being executed? They can't seriously have expected to win can they?"

"No, I think it's whatever story will come about them when they go."

"Oh, well they knew that would happen anyway. Even happens to finalists if you don't win."

"What's your secret? What Meena mentioned the other night?"

"Well, not anymore. I'm not even going to try to guess. I just told my grandmother everything I've done which she would be embarrassed about so there's nothing left. Couldn't care less what anyone else thinks."

Daniel didn't want to talk about the other night and was hopeful that Stephanie would take the hint.

"Bet that was fun telling your grandmother all that."

"Are you taking the piss?"

"Of course – I should have done that with my mum. Oh well, just have to wait and see what happens. I haven't killed anyone or done anything illegal."

Daniel raised an eyebrow.

"Well, I haven't done anything illegal which would be career limiting."

"That's more believable."

"So what's happening with you and Callum? Seems to have gone a bit cold."

"I'm not interested."

"In the outside world perhaps?"

"I dunno, he's ten years younger than me."

"I fail to see the point you are trying to make here."

Daniel didn't know how to respond to that so they just looked at each other for a moment and then started laughing. It was one of those infectious laughs that once it starts, you can't stop it. Tears were rolling down their faces and every time they stopped laughing they'd look at each other and it would start again. They were finally brought out of their laughing fit when someone asked them what was so funny – it was Callum.

Awkward!

As the time for the execution approached, everyone started to get ready for their moment on live TV. Those up for execution went all out. Frank and Judy were dressed like they were going ballroom dancing, as were Mike and Jamila – must be a hetero thing.

They took their places in the execution tubes. Daniel

remembered that feeling all too well. Mike and Judy had said their goodbyes. Frank ignored everyone and Jamila just said goodbye to everyone except for Callum and Daniel. If it was edited correctly, she would probably come across as a homophobic bitch.

Zelda was back on form and her usual chirpy self. No doubt she had had some sleep.

"Right, do our couples have any last words before we reveal the result of tonight's vote?"

Both couples shook their heads.

"Right, well let's get on with it then. The couple leaving us tonight are..."

The dramatic pause was even longer than normal as Zelda appeared to have her timing out. Either that or she was walking in slow-mo. Zelda put her hands on the big red lever and looked at both couples for a brief second before pulling the lever.

Frank and Judy disappeared from sight.

Bollocks.

The tubes lifted and released Mike and Jamila. He looked pleased. She looked mutinous and stormed towards Daniel, with her finger pointing.

"You're next you fucking cunt."

Zelda went into pure professional mode and turned to the camera, apologising profusely for Jamila's outburst. You can shag noisily, openly bully people, show erect penises and even cannibalism documentaries weren't unusual these days, but one thing is still a big no, no; dropping the C-bomb on live TV with no chance to warn people that it's coming.

Daniel chose not to react to Jamila. It wasn't that they were on live TV, it was just that he never saw the point in reacting to such aggressive behaviour in the same manner. Well, not since he was a teenager.

"You stupid fucking bitch, do that again and you'll regret it." Zelda snarled at Jamila.

Evidently the live feed had now been cut.

"Right, you lot. Enjoy your night and I'll see you in a few days."

Jamila still looked seething. Mike looked embarrassed. Claire had stopped groping Adrian now they weren't on live TV. Helen was moving slowly towards Meena. Sassy and Hope were giggling amongst themselves. Callum and Stephanie still look stunned, whether that was at Jamila's survival, her C-bomb or Zelda's response he wasn't sure – probably a combination of all three.

"Oh Daniel," Zelda shouted, as she was about to walk through the exit. "Frank and Judy got fifty-two percent of the vote. Good luck!" she smiled and left.

"Fifty-two per cent, the lying cow," screamed Jamila. "There is no way that we would have almost gone against those boring old fuckers."

"Honey, come on. Let's go upstairs so we can calm down." Mike tried to guide her upstairs.

"Keep away from me. This is your fault. *I'm* going upstairs. Just leave me on my own for a bit."

She stormed upstairs, leaving Mike looking crestfallen. Daniel decided to clear the air and asked Mike for a quiet word, which he agreed to. They went up to the single men's apartment.

"You don't need to apologise for anything, Daniel. It wasn't even you who put us up."

"It was my idea, though."

"I figured as much, but we put you up, so it's only fair and it is a competition."

"You two are both strong competitors. You know how this game works."

"Of course and it doesn't matter what anyone says, everyone wants to win that million quid."

"It wouldn't hurt, no."

"That's not your main reason for being here though, is it?"

"No."

"Do you want a beer?"

"Sure, there are some in the fridge."

Mike took out a beer for each of them, passed one to Daniel and asked him to sit down.

"I'm sorry you had to experience something like that, mate, must have been... well, I can't even think of a word."

"It's the guilt that still gets to me."

"What do you have to feel guilty about?"

"I survived and they didn't."

"Your friends?"

"It was my twentieth birthday and it was about eleven o'clock. I was having a boogie with my mates. There was a group of six of us. We had all grown up together. We were the four poofs in our year at school and we all gravitated towards each other, long before anyone came out. We had our two fag hags as well. We were like a clique. You ever watched an episode of that vintage programme *Friends* and wanted to have a group of friends who were that close and integral to each other's lives?"

Mike nodded.

"Well, we had that. It was very special and we were all out celebrating. I went outside to call my grandmother to wish her Happy New Year. It was the first birthday since my mum had died, but she understood I wanted to be out with my friends. I didn't want to wait until midnight as you can never get through to anyone. Well, you couldn't back then anyway. When I came back, I went to the bar. It wasn't even my round, but I was just feeling good after a shit year and wanted to enjoy the celebrations."

"Do you remember what happened?"

"Not really. Apparently I was thrown behind the bar, which is where they found me and I woke up in hospital. When I went back to the club a couple of days later, it had been levelled to the ground. The bomb took out the supporting beams that held the upper bar up from the main dance floor. Then the whole lot came down. That's where my friends were. They didn't stand a chance."

Daniel couldn't stop the tears. He then heard a noise and looked up. Stephanie and Callum were stood there. The look on their faces told him that they had heard most, if not all of what he had said.

The weeks following the bombing were the hardest. First, attending five different funerals within two weeks and then the way it was just tagged as a terrorist attack when there was never any link found between the bomber and any terrorist group. In fact there was very little known about him, still to this day. It was like there was a complete media blackout. The story was off the news within three weeks and there was a minor mention at the one-year anniversary and then nothing.

Daniel believed that people had forgotten or simply didn't care. That's why he was here. Maybe if it had some publicity, he would finally get some answers about why – that was the question that still wasn't answered. Why had Henry Parker, an eighteen-year-old art student from Essex, walked into a London gay bar on New Year's Eve and killed over a hundred people?

CHAPTER TEN

"That is never broadcast."

Felix walked away in disgust at the outpouring of emotion from his production crew. None of them were a worthy successor. They could never have a business mind when telling a story. They were too swayed by their emotions. People ruled by their emotions were destined for failure.

Felix passed the debrief room and saw Frank and Judy being interviewed by Zelda. This would later be released online. The live interview in front of a baying mob, booing for the sake of it was a thing of the past. It was easier to drop the contestants down a tube and give them a quick interview which could be edited to fit the story and released online later. People were notorious for not following the script, especially with live TV.

Once they were interviewed, the ex-neighbours were taken to a nearby hotel to wait for their lives to be completely destroyed from the press release – now *that* was entertainment.

Felix had to play it differently now, as the story of Frank and Judy's septuagenarian pornography and swingers club had

ked early in order to sway the vote and even then it
ı been too close. This left very little to release after
the execution. However, a researcher had struck gold and
earned a hefty pay rise and bonus to boot. Judy had participated in some low-budget German fetish porn in her twen-
ties, before she met Frank. Both of them had been married
before, very young; they had met and embarked on a scandalous affair. Well, for the time it was a scandal as Judy had
been in a position of trust at the local church and Frank had
been a parishioner. They had been together ever since. Not
really a juicy story in its own right, but the porn angle would
build on the previous story and make out that it was Judy
who had corrupted poor Frank. It wasn't Felix's best, but it
would do.

For that reason they had been briefed about what had
already been released to the press. Unfortunately, the lawyers
had said this was a must – people having legal rights was so
limiting at times. Their lives were still ruined, so giving them
an early heads up was only a mild irritant.

"Felix," shouted Desiree from behind as she scurried to
catch him up. "Let's talk in your office."

They walked in silence until they arrived at Felix's office
and shut the door. It was safe here and Felix knew that for a
fact as he had the place swept for bugs several times a day.
Some would call it paranoia. He called it strategy.

"We're going to have to get Frank and Judy out of the
country," remarked Desiree.

"Why? It's only a bit of porn and granny orgies."

"It's worse than that. You know those films that Judy did
fifty years ago? Well, one of them was a snuff movie."

"What – how did you find this out?"

"The *Daily Mail* just broke it."

"They did fucking what? Fire Jeremy immediately – no
severance pay."

"The Jeremy you just promoted and double॰
You want me to terminate him without notice? I
a tribunal claim?"

"Let him claim, we'll pay it off later. In fact, fire the entire research team. I should have known about this, not the fucking *Daily Mail.*"

"Don't be ridiculous."

"Excuse me," he grabbed Desiree by the throat. "Fine, well then you're fired."

"No she isn't. Put the girl down, Felix."

Mrs P was standing in the doorway. Felix let go immediately. Desiree gasped for breath and then quickly moved away from Felix.

"Desiree, go and sort yourself out and then see that Frank and Judy get out of the country. Apparently, Judy's friend lives on the Costa del Sol, so they think that would be good for them... I know, they were told that it was full of Brits, but they were adamant. Give them the full security compliment and I've briefed the pilot so they can go tonight on the jet."

"They're not going on my fucking jet," Felix spat.

"Quiet, Felix and don't use that disgusting language in front of me. Just go and get it done please, Desiree, and of course you're not fired. Must be a record now! How many times has he fired you?"

"This was lucky number thirteen," Desiree croaked, still holding her throat. "What about Jeremy?"

"Best to follow through on that one, but tell him we'll give him six months tax free on the new salary. He knows how it works here, he'll understand. Tell him that he'll still get a reference, but it'll need to come from you."

Desire nodded and left.

"Now, sit down Felix."

He was fuming that he had been trumped by another media outlet and had wrongly taken out his anger on Desiree.

she was one of the few people who really understood his approach to work and how successful it was. She also knew Felix's moods and how to handle them. She would have been re-instated in the cold light of day. She always was. What he didn't like was being emasculated in front of his staff by this woman stood in front of him. All five foot of her, with her white old lady hair, psychotherapist glasses, perfectly made-up face and old lady cardigan. She was the stereotypical grandmother and at eighty years old she was indeed a grand-mother, and yet she was the only person in the world who could control Felix and she still held a hefty stake in his media empire, a stake he had been trying to get her to relin-quish for years.

"I came back to sort out this mess you've created. You're losing control, Felix."

"I don't think so. It's running to script so far."

"Only because you keep changing the script. Adrian nearly left in the first week and Daniel North is the bookies' favourite to win."

"A minor blip. I'm all over it."

"The only thing you're all over is cocaine. How much have you had tonight? In fact, don't bother answering, it'll only be another lie. Felix, I only agreed to Daniel North being cast on this show because you said you could control it. I don't know why you had to bring him into this, especially when this was supposed to be Adrian's year. You're trying to do two things at once and you can't – typical man, unable to multi-task."

"I've got it under control. The sisters will be out next week and then we'll be in singles. It's easier to control the action then."

"Yes, but I'll be making some changes to ensure the sisters go this week. We're not missing the full impact of that story. So, we're not leaving anything to chance with a public vote."

"We can't rig the vote. You're the one who has always stopped me from trying to do that."

"We won't be rigging the public vote. We won't be having a public vote for the execution this week."

"But it's been published that there will be a public vote each week."

"I know Felix, I wrote those rules. I was very careful to say that it wouldn't necessarily be an execution vote each time."

"You've got my attention."

Felix walked into his apartment and threw the keys down on the side. He had been annoyed on the drive back from the studio that yet again he had allowed that woman to take control, yet the more he thought about her plan, the more genius he had found it.

Daniel's talk with Mike had been released online before he left and social media had gone crazy talking about Daniel's *emotional journey*. The press had jumped on it and published extracts from Daniel's blog. The story was also being picked up by international outlets and Daniel's popularity was soaring. This was exactly what Felix had wanted to avoid. It was all out in the open now and Felix had to be seen as driving the bandwagon, not slamming the brakes on.

Frank and Judy's story was already old news and it was likely that they could form a new swingers club in the Costa del Sol, have a new life and there was no nasty taste in the mouths of the public for destroying the lives of a pair of grandparents. Children and old people were still a no-go area for screwing people over.

Mrs P might be the only person who could quickly push all of Felix's trigger buttons, yet he still trusted her implicitly. There was a lot more work to do for this story to play out over its new course and it was imperative that nobody else would know what the new plan was, even Desiree.

Felix made an early start the next morning. They had a special live mid-week show to prepare for and he needed to focus. Unfortunately, his focus was pulled by something he saw unfold on the screens. As it was early the only person awake in the complex was Adrian who was doing his morning workout in what looked like his underwear. Still, it would appeal to the masses. One of the reasons Felix had paid an absolute fortune for the best fitness and diet experts was to get Adrian into the best physical shape of his life. This would guarantee him certain victory from a fickle, jealous and obese viewing public.

Adrian had finished his workout and was making his way back to the apartments when he passed the kitchen and saw Daniel making himself a cup of tea. Felix thought he would just keep walking, but he saw Adrian stop and then start walking towards Daniel. Felix ran into the main studio from his office to see there were only two staff manning the screens. He recognised them both as long-termers so when he told them to take a break they didn't question it.

"Morning Daniel, could we have a chat?"

Felix saw Daniel hesitate for second before nodding and then offering Adrian a cup of tea, which he accepted. Daniel busied himself making tea with the sound of the clattering teaspoon breaking the awkward silence. Once the tea was finished, he put it down in front of Adrian who was sitting on one of the breakfast stools. Adrian took a sip and commented on how good it was. Felix was getting irritated. The producers wouldn't be away for too long and this conversation needed to hurry the fuck up.

"First, I'd like to apologise Daniel, for being a complete prick the last couple of weeks."

What the fuck was he doing?

"I know we didn't get off to a great start and I'd like to explain why I behaved the way I did. I think then you might understand and hopefully we can get on better."

Shit.

"You see…"

"Could Adrian come to the Confession Booth immediately?" Felix bellowed into the loudspeaker.

"For fuck sake," Adrian snapped. "They do pick their timing well don't they?"

Daniel shrugged.

"Can you wait here? I won't be too long."

"Sure."

Adrian got up and made his way to the Confession Booth, still half-naked. The guy really had no body issues at all – maybe Felix had made him too confident. He would need to bring him back down to reality, with a bump.

It was a risk, but Felix had to talk to him. He waited behind the door, watching via his phone, which was linked to the studio cameras, and saw Adrian come through into to the Confession Booth alone and sit down on the Confession Couch. This had been Felix's idea after series one. It had paid off in series two when one couple had sex on it. They knew it wasn't private, although it was private from their respective spouses who were in the complex. That was until Felix had the footage beamed into the complex. It had been a huge scandal. The viewers had loved it. The only scandals on this series, so far, had been the post-execution press releases and subsequent fall-out. However, the surprise live show that Mrs P had come up with would give them some great headlines. What Felix had to do now was ensure that any scandal emanating from this series did not have Adrian at the epicentre.

He initiated the door lock so Adrian couldn't get out and killed the microphone and camera feed to the Confession Booth. He would literally have a couple of minutes before someone picked up on it and investigated. He burst through the door, grabbed Adrian by the throat and lifted him off his feet. Felix might be slightly shorter than Adrian, but he was a very strong guy. Adrian looked fearful, which was exactly what Felix wanted as he slammed him against the wall away from the eye-line of the camera, in case someone managed to turn it back on.

"What the fuck where you just about to say to Daniel North?" whispered Felix.

"I wasn't going to tell him about our arrangement."

"That isn't answering my question."

"I'm not homophobic and I don't like people thinking I am."

Felix let go of him, poking a finger into his chest so he stayed put.

"You're only playing a character. That's what everyone does on these shows. Nobody is genuine on them, ever."

"Daniel is."

"Really? There's a lot Daniel North hasn't told people about himself. He's just as guarded as the rest of them. So what were you going to say to him?"

"I was going to say that I thought playing the alpha male character would help me win. I wanted the money, but that wasn't who I really was. I still want to win the money, but I want to do it being the real Adrian."

"The real Adrian? Do you even know who that is? You

can't even see how much you've changed these last six months whilst you've been preparing for this show. Why on earth have you come to the Confession Booth with virtually no clothes on?"

"I didn't have time to change and I knew it was your voice calling me."

That was a worry as Felix thought he'd disguised it.

"You'll stick to the script you've been given, or the deal is off."

"The deal is not off. There is a new deal."

"Who the fuck do you think you're talking to?"

"I've got a backup plan."

"Really? Enlighten me," said Felix, removing his finger.

"I'm going to win this show on my own merit."

Felix laughed in his face. "Who's going to decide that?"

"The public."

Felix laughed again. "No, Adrian, I decide who wins this show. You have got some brains in that pretty head of yours, haven't you?"

"Well fine, then I'll take my execution on the chin like everyone else. If I don't win you can give me the money anyway."

"Are you taking the piss? You already turned the money down."

"If I don't leave this show with one million pounds in my pocket then those conversations we had, which were all recorded, will be released to the press. And, I'll tell them about the deal you had with my mother."

"What deal?"

"Well when she was dying, she said you owed her and you'd look after me. But she told me to protect myself and not to trust you. So I did."

Felix wasn't sure whether to believe him or not. As soon

as he left he'd have someone look for those recordings, if they even existed.

"And don't think you'll be able to find them. Those recordings are safely tucked away."

"And what? If anything happens to you, they'll be released to the press or sent to the police?"

"Don't be ridiculous, this isn't a movie or another one of your TV shows. This is my life. I need that money for a fresh start."

"Fine, but as soon as the house breaks into singles you're getting voted out. You can then have your money and piss off abroad like I originally suggested."

"So I'll be out of here at the end of next week."

"That's the plan, for now, but I don't want you chumming up with Daniel North."

"I'm not going to play the homophobic prick again either."

"You don't have to, just don't become his best mate. Keep it... cordial, and leave it at that."

"Why do you hate him so much? It's like an obsession with you."

"That's my business. Trust me, the less you know, the better."

"I better be out of here by the end of next week."

"You will be, just keep the clothes on. We have a lot of shallow viewers who would still vote for you even if you murdered a kitten as long as you were topless. Be distant enough and competitive enough to still get put up for execution. Leave the rest to me. Now wait a couple of minutes before going back."

Felix left through the side door and made his way through the camera run to the studio. He saw a group of producers crowded around the monitors. The one to the Confession Booth was still blank, so he went over to them to find out what was going on. He told them all to piss off and leave it to him; they dutifully complied. He waited a few minutes before turning everything back on. By this time, Adrian was back in the complex and had thankfully found some clothes.

He listened in as Adrian picked up his conversation with Daniel. It was as they'd agreed. They shook hands and Daniel went over to Stephanie with a cup of tea, as she was now awake and sitting on the sofa. Adrian sat for a minute watching them and then left the communal area, returning to his apartment, lying down on the king-sized bed. Felix watched him look up at the camera, hold up two fingers and smile. It looked like he was telling the camera to fuck off, but the real message was clear; Felix had two weeks to get Adrian out of the complex.

CHAPTER ELEVEN

It had been an irritating few days. Daniel and Callum had been snarled at by Jamila whenever she was alone with them. She had made it clear that they were next and would be up against the single women. Jamila claimed that even if the men survived the vote, Daniel would still lose his best friend and that would completely *destroy him*. Perhaps Daniel wasn't quite the drama queen his friends and family had pegged him as his entire life; Jamila was setting the bar very high for such a title. She also wasn't the most calculating villain, as now everyone knew her game plan and could develop a counter move.

The single men and women were now adamant that Jamila and Mike would be up again with the sisters as a buffer. Helen was less keen as she was still harbouring an unrequited love for Meena and in denial about it. She would throw in the odd reference to some man she'd had *intimate intercourse* with. However, these statements were becoming less frequent and for that Daniel was thankful. Hearing Helen talk about her heterosexual love-ins, whether made up or not, felt even more uncomfortable than the time his grandmother had asked him what rimming was.

Adrian was trying to show he'd had a character reversal, although Daniel didn't trust him. Callum was being a moody teenager and Daniel still couldn't get a handle on him. At times he seemed very mature for his age and at others he came across as just another entitled teenager who didn't like not getting his own way. He was sulking over the fact that he felt guilty over Frank and Judy's execution and that it was all Daniel's fault for making him put them up for the chop. Daniel had been clear that Callum was an adult who could have changed his mind if he wanted and he needed to own his decisions and not try to pass the blame to someone else. If he kept doing that he wouldn't get very far in life. The tough love advice approach had not gone down well and Daniel made a mental note to take more time to censor what he was thinking in future when it came to Callum. This younger generation might say what they think, but they certainly didn't enjoy being told a few home truths about themselves. Daniel wasn't sure how they were going to cope in the wild once they left the protective bubble of their family homes.

The only constant over the past few days had been Stephanie, who could easily hold her own in any confrontation. She never raised her voice or showed visible signs of anger. She must have tricked the producers into letting her onto the show. There is no way they would have willingly chosen someone as logical and considered as a neighbour; either that, or she was a latent sociopath.

Daniel and Stephanie now shared a bed every night and would be up until the early hours just chatting about their lives. Stephanie had three older brothers who were very protective of her and they were not, as Stephanie had put it, moronic meat-headed pricks.

.   .   .

It was still early, for them, so they were chatting in the lounge area of the apartment. They were both on the sofa, using the coffee table as a footstool, sharing a blanket.

"What do you think the Guvnorship challenge will be?" Stephanie asked Daniel.

"Dunno, they've done a physical and a mental. Perhaps it will be physical again."

"Well, something's going on because it's Tuesday night and we usually have the Guvnorship challenge on a Monday."

"They're probably trying to avoid a scheduling clash or something. Anyway, we know who everyone is putting up."

"Except the sisters," said Stephanie.

"If the sisters win then we're safe. You girls and the snake will be up."

"How do you know that?"

"Sassy told me," replied Daniel.

"And you believe her?"

"No reason not to and besides if there's a secret alliance we don't know about then it'll break the monotony a bit."

"Jamila and Claire seem to be out of their alliance."

"I'm sure there's still something going on there," said Daniel.

"Well, not if she puts us up as we'll go over you three. It's all women and poofs who watch this. We'll be finished. People vote with their groins and wanker or not, Adrian is hot."

"Well I wouldn't... actually who am I kidding, that he is."

They both laughed as Callum walked in.

"What's so funny?"

"Adrian," Stephanie replied.

"What's he done now?"

"Being a fuckwit and looking gorgeous."

Callum smiled, getting the joke. "Stephanie, can you give us a few minutes? I'd like to talk to Daniel."

Daniel hoped she would ignore his request as he didn't want to get into the whole *let's talk about us* melodrama right now.

"Of course," she replied, getting up. "I'll leave you boys to it."

Bitch!

Callum waited for a few seconds after Stephanie left and made sure that she wasn't eavesdropping, before he sat down. He put his hand on Daniel's leg which felt awkward and exhilarating all at the same time.

"We need to talk about us."

The next morning, Daniel felt a lot better. He had cleared the air with Callum. There had been a slightly awkward moment when Callum had moved in for a kiss. It was brief and Daniel was clear that he didn't want anything to happen whilst they were in the complex. He had come in for one reason and that's what he wanted people asking him about when he left, not his romance with some fit, young thing.

"You think I'm fit?" asked Callum.

"Well, yes of course, but like I said..."

Callum gently put two fingers on Daniel's lips to stop him talking.

"Well then, you can take me out for dinner in few weeks and I expect something top of the range, as you'll be able to afford it with your winnings."

"Don't be ridiculous."

"You don't think you'll win? Everyone else does."

"What?"

"Well, everyone who is not completely deluded."

"I'm not going to win. It's not why I came in here."

"Exactly – and that's why you're going to win."

"Like a sympathy vote?"

"Definitely not – it's because you're genuine and likeable, and funny. People like to laugh."

"Other people here are all those things. Mike will win, if he ends up as a single competitor, or you, or even Adrian. Stephanie would win over me by a landslide."

There was a knock on the door.

"You boys decent?" asked Stephanie, coming in with her hands over her eyes.

"Of course we are," replied Daniel.

"Shame."

"Stephanie," said Callum. "Tell Daniel that he's the one who's going to win."

"Of course, that's a no brainer."

"I don't agree."

"Well agree or not, it's fact, babes. Nobody else stands a chance."

"I think you will both finish ahead of me. In fact, I think you'll be the final two."

"Really?" asked Stephanie, smiling. "And who will be first and who will be second?"

"Fortunately, that's for the public to decide and not me."

"And you'll be third then I suppose?"

"No, I won't make the final. It'll be one of the villains."

"Not Jamila? I can't live with her for another seven weeks, I'll be on a murder charge."

Daniel laughed. "It could be her, or Claire, or even Adrian. What do you think, Callum?"

"Well, if you think Jamila might be in the final then Mike could well be the winner instead."

"Mike is a lovely bloke, so manly and rough, but he's a gentleman."

"Down girl," said Daniel.

"Oh, piss off."

"The lady doth protest too much."

"You know what I mean. Mike is a top bloke. He'll pull in votes. If he makes it into singles then he might win, although I'd prefer it to be one of you."

"Perhaps, but hopefully Mike and Jamila will be out next," added Daniel. "Shame, as I like Mike as well."

"He could do a lot better than her," snarled Stephanie.

"Oh I bet he could."

Daniel and Callum were both laughing.

"Are you two gonna behave? Look, we need to think about how this is going to play out and we need the numbers. If Jamila and Mike go next then there are nine, so we need another two on our side. So who do you think?"

"Well, I'm not forming an alliance with Adrian or Claire. I might catch something."

"We don't have to decide now," Daniel butted in. "But we do need to think about it before the next execution. Whenever the hell that is. It's after ten o'clock now so they won't do a Guvnorship challenge tonight. What are they playing at? I thought they didn't mess with the format anymore."

"Of course they mess with it, despite what they say. It'll be tomorrow now."

"Yeah, you're probably right. Anyway let's go and join the others so they don't think we've been plotting behind their backs."

They all left the apartment together and went downstairs to the communal area. Jamila was nowhere to be seen and based by the glazed look in his eyes Mike was nursing his umpteenth beer. The three sisters were present, Sassy and Hope were playing a card game on the table and howling with laughter. On closer inspection, they appeared to be playing snap. Helen was in the corner, in the snug area with Meena, having a very intense conversation. Helen's hand was stretched across the back of the sofa and slowly inching closer to Meena. It was very slow, like the minute hand on a clock and you had to look very closely to spot it. Claire was nowhere to be seen, either. That couldn't be a coincidence. Or perhaps Claire was being shagged stupid by Adrian again, although there were no vocal histrionics reverberating around the complex. Still, a night without the three villains, as they had now been dubbed, was not necessarily a bad thing.

The following evening, the claxon sounded for the start of the Guvnorship challenge and Daniel groaned. It was late, so that meant a live show. This should mean the challenge would be quick, and hopefully painless. Everyone made their way down to the communal area where Zelda was waiting for them.

"Welcome to your Guvnorship challenge," shouted Zelda.

This was unnecessary as everyone was about two feet away from her.

"We are going live in a minute. Just stay where you are and we'll do the big reveal once we are live, Live, LIVE."

It was hard not to get caught up in the moment. These high-stakes tasks got the adrenalin pumping and gave you a conversation piece for the next few days.

"Ladies and gentlemen, we are LIVE from the complex for a very special Guvnorship task. Now before I reveal your task, I have to tell you that in order to win, your entire team needs to get to the finish line. If any of you get to the end before your teammates you'll have to wait for them before you can step onto the victory platform.

"And in the balance of fairness, the teams of three can choose someone to sit out this challenge. The boys already have to bench Callum as he can't win a Guvnorship task two weeks in a row. Ladies and sisters, it's time for you to pick someone. You have thirty seconds to confer."

The sisters decide to bench Meena. She didn't appear to

have much say in the matter, as they didn't even confer. There was some gesticulating from the single women until Helen walked away from the group, sitting down next to Meena.

"The winning team will win a very special Guvnorship, but the losing team will also get a very special prize."

Why didn't any of that sound appealing?

"Are you ready?"

There was a murmur through the group.

"I said *are you ready?*"

The murmur became a polite whoop so Zelda would get on with the challenge. The doors slid back from a different place to the other tasks. It was a part of the studio they hadn't seen before and it was enormous. In front of them were rows and rows of hedges – it was a maze.

It looked about the size of two football pitches so not too horrendous, although Daniel's sense of direction left a lot to be desired. This would not end well. It looked like a traditional maze with ten-foot-high hedges so Adrian and Mike wouldn't have an advantage. Daniel assumed he would be able to work, begrudgingly, with Adrian to tackle the maze. Hopefully he did have a sense of direction. However, it was not be as Zelda instructed them to all take different corners of the maze. She explained the rules and said she would see them with their benched teammates in the middle.

Daniel was at top right corner of the maze with Jamila – that was not deliberate by the producers of course, despite Zelda calling it *random*. Mike and Adrian were at the diagonal opposite entrance. Stephanie and Sassy took another corner with Claire and Hope in the bottom left. The claxon sounded. Jamila shot off like a British holidaymaker at an all-inclusive buffet. Daniel was choosing to pace himself so he didn't tire too early if he hit lots of dead ends. Jamila was already doubling back on the way she came and raced past Daniel again with that determined look on her face. He could follow her or see why she turned back. He walked for a moment and then saw the dead end. Before turning back he stopped and remembered what Zelda had said…

"The only rule in the maze is that there are no rules. Get to the centre and don't be last."

He looked around at the hedges and saw one wasn't as tight as the others so he touched it, realising at this point that it was all artificial. He puts his hands in the gap and pulled them apart – it opened with ease. They said they were no rules so this shouldn't be cheating. Daniel climbed up the metal frame which connected the hedges and got his bearings for the centre. He then pulled the metal frame apart and headed in that direction using the same tactic all the way. Within less than five minutes he was at the centre of the maze with Zelda looking all excited and bouncy. Callum looked chuffed, as did Helen and Meena. Zelda asked him how he made it so quickly, so he told her what he'd done – it would be on camera anyway. She howled with laughter and said it was a brilliant tactic and hoped the others would take a similar initiative, as the live broadcast only lasted an hour.

Daniel sat down next to Callum. They couldn't do anything until Adrian was through the maze.

"You hopeful about Adrian making it through first?" asked Callum.

"Well, he's strong. He could even scale all the hedges if he wanted to, as long as he remembers that there are no rules."

Callum went to say something but was interrupted by Zelda.

"Someone's coming," she squealed.

Daniel and Callum stood up and moved towards the podium in the middle, in case it was Adrian who came out first, but it was not to be. However, if it couldn't be Adrian, then it being Stephanie was the next best thing. The boys sat back down and Stephanie went for her chat with Zelda before joining them.

"Shouldn't you be sat with your teammate?" Callum asked.

"I didn't want to intrude!"

They looked over and saw Helen's hand on Meena's thigh. There was some intense eye contact and low muttered conversation going on. The hand was on the move again and if another person didn't get out of the maze soon, it would be the first live broadcast of a woman being fingered by another woman, who claimed to have never met a gay person.

"Someone else is coming," screamed Zelda.

Helen was told to get her arse over to Stephanie so they could take the prize if it was Claire. The boys were ready for Adrian, but it was not to be – Hope was the next to arrive. Unfortunately, she was closely followed by Jamila. This was somewhat mollified by the look on her face when she realised that not only had Daniel and Stephanie beat her to the centre of the maze, but so had one of the sisters, meaning her team were the last to have their first person arrive.

Every team now got into position near the podium. Whoever was next through the maze would be on the winning team and have the power in the complex. After what seemed like an hour, but can't have been more than two minutes, there was that familiar rustle. Zelda's excitement went up a few dozen notches. Who was it going to be?

It was Mike!

There was a collective groan as Mike ran forward to his triumphant wife who looked like the cat didn't just get the cream, but the cow's udders were her personal source of protein. They ran forward and pushed the button.

"Like I said, you're next." Jamila looked straight at Daniel.

"Congratulations, Mike and Jamila, you are Complex Guvnor for this week and you win the special prize of immunity from next week's execution."

There was another groan from the rest of the contestants. The thought of Jamila having the power again and being immune for the next execution was too much to contemplate.

"There's definitely something going on. They've never given immunity before," said Stephanie who had sidled up to Daniel following Jamila's victory.

"You read my mind."

"What do you think it could be?"

"I've got an i—"

Adrian burst through the hedges looking very sweaty, in fact so sweaty that he had removed a few layers whilst working his way through the maze and was now wearing a tight white vest.

"You're drooling," whispered Callum in Daniel's ear.

"Piss off."

They walked forward to greet Adrian and then stepped onto the platform to push the button.

"Congratulations lads, you are safe."

Daniel looked at Stephanie as the realisation dawned. Although Daniel didn't want anyone to experience what was about to happen, if it had to happen to anyone who was left, then it had to be the sisters.

"What do you mean they are safe?" snapped Jamila.

"Someone else is coming," said Zelda, ignoring Jamila.

There was a rustle in the bushes again and Claire appeared. She had a cut on her cheek and looked dishevelled. Stephanie ran forward to help her and shouted at Helen to follow suit.

"Helen, you're on that team," Daniel snapped.

She quickly ran over and they helped Claire to the centre of the podium and pressed the button.

"Congratulations girls – you are safe."

"Why do you keep saying that? What does that mean?" barked Jamila.

"What do you think she means?" replied Callum.

"I think it means we are looking at a shock execution," Mike said to his wife.

"But that's not fair. I won, it's up to me... I mean *us* who goes."

She glared at Daniel and missed the look of disgust on her husband's face, clearly embarrassed by her behaviour.

It wasn't long before Sassy made her way through the hedges, being helped by one of the security crew. She didn't look good. There were no cuts like Claire, but she was clearly in a highly distressed state and was having difficulty with her breathing.

"Right girls, bad luck, please stand on the platform and claim your prize."

"Are you for real?" said Stephanie. "Can't you see the state she's in and you're just going to—"

"I'd stop right there, Stephanie. You are not the one presenting this show. I will give the commentary."

Daniel couldn't believe it when Zelda continued to insist that they move forward and *collect their prize.* Sassy was in no state to know what was going on. Hope was oblivious, well to everything in life really.

Meena knew what was about to happen, well she must have because she rushed forward to Helen, grabbed her face and kissed her on the lips.

There was a stunned silence – even Adrian didn't make a comment.

"Goodbye, Helen. I'll wait for you."

She then rushed over to her sisters and told them what was about to happen. They both started crying. Zelda screamed at them to press the button. There were no good-byes – it was brutal and cruel. Sassy was hysterical and Meena, always the quiet one, showed her true strength as her sisters made their way to the platform.

There was still a look of confusion on Helen's face, as she hadn't realised yet what was about to happen. Everyone else did. It was a horrible way to go, with no warning. Everyone's face showed a mixture of sadness, guilt and relief that it hadn't been them. Even Claire and Adrian looked rightfully distressed by what they were witnessing. Jamila seemed to only care about losing her power over who would be going home.

Meena whispered to her sisters again and Sassy's breathing calmed. Hope stopped crying. Meena stood in the middle, her sisters by her side, as she reached forward and pressed the button; the floor opened up beneath them and they were gone.

CHAPTER TWELVE

Felix looked around at the stunned silence from his production crew watching what had just unfolded. It had been sensational TV. He couldn't have predicted Helen and Meena's kiss, yet it all added to the drama.

It had all gone as planned. They'd had to move a few hedges to block Adrian's path so Mike could get to the finish-line first. Claire had to be literally told to go through the hedges, but this was off camera. Fortunately, her getting her top caught on the hedge and falling arse over tit and cutting her face was caught on camera and would soon be a trending GIF across social media. Jamila having immunity for the following week would make her unbearable and therefore great for ratings. Felix was back in control.

He looked up at the screens as he sensed something was going on. Zelda had started explaining the twist in the game and how the Complex Guvnor would work, as well as being split into singles. However, nobody was having it and everyone, bar Jamila, started dropping the C-bomb in unison – there was no option but to drop the live broadcast.

"Who the fuck started that? I want them gone," he snapped at Desiree.

"Not sure, possibly Daniel, but we'll know when we play the tape back."

"Oh forget it. It's all good for ratings."

"How do we let the public know about the singing contest?"

"Zelda can do a piece to camera, can't she?"

"But we've just cut the broadcast."

"Then film it and drop it in later."

"But we won't have our target audience watching."

"Jesus, fucking Christ, do I have to think of everything?"

Desiree's dog started yapping in her bag.

"And shut that thing up before I do. Now do what I pay you for and fix it."

Desiree hesitated for a second, about to say something and then thought better of it. She stalked off, comforting her little rat dog. Felix looked up and saw Emma watching him intensely. He almost asked her what she was looking at and then just smiled. She looked startled – he wasn't much of a smiler.

"Emma, can you help Desiree with getting Zelda to do a piece to camera? I'd like it to go out as soon as possible," he purred.

"Of course. I'll just ask someone else to go and give the sisters their debrief."

"Don't worry about that. I'll get it sorted."

Emma shrugged and went off after Desiree. Felix turned to the rest of the production crew who were all pretending to look busy. He decided to debrief the sisters himself – this could be fun.

As he walked to the debriefing room he removed his dark glasses as they would no longer be needed. He lit a cigarette – the vape wasn't doing it for him anymore. He opened the emails on his phone and scanned the prepared draft emails – one for each group, just in case. He never left anything to chance. He located the sisters' email and forwarded it to the relevant people. The press release had to come from him directly, for his paper to publish it. When the show had been so successful in its first series there had been various attempts from hackers to get fake stories into the press. Felix now released the story to his own news studio only. That was enough for it to break on every other channel. He would also run the execution on the front page of his newspaper the next day. This would then be duplicated by the other newspapers, giving an extra day's coverage. Despite their initial protestations of *been there done that* when the show started, this was now event TV and every media outlet wanted a piece of it.

He entered the debriefing room and saw the sisters, who were inconsolable. There was one of the medical staff checking them over. Hopefully she hadn't sedated them or it would be a very brief debrief. The medic nodded at Felix to indicate that there were all okay, physically at least. The psychiatrist would be here later, but for now they needed to be told what had happened and most importantly how their lives were about to be destroyed.

"Ladies, I am Felix Moldoon."

This snapped them out of their self-indulgent wallowing, except Meena who didn't seem to give a shit who Felix was. Shame, as it was her life that was going to be devastated the most.

"How are you feeling after your shock execution?"

"We're fine," smiled Sassy, tossing her hair.

Felix felt it was doubtful this young woman was flirting with him for some sexual motive. She was drawn to power and it was clear she would do anything to be famous. Hope was trying to look flirtatious as well, although it was clear her heart wasn't in it – she would fail in life. Sassy was different, he could see it in her eyes; the hunger. Meena was still blubbering about being torn away from Helen – it was hardly a romance that straight men were going to wank over.

"Right, well you'll be able to go in a couple of hours. You just need to be seen by the psychiatrist."

"I don't need no shrink," said Sassy in a manner which lived up to her name.

"Just procedure, and besides, your sister looks very upset."

"She'll be fine."

"Well, she's going to need your support now more than ever."

"How come?"

"Well, you know what Adrian said about Meena looking different to you two?"

"Yeah, but we get that all the time."

"Well, it turns out that it's true."

Felix was doing all he could to keep the glee out of his voice.

"What you sayin'?" asked Sassy.

"Your parents kidnapped Meena when she was a baby."

"What the fuck!"

Meena had stopped blubbering and was fully alert now. What was about to happen to this entire family would be spectacular on social media and for the ratings – Felix knew he'd probably have a hard-on if he hadn't taken so much cocaine that evening. Being able to feel the utter devastation emanating from them was exhilarating. Perhaps he would do all the execution debriefs in future.

"Your parents did have another baby, but she died shortly after she was born. Your parents took Meena from the hospital and ran. The police will want to speak to them of course, so you won't be able to go home just now. We have a hotel for you all nearby."

They were dumbstruck – it was incredible. Then the tears came and all three broke down in hysterics clinging on to each other. Shame there was no cameras in here – it would have made great viewing. He left them sobbing in some nauseating group hug. As he exited the room he saw the psychiatrist and suggested she come back a bit later. He called for security and had them posted outside the door. He wasn't taking any chances. They could do what they wanted once they'd left the care of the studio, but for now he had to keep them out of harm's way. Besides, nobody else was using his jet.

He walked into his office and shut the door. It was good to be alone; it had been a chaotic few days, but at least they had managed to get things back on track and the full impact of the sisters' story had played out perfectly. He now had to think about the order of play for the rest of the competition. He still wasn't sure who the new winner was going to be now that Adrian had made it clear that he wanted out. Mrs P had come up with the singing task for later in the week with a public vote attached to it. This might give him a steer as to who could be the new chosen one. There was no way Jamila or Claire could ever win over the public and Daniel North was definitely out as a winner, in spite of how popular with the public he was. Whoever Felix chose as his champion would need to be able to beat Daniel in a public vote so it would have to one of the other guys – Callum or Mike. Neither of which excited Felix as a potential winner; this series could end up being a bust now the big stories had been released to the press. There were still a few dark secrets about those who were left and it was usual for the dynamic to shift once they started to compete as singles, so the main source of drama would now come from inside the complex.

His priority for the next week was to ensure Adrian was up for execution and that he lost the public vote, so he had to go up against one of the guys as none of the women would survive a public vote against him. The logical person was Callum. If Daniel was up against Adrian, Felix wasn't sure he would be able to stick to the plan; it would be too tempting to get Daniel out. After Adrian was gone Daniel would be the next up for the chop and then perhaps Felix would leave Desiree to run the rest of the series and let the public decide for real this time – he needed a holiday.

He was tired. This show sapped his energy in a way that none of his other programmes did. He opened the desk drawer and took out a mirror with pre-prepared lines of cocaine and sniffed two, one up each nostril in quick succession, rubbing the remains around his gums. He leaned back and closed his eyes, waiting for it to properly kick in.

"I wish you wouldn't touch that rubbish," came a voice from behind him.

Mrs P walked from the back of the room and sat down in front of Felix's desk.

"What are you doing here?"

"I see the first part of the plan worked as agreed?"

"Yes, the sisters are on the way home, well what's left of their home, and the rest are now all competing as singles."

"Shall we get Adrian out next, then?"

"We don't have a choice now."

"Good. It should never have come to this. You should have just forced him to take the money. It's too big a risk that someone is going to start digging into his background."

"How can they? We gave him a full fake background, even changed his surname, not to mention the cost of those elocution lessons to change his accent."

"And would that stop you if someone on a rival show had done the same?"

"No."

"Exactly, you should have just told him no, in the first place. You don't owe him anything. You didn't even know he existed until a year ago."

"He said he wanted to earn the money."

"Wonder who he gets that from?"

"Well not his mother, the money-grabbing whore."

"Please, Felix, the woman is dead."

"And she kept my son from me."

"Well you know him now, even if you've decided not to tell him who you are."

"I think that's best for him. This money will give him the opportunity to set himself up with a future."

"You mean, because his father is a billionaire and could give him a hundred times as much if he wanted to."

"Exactly. Anyway, we need to get him out. It's what he wants. It's why I ensured Jamila had immunity so she can't go up against him and screw it up."

"Since when have you allowed anyone to tell you what to do?"

"Whenever you speak!"

She tittered. "So who do we put him up against to ensure he goes?"

"Any of the other men. We can't take the risk on one of the girls, given the voting audience all want to mount him."

"Such a delightful turn of phrase, Felix. Right well, I'll be off. I think it's time I headed back anyway. I know it's easier for you when I'm not around"

"I'll speak to you tomorrow, then. Safe flight."

They both stood up and he kissed her on the cheek before she left.

CHAPTER THIRTEEN

Daniel looked up at Stephanie, giving her a look that implied it was someone else's turn to take over. Helen had been sobbing on his shoulder for over an hour. She was completely distraught over what had just happened. Daniel really felt for her, but he needed a break.

Jamila and Mike had argued shortly after the execution. Mike had seen how distressed Helen was and had popped in to check on her. He was closely followed by Jamila who accused him of *fraternising with the enemy*. The guy deserved a medal for his patience, although this time it appeared he had been pushed too far.

"Perhaps, if just for once you could show that you have some warmth and compassion then I might consider..."

"Consider what? Who the fuck do you think you are talking to?"

Daniel had noticed that when Jamila swore her Mancunian accent became even stronger and she came across as very coarse and unattractive. Given how she dressed and presented herself, it didn't align with the image she sought to convey. Jamila had the misguided view that she was above everyone else in terms of social standing, when in fact she was just another rough northerner on a Reality TV show.

Mike had backed himself into a corner now and Daniel wondered if he would take the sensible option and retreat to the safety of submissiveness.

"I might consider having a family with you," he added.

Alas not.

"You heartless cunt!"

She slapped him hard across the face, although he didn't flinch or react. Just took the slap and maintained eye contact with her. It was incredibly tense. Even Helen was now more interested in what was going on, over her own drama.

"Would Jamila come to the Confession Booth immediately," bellowed the voice over the tannoy.

"If I get executed because of you we're finished," she snarled at Mike before she stormed out.

Physical violence was usually grounds for immediate execution from the complex, although the previous series had been a little inconsistent with that rule depending on who the producers liked. Daniel hadn't even had a warning for his little rumble with Adrian so she'd certainly use that as ammunition if they tried to get rid of her. Unfortunately, Daniel was certain that Jamila wouldn't be going anywhere.

It was all very awkward as nobody knew what to say to Mike. The silence just hung there for what was probably just a few seconds, although felt as long as a commercial break on one of those shitty cable channels that gets about six viewers.

"I'd like to apologise for my behaviour. I was wrong to say such a thing in public."

Daniel wasn't sure what to say, although it didn't matter as Mike quickly left looking embarrassed.

"I'll go and see that he's okay," said Stephanie.

"Do you really think that's a good idea?" replied Daniel.

"He needs a friend right now."

"Okay, so the first thing his wife will see when she comes out from getting a bollocking or whatever they say to her in the Confession Booth will be you cosying up to her husband."

"Don't be ridiculous, we're just friends."

Her inability to maintain eye contact and the slight swelling of her cheeks gave away what she was really thinking.

"Besides, he's married."

"Exactly."

"I'll be back in a bit."

She left Daniel with Helen, who was still a bit weepy, so Daniel couldn't leave her on her own to go after Stephanie. He just hoped that Jamila didn't find her with Mike, or even worse, that Mike would tell Stephanie to piss off as he didn't look like he wanted any company. Then he'd have two women needing comfort. This had not been part of the sales pitch in the audition process.

"I very jealous of you Daniel," said Helen

"Why?"

"You very honest about who you are. It is not so easy for me."

Daniel suspected he knew what was coming, but knew she had to say it herself.

"I like girls," she whispered.

"The hardest person to admit it to is yourself."

"I think, maybe my father is more difficult."

They both smiled. It was only subtle; an intimate moment between two friends who could relate to each other in a way that many people can't.

"Was Meena the first girl you've felt this way about?"

"She is the first who is special, do you know what I mean?"

"Yes, I know exactly what you mean."

"There have been others. I fool myself it is just something you do when you are young, but now I not hide my feelings anymore, not after meeting her."

"When you meet someone like that, you just have to go for it."

"And you do same with Callum."

"That's different."

"Why different?"

"That's just lust."

"I don't agree. I see the way he look at you. It more than just sex to him. This why he respect your wish for no sex on TV."

"You don't miss anything, do you?" he smiled.

"I watch. I listen."

"It's different with men."

"What you mean?"

"It's hard to explain."

"I tell you what I think. Men like to show they are strong, even if it is men who like other men. Feelings are not something you talk about so easy. You also like sex, lots of sex. Men do not keep the two separate. You will not look at a future with Callum as you think he just want you for sex. You want sex as well but you not do it because of your grandmother. So until you get rid of this, what is the English word..." she wrung her hands together.

"Tension?" Daniel smiled.

"Yes, that is it. Until this tension between you is gone then you will not look past that. It is the same for all men. Sex first and feelings later."

A rather blunt, but accurate assessment of the entire male gender, by a German lesbian – perhaps Helen would get her own talk show after this was all over.

Daniel went to speak, but Helen stopped him and said she had to ask him something urgently before anyone came back. He listened to what she had to say and promised to do all he could to help her. It went against every logical argument in his head, yet he knew sometimes you just have to do the right thing,

Daniel spent the next morning with Stephanie. She didn't mention Mike, so he didn't bring it up. Nobody knew whether Jamila had received a warning or not. She had emerged from the Confession Booth after an hour. According to Callum, it was clear she had been crying, although she spoke to nobody and went straight to her apartment. The game had changed as they were now competing as singles. With the sisters gone they had an alliance to form, and Daniel didn't want to waste any time in securing his future in the complex. He knew he wouldn't win, although he was certain that when he left, it would be when he was ready.

"We need five to hold the balance of power," Daniel said to Stephanie.

"Well, we can forget Jamila and Claire as they must still be in an alliance."

"We can rule out Mike as well."

"I'm not so sure."

"I'd not get your hopes up that he's going to vote out his own wife."

"No, but he could side with us to get rid of Claire and Adrian."

"Speaking of Adrian, I think we need to get him onside."

"After the way he was with you at the beginning, do me a favour. I'd rather chummy up with Claire. At least she's always been consistent with being an arsehole."

Daniel laughed.

"Well we definitely have Callum, even if he is in a mood with me again."

"Trouble in paradise?"

"Just a horny teenager with no patience. Had to bat him off again last night."

It was Stephanie's turn to laugh.

"We've got Helen onside as well," said Stephanie. "You're the only person in here that she's close to, especially with Meena gone, so she'd back you."

Daniel decided not to mention his conversation with Helen. It may not come to anything and he didn't want to worry Stephanie unnecessarily. She was oblivious, but Daniel was not the only one who had noticed her interest in Mike and should Jamila win the Guvnorship again, Stephanie could well find herself on the chopping block, probably up against Daniel – that was his worst nightmare.

The neighbours were all having lunch, although it was a fairly silent affair when there was a request for someone to go to the Confession Booth to receive the instructions for this week's *special* Guvnorship challenge. The emphasis from the producer on the word *special* made Daniel shudder after what had happened the night before. Stephanie had finished her lunch so went to get the details. Jamila was still subdued, as she would usually have run to the Confession Booth, so she could be the one to know something before everyone else. This was her usual for daily tasks, although this was the first time a Guvnorship challenge had been announced in this way. Usually Zelda was on hand to provide them all the gory details.

After about five minutes Stephanie came back looking like she had won the lottery.

"It's a singing contest," she beamed.

"A what?" spluttered Daniel, who had just taken a big gulp of water.

"A singing contest. We all sing live on Saturday night and the winner is voted for by the public and they will be Guvnor."

"Oh, so not a signing contest. It's a test to see who is most popular with the public then."

"You're such a pessimist."

"It's called realist."

Stephanie scowled at him. He needed to shut up and he did. This was a big deal to her. She wanted to be a pop star and this challenge would allow her to showcase her talents on live TV. Daniel just hated singing. He'd been told he could hold a note, but that had been by an ex-lover and people will say anything to flatter you if they could get rewarded with sex. The guy had then suggested Daniel audition for one of the TV talent contests, so Daniel had rightly assumed they were definitely taking the piss. Besides, whether he could sing or not, if your heart isn't in something then why would you bother with the stress? However, he'd feign enthusiasm for Stephanie, because that was what friends did for each other.

"So what are you gonna sing?" he asked her.

"There's a list to choose from."

"Who gets to choose first?" asked Daniel.

"It doesn't matter as we can all sing the same song if we want, although that could then give you an advantage if you sing it better. Knowing what happened the other night, they'll probably execute the person with the lowest votes."

"Is that what they said?"

"Well no," Stephanie replied. "But then they've never done an execution mid-week before without a Guvnorship challenge, so I'd say all bets are off now."

"Well we have immunity and you can't have the Guvnorship twice in a row, so nothing for us to worry about," said Jamila.

"That's another thing. As we're now singles, you can win the Guvnorship back to back."

"What? Is that just this week?"

"No, for the rest of the game."

"And you didn't think to mention that?"

"Thought I'd share the news that was relevant to most the people here first."

"Give me the list?"

"No, you can wait your turn."

Jamila stormed off and then barked at her husband to follow. He hesitated for a second and then dutifully complied.

Claire was also delighted about the singing contest. She sat down next to Stephanie and asked if she could look at the list with her, which she agreed to. They started pointing at songs and whooping with delight. It was the most surreal thing Daniel had ever seen; two women, who had barely spoken to each other in almost three weeks, were now kindred spirits.

"I no like singing," said Helen.

"I hate singing," Daniel replied.

"I'm not keen either," added Adrian. "What about you, Callum?"

"I'll do a bit of karaoke when I've had a few. Maybe they'll let us get pissed before the contest."

"Hopefully," said Daniel. "Or this challenge is going to be mortifying."

The next day felt like the longest day of his life; Stephanie, Claire and Jamila all tried to outdo each other with their vocal ability. Stephanie and Claire had become very chummy in their dislike for Jamila, although it was clear they still saw each other as a rival for the prize.

The men and Helen didn't bother practising at all. Daniel had seen a song on the list that wouldn't be too horrendous and so had put his name down for that. All they had to do now was wait for the task to come around so they could get it over with.

The slightly concerning thing was that Jamila could sing very well. If this was just based on singing ability then she was a contender for sure, but the fact that she was a complete bitch made Daniel certain that she wouldn't win. Stephanie was definitely the favourite amongst the others. It was hard to separate them vocally, something Daniel kept to himself, so it would be the personality which pushed people towards Stephanie, namely because she actually had one. The rivalry between the women was steeped up a notch when Claire had paid Stephanie a compliment after another rehearsal.

"That was amazing. You sound like Beyoncé."

"Yeah, she also looks like she ate the rest of Destiny's Child," said Jamila.

This had resulted in an almighty row and fearing for their own safety, all the men and Helen had made a quick retreat.

The night before the contest, it was agreed that there would be no more practice and hopefully no more arguments. They all had dinner together, just in case there was a twist and someone else went home the next day. It was Mike's idea, no doubt to try to break the tension between his wife and everybody else she was living with. The evening went without incident. They had worked together very well on the daily task and made sure that they ordered a takeaway which would meet with everyone's dietary needs. This was a lot easier with Sassy no longer being in the complex, who had claimed to be allergic to salt. The conversation stayed off the game, which meant Jamila barely spoke, which was no bad thing. People mainly talked about their family lives and their day jobs, those that wanted to. Nobody was forced to talk. It was a really pleasant cordial evening; something which had probably resulted in the producers ripping their hair out wondering who would be in the firing line from Felix Moldoon – something he was publicly well known for.

CHAPTER FOURTEEN

The last few days had been nothing special; in fact, they had been fucking boring.

The row between Mike and Jamila was something, in spite of Jamila's propensity to drop the C-bomb. Felix had ordered the footage to be broadcast in full and would simply pay the fine from the regulator – they needed to show something.

The only other thing which had really happened was Helen finally admitting she was a lesbian – this was such a non-event Felix didn't even want it broadcast. However, there was literally nothing else and it was so interlinked with the Jamila and Mike blow up that he let it through. Their group dinner was the most nauseating thing Felix had ever witnessed and three people had been fired for even suggesting that it be added to the nightly show.

Felix was hopeful that tonight would go as planned and Stephanie would win the singing contest. She had competition from the other women; Helen didn't count, as she was barely female. Felix was convinced, due to the social media coverage, that Stephanie's popularity would see her victorious. She would then almost certainly put Adrian up and her suggestion to Daniel and Callum that she put Claire up as well would be tricky as that wouldn't definitively secure Adrian's execution, but Felix could work with that. He'd just tell Adrian to treat her like shit – that was a guaranteed execution. He wouldn't like it, but he'd need to do as he was told if he wanted out of the complex, with a million pound in his back pocket. However, the whole thing would be a lot easier if Adrian was up against any of the other men.

The worst outcome for Felix would be if Helen was on the chopping block. There was an online campaign to have her executed so she could be reunited with her family. People were feeling guilty after slagging her off on social media about how butch she was during the first few weeks of the show. It had happened countless times with Reality TV stars who visually play to a stereotype, and then once their real persona is revealed, the public feel remorse and instead of admitting they were just twats driven by their own biases, they feel like they have to make amends in some way with an online campaign – it was pathetic.

Helen's father had also been doing the media circuit about how much he loved and supported his daughter. It was nauseating and Felix had no choice but to have him on his news channel; better than having the competition hogging the glory.

The one benefit from the *Free Helen* campaign was that it had taken attention away from the sisters' execution which had not landed well with the public. The exception seemed to be Sandra, although she was also now in an online spat with Treehugger.

———

Best Twist Ever!!!

Sandra304: OMG!!! How amazing was that twist with the sisters going? That has to be the most exciting piece of television I have even seen in my life!!!

CNFanboy: I know! It was absolutely awesome!

TreeHugger23: This is the most despicable thing I have ever seen in my entire life. Television has now sunk to new levels of depravity

Sandra304: You need to chill ya boots mate. It's just a TV show!!!

TreeHugger23: Felix Moldoon should be in prison

Sandra304: Oh f**k off and go and hug some trees!!!

TreeHugger23: How juvenile to result to insults. What does 304 stand for? Is that your weight?

Sandra304: *This post has been removed as it violates the rules of the forum.*

———

"How's Adrian doing today?" Felix asked Emma.

She was in Felix's office to discuss the evening's live show. Desiree had some emergency with her dog – hopefully it had died.

"Well he's being very polite to everyone, but keeping himself to himself. He's quite boring really when he's not trying to get attention."

"Good, boring people get voted off."

"There's no chance of him winning tonight is there?"

"Jesus Christ, no – have you been smoking something?"

"I know he can't sing, but he might decide to take all his clothes off on live TV and you know how fickle the viewers are for a bit of toned flesh."

"I thought he'd stopped walking around with barely any clothes on."

"He has, although he still works out in that tight vest and those little shorts which leave nothing to the imagination..."

Emma looked off into the distance and her eyes glazed over.

Felix clicked his fingers. "Emma, are you still with us?"

"Sorry, sir."

"We're not broadcasting any of Adrian's workouts are we?"

"No, they aren't being shown on the live feed either. That's what you instructed."

"Excellent. Sooner he is out of there the better."

"Hard to believe he was the chosen one at the start."

"Three weeks is a long time on this show, Emma."

"I didn't think you backed losers."

"I don't."

"I didn't think you changed your mind either."

"I don't... often."

"You got this one wrong, didn't you?"

"Excuse me?"

"So are you going to enlighten us on the new chosen one?"

"No. You can leave now."

She smiled and walked out, leaving Felix seething at her brazenness.

Felix knew that the singing contest would be a straight-out battle between Stephanie and Claire, although Stephanie was still more popular with the public. Claire had experienced a slight lift in her popularity over the last few days, although she was starting from such a low base that she probably wasn't a realistic contender. Jamila was excellent, much to Felix's surprise, but she could be the best singer of all time and there was still no way she was going to win any public vote, except when it was her turn to be executed.

Felix saw this little singing exercise as a way to test out Stephanie and Claire on the public. If the reaction was positive, he'd be the first in line to sign them up to his talent show. He had first dibs, it was in their contracts. From the day they walked into the complex until New Year's Eve, if they even wanted a sniff of celebrity, he owned them all. If they waited the twelve months until they were out of contract there would have been a new wave of Reality TV stars and any management company wouldn't be interested; it was a foolproof business model.

Felix arrived at the main production suite to check on preparations for the Saturday night live show. Each contestant would sing a song of their choice – well, from a pre-approved list for licensing reasons. The phone lines would then open and the show would come back on air an hour later and reveal who had won the contest. That person would then choose who would face execution in seven days' time and it would all be live – what could possibly go wrong?

"Ladies and gentlemen we are LIVE. Please don't drop the C-bomb!"

Zelda was back on form, and sober.

"Now, are you each ready to perform? We're going to call your names randomly and you have three minutes to wow us with your vocal talents in the recording booth. We'll then open the vote to the public and see who will be the next Complex Guvnor. They will then have no chance to think about it as they'll decide who faces the next execution, LIVE."

First up was Mike, who was so out of tune the sound guy was wincing constantly. Next up was Callum, who wasn't much better, although he'd had a few beers so was like most people on karaoke in that he assumed he was awesome. Daniel politely applauded. The whole awkward moment of him asking Daniel how he had done was captured on camera. Although, Felix thought he'd handled it very well by saying things like, *you sang passionately,* and *you looked like you were enjoying yourself.*

Claire, one of the heavy hitters, was up next and she'd chosen a big Celine Dion ballad and it was excellent. The notes were pitch perfect. Why she hadn't got some form of record deal in the past was probably down to her being as likeable as an ultraviolet light in a brothel. With the right marketing and songs, she could make a shitload of money for whoever represented her – which would be Felix, of course.

Next up was Stephanie and she was sensational – a big belter of a voice. She had chosen something more up-tempo, so to Felix, she sounded much better than Claire. He wasn't keen on pop-open-a-vein-style ballads. Felix was impressed by Stephanie and could see her doing well on one of his other TV programmes which was scheduled for the summer. He doubted she'd turn down the opportunity to sing on live TV in front of ten million viewers.

Everyone was whooping and hugging Stephanie when she came out of the singing booth. Claire looked mutinous and Jamila just gave a slight smirk and told her husband to be quiet when he went to say something.

Adrian was next up, followed by Helen; the less said about either the better.

Jamila was the penultimate performer and surprised them all. First she was singing the same song as Stephanie, which couldn't be a coincidence from a list of over a hundred songs. It was a different version, slower; more acoustic and rough. She was much better than she had indicated in her practice, where she already sounded very good. In fact, she was phenomenal. She did a lot of vocal acrobatics though, so Felix was hoping that wouldn't appeal to everyone. Given she was at the bottom of the popularity poll, it would still be a miracle for her to be high in the voting, no matter how good she was.

Daniel was the last to sing and then the votes would open. Felix was thinking about how he could use the substitution challenge should the vote not go as planned. He was then snapped out of his thoughts by the sound of Daniel's voice. It was like nothing he had ever heard before. The pitch and tone were absolute perfection, the vocal range for a man was sensational and when you saw him singing, he made it look so effortless.

Once Daniel had finished his song, the camera panned back to Zelda who had been so mesmerised by the performance that she missed her cue. In fact, the complex was so silent that you heard someone scream the cue again into Zelda's earpiece. She recovered quickly and announced the phone lines were open for the public to cast their votes for the winner of tonight's contest.

When Felix had heard Daniel sing, his heart rate had risen with the excitement. If this was a cartoon, pound signs would have just appeared in Felix's eyes. There was money to be made here and a lot of it; was Felix prepared to take such a big risk?

After fifty minutes, Desiree walked into Felix's office; he had been having a little sleep. She wasn't carrying her dog, although Felix didn't bother to ask how he was. It would be difficult to not smile if it really had died.

"Results are in," she said.

"Who won?"

"Daniel, with half the votes."

"Half?"

"Yep, Stephanie second and Claire third."

"Not Jamila?"

"She came last."

"She what?"

"She came last."

"How is that possible? She was brilliant?"

"Brilliance doesn't always win votes."

"Too true. So her husband beat her?"

"Yes, he beat Adrian as well. Here, have a look."

She passed him the results. They were good voting numbers. Five million votes in under an hour was impressive, even by this show's standards.

Daniel – 50%

Stephanie – 18%

Claire – 11%

Callum – 7%

Mike – 6%

Helen – 5%

Adrian – 2%

Jamila – 1%

Felix looked up. "Announce all the results in reverse order."

"What?"

"Are you questioning my decision, Desiree?"

"Yes. There'll be a bloody riot and we're live. Have you seen the number of fines we are in for? Do you want to be bankrupt?"

"Stop being a drama queen. I'm not sure I like this new approach people seem to be taking. That Emma's rubbing off on people with her bolshiness. Get rid of her."

"What?"

"Is that all you can say? I said get rid of her."

"But she hasn't done anything wrong."

"Fine, I'll deal with it myself."

"No that's alright. I'll take care of it. Just let's get the show out of the way. I'll let Zelda know as we'll need to be quick if we're going to list all these results."

"Can't you just reveal them on a screen or something?"

"Not when we're live in less than ten minutes."

"I don't like problems, Desiree. I pay you to solve my problems. Now piss off, before you become a problem."

She scuttled off and Felix sat back and turned on the monitors which showed the complex. He would watch it all unfold from here. Daniel North had proven to be something of a surprise and Felix knew there was a lot of money to be made here. However, Daniel would not be easy to manipulate as he was not hungry for fame, yet there was something about him that made him stand out from the others. Deep down everyone wanted to be famous for something, Daniel didn't and Felix knew that was a genuine sentiment. He knew when people were lying. The online response to Daniel during the show and now after his performance validated just how popular he was. He might not want fame, but fame wanted him.

There was only one way that Felix could have complete control over Daniel, so he would have no choice but to let that fame consume him. Daniel had to become the new *chosen one* and the next winner of *Complex Neighbours*.

CHAPTER FIFTEEN

Daniel was rooted to the spot. How could he have won a singing contest? He hated singing and had a mediocre voice at best. He had a row of people looking at him expectantly. What were they waiting for? A victory speech? This could be awkward.

"Daniel, can we have your decision," boomed Zelda.

He looked at Stephanie, expecting her to be mutinous – singing was her thing; she was beaming. That was a relief. Now he had to decide who would face execution. He'd made a promise, yet here was a chance to get rid of Adrian. Things may have become more cordial between them, although Daniel would still prefer it if Adrian left the complex. The first one was a no-brainer, especially if it meant breaking up an alliance.

"My first choice is Claire."

"Reason?"

"I'm not sure we have enough time!"

This caused everyone to laugh, even Claire.

"And your second choice?"

Daniel scanned the faces of his fellow neighbours. Jamila

and Mike were safe, unfortunately. Adrian simply shrugged when their eyes met, resigned to his fate. Callum was avoiding eye contact. He couldn't seriously be expecting to be chosen? Helen had a pleading look on her face, hoping Daniel would deliver on his promise; a promise he never thought he'd have to honour. Finally, he came to Stephanie, who glanced at Adrian and Helen, gave a simple smile and slight nod of her head.

"My second choice is..."

Later that night, Daniel was alone. It was his night in the big bed; Callum and Stephanie were in the two-bed room. They had started rotating around each night so everyone got some privacy every third night. Daniel thought about having a wank, and then decided against it. He was nice and snug and couldn't be arsed getting up to clean the mess.

Daniel thought about his fellow neighbours. Half of them had gone, in just three weeks. There was still six weeks to go so a lot could happen. At the beginning he had assumed that this would be the eight who would break into singles. He had then realised that Jamila was a complete bitch and changed his mind, although he had been right at the start. Was he right about who would win?

He hoped he would never have to pick between Callum and Stephanie when it came to executions; with immunity and other twists, it was certainly a possibility. It would also make great TV, so it was inevitable that at some point he'd have to make that decision. They were his closest friends in this bizarre little world, and he hoped that they would be just as close when they left and returned to normality.

Daniel wanted either Stephanie or Callum to win and he truly believed that one of them would. Stephanie for the opportunities it would give her and Callum had said he needed the money for his family. Daniel knew that once they were away from the cameras that he and Callum would deal with the *tension*, as Helen so eloquently put it. After that who knew – perhaps it was time to stop pushing people away.

There was a tap on the door.

"Come in."

Stephanie popped her head round the door.

"Want some company?" she asked.

Daniel knew what she really meant was that she needed some company. Callum was probably already asleep; besides, teenagers could be far too ideological and sometimes you just needed a chat with a fellow cynic.

"Sure," he said, lifting back the bed cover and shuffling along so she could get in next to him.

"What you thinking about?" she asked.

"Who's going to win."

"And?"

"You or Callum, I think."

"Well you know who I think is going to win."

"I wouldn't rule out any of the others though just yet. You know with this game that anything could happen."

"Well there's no way Helen will win," said Stephanie.

"Well hopefully the public will do the right thing and send her home."

"That was a very kind thing you did."

"I just did what was right."

"I agree, but anyone else would have used it as an opportunity to get rid of Adrian."

"Well he won't win anyway. He's done too much damage, so who cares how long he stays. His heart doesn't seem to be in the game anymore. He's been quite subdued and avoiding Claire."

"Do you think Claire might go instead?"

"It's possible. We all thought Jamila and Mike would go over Frank and Judy."

"That feels like a lifetime ago now."

"I know and it was only a week ago. That mid-week execution's thrown me with what day it is."

Daniel believed Helen would go home this week. He'd have liked her to stay, certainly over some of the others, but he knew she would never quit and this was the only way to send her home. Hopefully, when she was back with her family she could pick herself out of the depression she was in and look back on the whole experience more positively. Daniel would watch her when she thought nobody was looking, the mask would slip and show how incredibly unhappy she was.

Helen was probably wondering what her family would think of her. Although some people have horror coming-out stories, especially since the whole gay marriage is illegal and now its legal again period – it was astounding what damage those five years had done to set back social attitudes. Daniel had known his mother and grandmother would be supportive when he came out, although he'd had that niggle in the back of his mind that they might reject him – of course they didn't. His grandmother's *you took your time* was all it took to put an end to any doubts. Although, he was lucky as he'd come out when social attitudes were at the height of acceptance; today it was back to reluctant tolerance.

"Do you think Jamila could win?" he asked Stephanie.

"Villains have won these types of shows before."

"True, although not many of the women villains have. Besides, it's obvious she isn't popular with the public with her coming last in the singing contest. She was one of the best singers."

"Excuse me?"

"Well, she was."

"Annoyingly, yes she was. Is there nothing that woman

can't do? I still don't know why Mike bothers with her. He
could do so much better."

"Like you, you mean."

Stephanie just smiled but said nothing.

Daniel thought more about Mike and Jamila. Could either
of them really win it now? Jamila might get to the end, but
then she'd pay for it. People like to be entertained and they
respect people who play the game, but there was a line and
Jamila had not just crossed it, she'd wiggled her arse on it and
called it a cunt. Mike was different. Without her, he could do
it. He was a traditional Reality TV winner, the affable straight
white male, although now it usually went to the person who
had been on a *journey*.

Claire didn't stand a chance. She was pushing forty and
wore her sexuality out and proud. The female voters would
punish her for it. She also wanted to be famous and was not
quiet about it. Stephanie was honest about her fame aspira-
tions yet didn't bang on about them.

"What about Adrian?" Stephanie asked.

"Well he won't be short of work, regardless of when he
gets out of here. We'll no doubt see his crotch on billboards."

"There's worse things to look at over your morning
coffee."

"Very true."

"Would you?"

"What, with Adrian? He's straight."

"I mean if he was gay."

"There's that personality though."

"Yeah, but like I said, you don't..."

"You don't fuck a personality. I remember. As a one
nighter, definitely. Mainly so I could boast about it to
everyone I knew."

Stephanie laughed.

"Not more than a one-off?" she asked.

"I'd be too paranoid, dating anyone that beautiful. Knowing that everyone was looking at us and thinking that I was probably rich, as there'd be no other way he'd be with me."

"You think he could win? He fits the classic profile."

"I doubt it, he's going to have pissed off a big chunk of the audience, but then it depends what they've broadcast doesn't it."

"As soon as I'm Guvnor, I'm putting Adrian up against Jamila," said Stephanie.

"Adrian would win over her."

"Exactly. Imagine how nice it would be if the final three was us and Callum? It would be such a nice last week."

"The three of us all getting on well – yeah, that'll be fascinating for the viewers! I doubt Felix Moldoon will let that happen."

Daniel wasn't sure who would win. He knew Jamila would make the final three, the producers would see to it as she caused the most conflict. Callum and Stephanie seemed to think that Daniel would be there until the end. Was it possible? He had won the singing contest and he was far from the best singer. He'd said himself that it was just a popularity contest and he'd won it. Could he really win the whole show?

The next morning, Stephanie had risen early, so Daniel was hoping for a lay-in when the claxon sounded for the daily task. There were different sounding claxons. The loudest meant there was a Guvnorship challenge and then there were two daily tasks – one sounded more like a laser and this was an optional task, although most people took part for something to do and to ensure Jamila didn't win. She entered everything and would no doubt be on a rampage after coming last in the singing contest.

The claxon today was more like a door buzzer which meant it was a mandatory task. Daniel dragged himself out of bed, pulled on some jogging bottoms and changed his t-shirt to something which was mildly less creased. It was early morning so there was no way they'd be live – well, hopefully not. He looked in the other bedroom, no sign of Callum; he must have gotten up early as well.

Everyone was assembled downstairs in a much better state of dress than Daniel. How long had he been asleep? The only exception was Adrian who had evidently been working out again. He reminded Daniel of those fitness buffs on Instagram who exercise with no top on. Normal people tended to workout in billowing t-shirts that hide any bounce when running on the treadmill. Well, at least Daniel had for the six times he had been to a gym in his entire life.

The side door opened and Zelda came out announcing that it was their first substitution challenge. Jamila looked like she'd had an orgasm in her pants. Was it Daniel's imagination or was Mike standing a safe distance from his wife and giving her a look of contempt?

The substitution challenge usually came in at this part of the game. The challenge was similar to a Guvnorship task, only shorter and less intense. The winner could remove themselves or someone else from possible execution and the Guvnor would have to replace them.

"Would anybody not like to play?" asked Zelda.

Daniel had to ensure that everything stayed as it was, so knew he would have to compete.

Helen stepped forward and Daniel quickly went over to her.

"Helen, if you don't play somebody else could win and change things whether you like it or not."

"But I want to go home. I must speak to my family."

He put his arm round her and whispered to her.

"I know, and that's why I put you up. But there are a few people here who will change things and that could mean you have to stay another week and if Jamila wins next week she won't be interested in helping you, she'll be only interested in eliminating her competition."

"Are you participating, Helen?" asked Zelda.

"Yes, she is," Daniel replied.

"Right, well, the task is simple."

Zelda did her usual flourish with her hands as the door slid back and revealed an obstacle course.

"The quickest time will win the substitution challenge and have the power to force the Guvnor to change one of the people facing execution this week. The individual who completes the obstacle course with the least amount of errors will win immunity from being the substitute. Are we all clear?"

"Yes," they shouted.

It was a faux enthusiastic response, in order to move things on. Today was a Sunday and this was not what people should be doing.

"As our current Complex Guvnor, Daniel will go first. Now pay attention as Baz shows you how the course works."

A very fit military guy with tattoos and wearing combat fatigues and a tight black vest came out of the door. This seemed to perk a few people up. Baz ran through the course and explained it all very quickly – a bit too quickly. The gist was that you had to complete each section perfectly. There were five sections: tyres on the floor, monkey bars, a balancing beam, a climbing net and a slide at the end, which you had to go down head first – into a mud pit. If you flunked on any section, you had to redo that section until you completed it successfully. You then kept going until you got to the end of the course.

Daniel was told to take his place at the start. Even though

he knew he had no chance of winning this against people like Mike and Adrian, he had to show willing. He would go for the perfection element instead. That went to a pile of shit straight away as he tripped on the first tyre and went flat on his face – he heard laughter behind him, yet chose not to look at who it was. After three attempts he was through the tyres and onto the balancing beam which he did first time. The climbing net was also fairly straight forward. The monkey bars however were not – it took ten, yes ten attempts, to complete the things. Finally it was the slide into some very questionable mud, which stunk and made Daniel retch. The completion time was taken from the point you land in the mud. Despite it feeling like he had been on the course for about a year, he had completed it in just under five minutes.

This feeling soon abated when Adrian completed the course faultlessly in less than two minutes. Stephanie was worse than Daniel, which was something of a blessing, and came in at seven minutes. Claire was even worse at just under nine minutes. Callum took three minutes, thanks to the climbing net being his nemesis. He swung across the monkey bars in a nanosecond, though – very impressive. Helen shocked them all by beating Adrian's time and only having a stumble on the balance beam. She was in the lead with just Jamila and Mike to go.

Jamila went first and was faultless through the tyres. However, her confidence got the better of her as she could not get over the balance beam.

"Fucking piece of shit," she screamed.

"Just breathe and take your time, baby," said her husband, trying to encourage her.

"Don't fucking tell me what to do!"

Mike's face flushed. Daniel felt sorry for him. He noticed a look on Stephanie's face as she gazed at Mike – she was getting herself into a dangerous situation if she didn't stop being so obvious.

Jamila having successfully completed the balance beam was now stuck in the cargo net – literally. She was effing and blinding as she struggled to make any headway and in the end Beefy Baz had to come and help her out.

"That's ten minutes, Jamila. You are out of this substitution challenge."

"But I want to finish it," she screamed.

"You can have a go again later when we all go for dinner," piped up Adrian.

This caused everyone to laugh, even Zelda. Jamila stalked off back towards the main complex, muttering under her breath words which could not be broadcast.

"Aren't you going to see if your husband can win?" asked Zelda, now she had stopped laughing.

Jamila turned and walked back over to the bench and sat down pulling one of the blankets around her, even though she hadn't even had a dip in the freezing cold mud bath.

"Right, Mike you're up, best of luck," remarked Zelda.

It was questionable what Zelda was actually wishing Mike luck about.

The whistle was blown and Mike flew through the course faultlessly and in a record time of seventy-two seconds.

Jamila soon perked up and was jumping up and down with delight.

Zelda asked Mike to get his breath and then reveal his decision about who he would be taking off the block. She stated that Adrian could not be a replacement as he had completed the course without any faults. If Daniel wasn't mistaken, he saw a flash of anger across Adrian's face, although he recovered himself very quickly.

This meant that if Mike made a change then Daniel would have to choose Stephanie or Callum as a replacement –

the thing he never wanted to do. He could feel his heart hammering in his chest as he thought about the choice he would have to make. He knew what his choice would be; he just didn't want to make it.

Jamila, no doubt having worked out the dilemma Daniel faced, ran over to her husband and went to whisper in his ear, making sure he followed through with whatever her plan was.

"Don't tell me what to do," he said, moving away from her.

Jamila looked like she had been slapped in the face.

"I choose to make no substitutions, Zelda."

CHAPTER SIXTEEN

For the first time in his life, Felix was genuinely lost for words.

Felix was conflicted between what would make great TV and the fact that they'd veered off plan and Adrian would be in there for at least another week. He was also pissed that they hadn't gone live with the challenge, although that was soon alleviated when Jamila had launched into a foul-mouthed rant – he'd never known *cunt* be used as a preposition before.

The big problem was Adrian. They had a deal and now Adrian would see that Felix had gone back on that. The easiest thing would be to talk to him directly, but he'd need to wait for the right opportunity.

"Desiree, get that packaged up so it can go out tonight and initiate the lockdown protocols," Felix whispered in her ear.

The lockdown protocols meant that nobody could leave the studio until the show went to air. Nobody was permitted their personal phones in the studio, other than Felix. The Wi-Fi signal would be blocked for all mobile devices, as would outgoing calls; in effect everyone was cut off. This meant the show could go to air and be a great surprise for the viewers, rather than spoilers leaking in advance. Unlike other broadcasters, he didn't feel the need to pre-warn viewers of the twists and turns to have them tune in, he already had them – the online reactions afterwards would bring in more viewers to the next show.

Felix briefed staff on the lockdown procedures. The majority had only been working for him on this series so had not experienced them before. Only a few loyal soldiers, who toed the line, had survived more than one series. Following the update he left the studio, asking not be disturbed until the show was ready for pre-broadcast review. He had Mrs P to deal with, who would not be pleased that Adrian wasn't leaving. Hopefully she would stay where she was and leave him to sort this out, although somehow he doubted it.

Once the lockdown was all in place, Felix covertly entered the camera run. He couldn't risk calling Adrian to the Confession Booth again, so he was going to have to go into the complex and speak to him. There was only one place Adrian would be now and that would be the gym; hopefully alone.

He made his way down the long camera run which went right around the complex and found the stairs down to the basement. He managed to stay out of sight from some of the cameramen who were about to have their changeover, so he would have around five minutes to talk to Adrian.

He was outside the gym and could see Adrian working himself into exhaustion. This was not a good sign. Felix had seen Adrian get into this state during his preparation for coming into the complex; he was close to the edge.

Felix waited for Adrian to come near the fire-exit door before he opened it slightly, hoping it would pique his interest. It did; Adrian, still holding a dumbbell, opened the door and poked his head round.

"Adrian, get in here."

"You? Fuck off."

"Don't you want to hear what I've got to say?"

"Fine," he said, throwing the weight on the floor so forcefully that the ground shook.

He fully entered the camera run. As Felix closed the door, the claxon sounded for a food task. He'd forgotten about that and now knew that they wouldn't have much time. Felix kept his voice to a whisper.

"Nobody could know that Mike would do something like that. It was all geared up for Jamila to win, but her impatience blew it for her."

"It's your show, you're supposed to know everything."

"It doesn't matter who won though, does it? What the hell where you playing at in that contest? You won immunity, so you would never have been a substitute."

"Yeah, well that was just instinct. Maybe you should make things a bit more challenging."

"Well maybe rein it in next time, or do you really want to stay?"

"No, I want out – now."

"Okay, well go to the Confession Booth and tell them you want to quit."

"I don't quit."

"Good, just suck it up. It's only another week."

"And how do I know there won't be another fuck-up and I'll be here to the end. I just want my money," he shouted.

"Keep your voice down."

"Fine, just make sure I'm up next week."

"Don't worry, we'll make sure Jamila wins."

"Great and she'll put up her husband with Daniel."

"Just leave it to me."

"Fine, but you owe me something else."

"Like what?"

"Get rid of the lesbian. At least with Claire here I can keep myself occupied."

"I thought you had stopped going there?"

"Needs must and I'm bored shitless in here. Just get me out with my money and until then make sure I keep getting laid."

"Fine, the lesbian's a gonner."

This was perfect as *#FreeHelen* was building momentum online, so it was likely that the vote would go that way. It would appear that Felix had delivered on one of his promises to Adrian. There was a sudden bang and shuffling noise behind them.

"What was that?" asked Adrian.

"Just be one of the cameramen. Now get back in there."

Adrian opened the door and walked in without looking. It was a stupid mistake. Luckily Felix was out of sight, although he could hear what was being said.

"What were you doing in there?"

Shit, it was Daniel.

"The door was open, so I thought I'd be nosey. Cameraman told me to get back in here."

"Well we've got a food task."

"Another one? Is it mandatory?"

"No."

"Well I'll just stay and finish my workout then. Thanks though."

"Okay, I'll let the others know."

Felix heard the door shut and knew Daniel must have left. He looked through the one-way glass and saw Adrian lifting weights. He was currently on the bench press with his crotch pointed at the camera – the boy knew how to play to his strengths. Looking around when he heard another noise, he knew he had to get out of the camera run. He walked past the gym, further away from the main studio, until he came to some stone steps with a coded door at the top. He stopped for a second; he was convinced someone was watching him, although he couldn't see anybody there. He went through the door into a secure room which he used for private meetings. He could now walk normally, so he made his ways across the room, past the boardroom table and through another door, up some steps and then through a final coded door which lead into his office. This must have been how Mrs P had entered his office the other night; she was the only other person who knew the code.

Felix was sitting at his desk, tired from the exertion, which couldn't have lasted more than fifteen minutes. His adrenalin was pumping and he had found the secrecy exhilarating. He thought about the upcoming execution and with the *#FreeHelen* bandwagon he knew this was one of these unique times when it was best to just let the public do their thing without any manipulation – a novel concept.

Once Helen left, the main story would come from her attempting to be reunited with Meena, although that was another shit-storm that had bubbled up again and the legal team were now getting in a tizz about it. The latest online spat between Debbie and Treehugger had summed up the situation perfectly.

––––––––

More lives devastated in the pursuit of ratings

Treehugger23: Felix Moldoon has now sunken to new depths of depravity. The outcome of his latest, "We destroy you with one tweet," is the most cruel and barbaric yet. Poor Meena finds out that she was stolen from her real parents and instead of a happy reunion they reject her because she kissed another woman. Then because she wanted to know her birth parents, her fake ones have also rejected her from their prison cells. Then her sisters, who said it would change nothing on the day of their execution, have now sided with their parents. Poor Meena now has nobody. When will this man stop running people's lives for his tacky TV programmes?

DeliciousDebbie1985: You're such a drama queen! This was a serious crime these people committed and it was only right that it was brought to people's attention.

Treehugger23: Agreed, but the authorities should have been told, rather than the press. He must have known before they went into the complex. What if she had won, would he have kept it quiet forever?

DeliciousDebbie1985: If she had won? Are you completely deluded, none of the sisters would have won! It's always one of the singles who wins.

Treehugger23: Exactly, that proves the show is rigged. I don't know how people can waste their money voting for this rubbish thinking they have a say. It's clearly all fixed.

DeliciousDebbie1985: Don't be ridiculous. It is independently adjudicated by The Electoral Commission. They can't rig the vote. You'll probably be getting hysterical next week when Helen gets executed. #FreeHelen

Treehugger23: Well it shouldn't be Helen. That Claire is a nasty piece of work and a fame-hungry whore.

DeliciousDebbie1985: Don't you think it would be nice for Meena to have someone out there who cares about her and besides Helen has been miserable since she left and needs to be with her family. Her dad is absolutely lovely – did you see his interview? #FreeHelen

Treehugger23: Yes, I saw it, so she'll be fine when she

leaves the show. We should use this opportunity to get Claire out. Adrian might have a chance to shine then.

DeliciousDebbie1985: Claire mixes things up and keeps the tension up. It would be boring as f*** if her or Jamila left too soon.

Treehugger23: Don't even get me started on Jamila. I still can't believe she survived that vote. Another reason that proves it's rigged. Look at all that stuff in the press on the old couple. That was convenient.

DeliciousDebbie1985: Here you go again with your conspiracy theories. Anyway I thought you said you didn't watch the show. You said it was beneath you and only appealed to the unintelligent masses!

DeliciousDebbie1985: And he goes silent again!!!

―――――

Desiree ran into Felix's office, indicating that something was wrong.

"What is it?" he asked.

"The story is already out."

"Who?"

"Erm..."

"Who the fuck was it?"

"Emma."

"I told you to get rid of her."

"I've been a bit busy. I can't do everything you know."

"Have you lost your mind talking to me like that?"

"I'll deal with Emma now."

"Bring her to me."

"I can get her out of the building. You don't need to see her."

"I said bring her here – NOW."

"I'm already here," said Emma as she walked into the office.

"Do you not know what lockdown protocol means?"

"I made an executive decision."

"Did you now? Desiree, get out."

She hesitated.

"OUT!"

Desiree left the room. Emma didn't seem in the least bit concerned by what had happened.

"Do you want to see my proposal then?"

"Fuck off, you're sacked and you'll never work in TV again."

"I don't think so." She turned and shut the office door, locking it from the inside. "Best we aren't disturbed, don't you think?"

"Excuse me?"

"Well, you see. I have just had a very interesting few minutes."

"Don't piss about, if you've got something to say then just say it."

"Why don't you sit down like a good boy and we can talk about your little chat just now with Adrian." She waited a beat. "I said sit."

Felix sat down. It was like Adrian had said, instinct.

"You see, I think it would be interesting for the public to know just how much manipulating you do behind the scenes."

"Is that it? Every Reality TV producer manipulates things behind the scenes."

"True, but do they have secret deals with contestants and then offer them one million pounds even if they don't win the show?" Another beat. "You see Felix, I want Desiree's job and you're going to see that I get it."

"You don't dictate terms to me," snapped Felix standing up.

He walked right up to her; she didn't flinch.

"Ah well, that is where you are wrong," she said, pacing around the office. "You see I did a little investigating after I witnessed one of your earlier little chats. Your real name isn't even Felix Moldoon is it?"

"Lots of people have a different professional name, especially in this industry."

He tried to control his breathing. He was seething with such anger and hatred towards this woman. She could ruin everything and just because she wanted to be a producer on a Reality TV show. It wouldn't stop there though, would it? She would want more and always have this hold over him.

"Very true, but you have a slightly different reason though, don't you? Like Adrian being your son."

Felix smiled and walked over to his desk and opened a drawer. Emma's brazenness faltered for a second as she was clearly concerned he was going to pull a gun out or something. Instead he took out a folder; a little parting gift from Mrs P.

"What's that?" she asked.

"Have you finished your little speech then? Anything else you found out in your little investigation?"

"I think Adrian being your son is damning enough."

Felix threw down the folder and suggested she review the contents before she said anything further. She hesitated and then picked up the folder and opened it; the colour drained from her face.

CHAPTER SEVENTEEN

"Daniel, you try and come across as a guy who is on this show for moral reasons, but I think you're a sneaky fucker who is only out for himself.

"Steph, I mean what it is it with this Stephanie crap, you make out you want to be famous, but in actual fact all you are, is desperate to be liked."

Claire was on a roll. She believed she was just about to be executed from the show. Helen was already stood in her tube, but Claire wanted her say first.

"Callum, running around like some love-sick puppy just makes you come across as pathetic. He's not interested in you, only himself, so give it up."

Callum genuinely looked hurt by her comments. Daniel wasn't sure why – she was just ranting.

"Mike, you're a pussy. Grow a pair and leave that snake. Jamila, you're a cunt!"

Zelda was about to offer a quick apology to camera, but based on how she jumped into the air, a producer had clearly screamed into her ear to stay on Claire – this was no doubt

TV gold and there could be only one reason why. This was going to be awkward.

"Adrian, you might have a big knob, but you know you actually need to do something with it. You are the most vain, egotistical twat I have ever had the misfortune to meet and the worst fuck of my entire life."

Didn't stop you going back for hundredths, thought Daniel.

"Finally, Helen... you... are actually the only person here I like as you're the only genuine one. I'm sorry I was so rude to you to begin with and wish I'd had chance to get to know you better."

And with that Claire turned with a sashay and hair flick and walked into her execution tube. It closed around her. Helen's had been closed for about a year, whilst Claire had her rant. Good job she wasn't claustrophobic.

"Claire and Helen," Zelda began. "The public have voted and I can reveal that with sixty per cent of the vote, tonight's execution is..."

Daniel looked at Helen, he blew her a kiss and she smiled. He knew that when it came down to it, the British public would not like to see someone suffering... unless they deserved it.

The lever was pulled and Helen disappeared from sight. This is where the awkward bit came in, as the tube lifted from around Claire, the look on her face said only one thing... *fuck!*

Daniel woke up the next morning feeling very fresh. It was the first morning after an execution night when he didn't have a hangover. The atmosphere in the complex last night had been so horrendous that he'd opted for an early night. After Claire's rant the immediate reaction from people was anger once she stepped out of the tube, yet she was adamant she wasn't going to apologise for what she said as it was the truth. Daniel reflected on what she had said and questioned whether his motivations for being on the show were entirely honourable. He had been so driven by a sense of justice, that had now thrust him into the spotlight and he hated to admit it, but a part of him enjoyed being at the centre of attention. It reminded him of something his mother had told him when he was a teenager...

"You're an introvert, trapped in an extrovert's body."

"What does that mean?"

"You don't want to be the centre of attention, but you can't help yourself."

There was a loud grunt and snore to his left, so he got up and decided to go and sit in the apartment lounge. Mike was asleep in the next bed. He had moved into the single men's apartment after the substitution challenge. Stephanie had the king-sized bed to herself and Callum was off sulking somewhere. Mike would be hungover as he'd stumbled in at four in the morning wanting to chat. Daniel had pretended to be asleep; something he was, until Mike walked in.

He pulled on his jogging bottoms and walked out of the apartment, looking down at the communal area. Nobody else was up yet. He walked down the stairs and decided to have a cup of tea in the open-plan area. It was rarely this quiet and he would enjoy it for a bit before the drama bubbled up again. It was Sunday so people would likely sleep in, hopeful there wouldn't be a task until later in the day. They received their main shopping today and it always included ingredients for a roast. With Helen's departure there were no vegetarians left, so they could do the full works.

Everyone usually mucked in with cooking the Sunday dinner, and they ate together. It was the only night of the week they really did that because there was a lull in the game, before it started back up again on Monday with the Guvnorship challenge. The substitution was usually on a Wednesday once the routine was back to normal after the sister's midweek execution had thrown it all off. In time the weekend would be here again along with another execution.

Daniel went into the larder and it had already been fully stocked. The fridge was also packed. A huge joint of lamb dominated the middle shelf of the American-style fridge freezer. There were half a dozen packs of bacon and there was fresh bread in the larder. Daniel thought he'd leave it for a while as he didn't want the smell of bacon waking anyone up. He wanted to enjoy the peace and tranquillity for as long as possible.

"Can we talk?"

That blew that out of the water. "What do you want, Claire?" The words came out crueller than intended. He sighed. "Let's be very British about this. Can I get you a brew?"

"Yes please," she smiled.

Daniel made the tea and gestured for her to sit down at the dining table, which now seemed overly large, given there was only seven of them left.

"Did you think Helen would get executed?" she asked.

"Yes, she was unhappy and the public are only cruel when someone deserves it. I'm guessing you certainly didn't think it would go that way?"

"Of course not. Look, I could go round everyone and apologise for what I said but nobody would believe it."

"Fair point! Maybe what you apologise for then is…"

"How I executed it?" She laughed uncomfortably.

"No." Daniel smiled politely. "No, you apologise for not being honest and saying these things to people at a time when you could have a proper conversation about it. Take what you said about me, for example..."

"Do, we have to?"

"Yes, but you didn't say anything I'm not aware of. It was helpful to know I come across as sneaky as that is not my intention. I've had to deal with a lot of shit in my life and I see myself as just being guarded to protect myself. I doubt you're the only person that sees me in a different way. It's helpful feedback, just not screamed at me when I can't discuss it with you."

"I doubt the others will be so understanding."

"Don't write them all off. There's some good people living in this complex."

"Where do I start? With the most difficult and work backwards?"

"Normally, I'd say that, but you may need a few allies before tackling Jamila."

"She'll have me on the chopping block this week anyway, she's due a win."

"Oh, I think you'll be safe. It's me she's gunning for. Can't think why," he smiled.

"How am I going to tackle Adrian?"

"I'd leave that one in the too hard basket."

He then raised an eyebrow, causing Claire to laugh.

"What the fuck is so funny?"

What was it with everyone sneaking around this morning?

"Morning, Adrian. Do you want a brew?"

"Why the fuck are you talking to her?"

"Like it or not, we have to live together."

"What a surprise, Daniel North, the calm and rational one."

"I make my own choices, Adrian. We've not all had such a privileged upbringing."

"What the fuck do you mean by that?"

"The posh voice? Why, what did you think I mean?"

"Who knows in this place – people are back-stabbing twats."

"Should I leave you two to talk it out?" Daniel asked.

"I ain't fucking talking to her ever again."

"I dunno why you're worried, she just told millions of viewers that you've got a big knob. Take the compliment and forget the rest."

"Typical of you to just focus on that."

"Yes, Adrian. I only think about cock, I'm so shallow. I best go to my room now so I can be alone with my lustful thoughts."

Daniel picked up his tea and started walking away.

"You're not leaving me alone with her, are you?"

"You're a big boy... apparently. I'm sure you'll cope."

The rest of the day was tense and awkward as Claire did the rounds and made her apologies. Most people were amenable, to her face at least. Stephanie was too hungover to care, so it was likely she would have a different view come Monday morning. Mike was his usual affable self and said she had a fair point. It looked like Mike and Jamila's relationship was completely broken. Jamila had accepted Claire's apology which Daniel was still reeling from, until Stephanie reminded them of their early alliance and that Jamila's behaviour was no doubt to give her an ally so she wasn't completely isolated. Even Adrian was softening, or perhaps he wanted to prove a point. The evening came around and the drink started flowing, except for Stephanie who stuck to fizzy water. It was unfortunate as she kept burping constantly and

Daniel had added a lot of garlic to the roast lamb he had cooked – one of his grandmother's recipes – and therefore those burps were not pleasant. Claire was starting to get a bit handsy with Adrian again, and although she wasn't back to straddling him, he wasn't batting her hand away either.

The only person who was having a real issue was Callum. He point-blank refused to talk to Claire. In fact, he barely spoke to anyone and just sat there sullenly stabbing at his food like a stroppy teenager. However, he was also knocking back the booze like a student during happy hour.

After they had finished dinner, Callum took a six pack of beers and went back to his apartment. Daniel left it a reasonable amount of time before following. He thought about knocking and then decided against it and just walked in. Callum was sat on the sofa draining the dregs of one of the bottles. He wasn't too far gone yet, so hopefully he would remember this conversation in the morning.

"Come in Daniel, have a beer with me."

"I'm alright thanks. I came to talk to you."

"Sit down with me then," Callum replied, patting the sofa beside him.

Daniel was going to sit in the chair opposite but he sat where he was asked. Callum's hand immediately went on Daniel's thigh. He let it slide – just not too far north.

"I want to talk about last night," Daniel started.

"You talk a lot, Daniel North."

Callum leaned forward and Daniel was expecting some drunken slobber, but instead it was the gentlest, softest kiss. He didn't resist for a few seconds, which became a few more seconds. Apart from the beer breath, it was the perfect kiss. Callum's hands then started travelling north, so Daniel gently broke away.

"Not here, but when we get out of this place, I'd like to see what happens."

Callum still had his faculties enough to know that Daniel wasn't saying *no*, it was simply *not now*.

Daniel stood up and then leaned down and kissed him on the forehead, suggesting he get some sleep. He stroked his cheek, picked up the remaining beers and walked out, looking back as he was at the door to see Callum smiling at him. It had been a long time since somebody had smiled at him like that; it felt good.

After the eventful weekend, it was time for another Guvnorship battle and it was another endurance challenge. They were outside in the middle of winter and had to stand on a log barefoot, in shorts and t-shirt. The longest to stay there would win. Stephanie gave up straight away as she was suffering from a two-day hangover. Daniel also gave it up early on as he knew Jamila would see this one to the end. It was already starting to drizzle, so he saw no point in making himself sick. He made some hot chocolate with cream and marshmallows. It was another of his grandmother's recipe which involved blending melted chocolate with the milk before heating it. They had become popular in the complex, so Daniel made them sparingly.

Mike jumped down from the log and walked over to join them.

"That's not built for a bloke my size. Can I get one of those?"

"Of course, take this one," Daniel said. "I'll make another."

He then left Mike and Stephanie in an awkward silence. He knew Stephanie was sweet on Mike. To date, she had lusted from afar so had been able to converse with him without making a tit out of herself. He was married and therefore off limits, although now perhaps there was a glimmer of hope. Who knew – a lot of crazy things happened in this place.

Daniel left it as long as he could before returning to join them in watching Jamila, Claire, Callum and Adrian battle it out for Complex Guvnor. Daniel knew that a victory for Callum was the only way he could be guaranteed to be safe from execution for another week.

After an hour and another hot chocolate, it was down to the two women. The tall men had succumbed to gravity and were also enjoying a hot chocolate.

Daniel walked over to Zelda with a cup of his speciality. She hesitated for a second and then gratefully accepted.

"You may as well sit with us. Look at the determined look on both their faces. This is going to be a long afternoon."

She nodded and then joined them on the bench. Daniel wondered if there were going to be any tricks to force them off. Perhaps this was a low-budget week and they were saving the pyrotechnics for later.

It was almost four hours, and they'd moved onto mulled wine, before something happened. Unfortunately it was Claire who finally lost her balance and Daniel knew his fate was sealed. The question was, who would he be up against?

Zelda got up, a little bit merry, remembering she had a job to do.

"Jamila, congratulations on your second Guvnorship."

There was no polite applause.

"Can you give us your decision?"

"Yes, Zelda. Claire, I think you put up a great fight so there's no way I could put you up. No, I think this week we should have two of the men battle it out. I choose Daniel, for obvious reasons, and..."

Here we go, thought Daniel.

"Adrian."

Well, fuck a duck!

CHAPTER EIGHTEEN

There was a press frenzy around Daniel versus Adrian. Felix wanted Adrian out of the complex, so hopefully this would work in their favour. The bookies had already stopped taking bets on Adrian being executed due to Daniel's overwhelming popularity. Daniel was the most popular contestant the show had ever had. There was something about him that the public seemed to take to – he could be bitchy, yet he was vulnerable; he could be calculated and a real game player, yet he was sensitive to others. Well, this was Desiree's summation anyway. She tended to be able to read the public mood better than Felix, not that he would ever admit that to her, or anyone else. The power base had to remain as it was.

Daniel North was a very unique individual – completely flawed, yet utterly likeable. There was a way to make money out of this man, before Felix ensured he disappeared back into obscurity. He had requested Desiree come up with a task that Adrian or Jamila couldn't possibly win. They were the only two who could take Adrian off the block – Jamila would have a strategy and she had become very guarded about her plans, even in the Confession Booth. Adrian was too unpredictable and Felix wouldn't be surprised if he saved himself and then blamed Felix for not rigging the substitution challenge against him. He couldn't take the risk of talking to him again, even with Emma now out of the picture. Mrs P had done a fantastic job. Felix knew they'd never hear from her again.

———

The Battle of the Century

Sandra304: This weekend sees the battle of the century when Daniel faces execution against his nemesis Adrian. This promises to be the TV event of the year!!!

Treehugger23: Hardly the TV event of the year. It's a slam dunk Daniel will win, so it's hardly going to be gripping TV when the outcome is already known.

DeliciousDebbie1985: Ignore him Sandra, he's just a troll and should have been banned for what he said about you. You're right though, this execution is going to be EPIC! Do you think Adrian believes he can win?

Sandra304: Adrian thinks he's god's gift and will get all the female votes!!!

DeliciousDebbie1985: He is one fine looking man, but Daniel is good looking as well. Besides, Daniel is a really decent guy as well and dead funny – love him!

Sandra304: You're right, they've done well good with the eye candy this year. Adrian, Daniel, Callum and Mike are all fit – even one of those brothers was hot!!!

DeliciousDebbie1985: I'd forgotten about the brothers. Nobody remembers the ones who went first do they? Haha!

TreeHugger23: I'm sure the families of the people who

were murdered haven't forgotten the three brothers. You should be disgusted with yourselves!

DeliciousDebbie1985: Oh, he's back with his self-right-eous opinions. The man who never watches the show, yet seems to know more about it than anyone else. So who do you want to leave the complex then @Tree-hugger23?

Sandra304: I bet he's an Adrian fan!!!

DeliciousDebbie1985: Yeah, definitely.

TreeHugger23: #DanielToWin

Sandra304: Boom!!!

DeliciousDebbie1985: Woohoo! #DanielToWin

———

Felix had arrived early for the briefing, before everyone else, and had been reviewing the latest social-media reactions. It was mildly entertaining to see a slight look of panic on people's faces as they arrived, checking their watches. He didn't do it often, mainly because he didn't have to be on time; he was the boss. He hadn't slept well and was keen to get the meeting over with so he could get on with the rest of his day.

"Right, now everybody is finally here, let's run through things shall we," said Felix.

The fact that the meeting was starting promptly for the first time this series was irrelevant. Felix had been made to wait. Desiree usually chaired the meetings, as Felix was always late but today he decided to run things.

"First up," he said, looking at the agenda which had been passed to him. "Storylines for tonight's show – one will need to focus on the execution, what are the other two?"

"We have a few choices," said Desiree. "The Mike, Stephanie and Jamila love triangle is a strong contender."

"Is a bit of low-key flirting classed as a love triangle these days?"

"Well if it does become something then it could damage Stephanie's likeability, as it will look like it came from nowhere."

"Fine, go with that. What's happening with the Callum and Daniel thing?"

"Just friends still."

"For god's sake, I've never known two gay guys take it so slow. And I suppose Adrian and Claire are back at it like rabbits?"

"Yes, he seems to be making a lot more effort. He keeps seeking reassurance before, during and after now."

"Well, just weave those two couples into the execution story if we're able to make it vaguely interesting. Have we got anything on Jamila, other than her husband flirting with someone else at a pace that means we'll all be dead when we get a first kiss?"

"She keeps trying to connect with Claire, but she is enjoying Adrian whilst she can. Adrian has convinced her he is leaving this week and she seems to have bought into that. Viewers think he is manipulating her for sex."

"Good, that means the bookies won't be wrong then. Is Adrian still twenty to one on?"

"Drifted to fifty now," piped up one of the others.

"Okay, well nothing is ever certain. What's happening with the substitution? Still scenario testing?"

A few people nodded. He instructed the team to come up with a substitution challenge which would see Daniel victorious. That was the ideal outcome. Whoever did that and ensured victory would get a bonus. They all scurried off to try to outdo each other. That was the way you managed people – a combination of total dominance and having them compete against each other.

. . .

Felix was watching the proposed footage for the nightly broadcast. A regular segment was the late-night chats between Daniel and Stephanie. Felix found them to be absolute drivel, but the viewing public loved them so much that they had their own discussion forum. For that reason Felix allowed them to stay in. He usually only skimmed over this section, but this time was different.

Stephanie and Daniel were sharing the king-size bed and both still sat up chatting. They were drinking wine and still dressed. This was a break from their usual routine when they were both in their pyjamas with a cup of Daniel's homemade hot chocolate looking like a couple who had been married for fifty years. Tonight, they were acting their age and it was clear that they were both a little merry.

"Still no joy with you and Callum then?" asked Stephanie.

"No, and there won't be. Not in here anyway."

"So when you get outside you'll be straight in there," she laughed.

"Who knows, but I'm not looking for anything serious."

"Have you ever had a boyfriend?"

"Of course, there's been a few. Nothing longer than a few months, though."

"Did you ever meet someone who you thought was the one?"

"There was a special guy once, but that's a long story."

"Well I ain't tired."

Daniel appeared reluctant to tell the story although Stephanie topped up his glass and looked at him like she was interested in hearing nothing else.

"I suppose I'd better set some context. About five years

ago, I couldn't get any work because of the recession. It didn't help that I wasn't really qualified for anything as I'd done so many different jobs. Anyway, I was online one night and started chatting to some guy and it sort of went from there."

"What, was that the guy who you thought was the one?"

Daniel took a very large swig of his wine. "No, that was the first guy who paid me for sex."

Stephanie screamed with delight that she was now getting a juicy story. This was not news to Felix. The researchers had uncovered this in Daniel's past and it was to be his execution story. That wouldn't matter now as he was going to win the whole show, but Felix didn't like to not have a back-up plan. He had learnt that when dealing with the public you couldn't assume everything would go your way, although it usually did for Felix. However, Felix wanted to see where this story was going to go. If it didn't go anywhere then they'd cut it from the show in case he did need to use it later.

Stephanie had gone to get more wine and when she returned Daniel told her of how he'd worked for almost a year as a male escort when he met a new client one night. That was when everything had changed.

"What was his name?"

"Best save that one for when we're not on national TV, babes."

"On yeah," she laughed. "I always forget."

"Well I went round to this guy's place and when he opened the door I thought I had the wrong place. The guy was drop-dead gorgeous. You know, the kind of muscled hairy daddy look."

"Nice."

"Exactly and he looked like he was only ten years older than me."

"Why was he paying for it then?"

"That's what I thought. I was a bit cautious as I had been

robbed a couple of times before and they were usually the younger clients."

"You were robbed?"

"Occupational hazard, I only got physically attacked once."

"Oh my god!"

"That's a story for another day. Anyway, I met this guy. Turns out he was in his late thirties. He had a high-powered job and just wanted to get his end away with no strings attached."

"Isn't that what most gay guys do every weekend?"

"He also didn't want to spend time looking for the perfect guy and I was exactly what he was looking for."

"So what happened?"

"We had a great time. Easiest money I have ever earned in my life."

"Oh my god, you still charged him?"

"Of course. I stayed the whole night as that was the deal and then in the morning I left with a grand in my wallet."

"A grand for one night's work? Jesus, I've been doing something wrong all these years."

"Well, that was the going rate. They probably get more nowadays. Anyway, we stayed up all night chatting and having sex. I could talk quite openly to him. He asked me about some of the scars on my back and I was just honest and told him about the bombing. I have no idea why. I just felt I could talk to him. No idea what it was, there was just something about him. Anyway, he called me a week later and said he'd like to see me again. I don't know what possessed me to do it because it was easy money, but I just said he didn't need to pay me next time and it kind of went from there."

"How long did you see him for?"

"Six months."

"Did you keep seeing other clients?"

"At first. I needed the money and then he helped me get a proper job so I stopped. It was only a stop-gap and besides when I was doing it I only spent the bare essentials so I had enough money for a deposit on my own place."

"In a year? Bloody hell, what was your hourly rate?"

"I didn't have one. I only did overnight stays and two or three of them a week for a year soon adds up."

"So why didn't it work out?"

"I went into self-sabotage mode. Screwed the whole thing up because I have some fucked-up view that I don't deserve to be happy."

Stephanie smiled.

"What?"

"You and me are exactly the same. Well, except for the fact that I'd charge two grand a night for anyone to get a piece of this," she said, running her hands over her body.

This resulted in more laughter from them.

Felix turned off the footage.

Later that day, he tasked Desiree with tracking down the mystery man. Mrs P had not been keen on Felix's decision for Daniel to now be the winner, so he wanted her to stay out of the way. She thought they should just let a nobody win and put this series down to experience; there was little chance of that happening. They needed to find this guy, as the last thing they needed was a kiss and tell in some second-rate tabloid. The footage of Stephanie and Daniel's chat wouldn't be broadcast. It was best if nobody knew anything about this part of Daniel's past, although he suspected the die-hard fans wouldn't care. There was always the possibility that there was more that Daniel wasn't sharing; Felix had to go against every natural instinct and do all he could to protect him.

CHAPTER NINETEEN

It was time for the substitution challenge and everyone was up for this one. They all wanted to change who faced execution this week. Daniel suspected that the primary reason for people wanting to change things was to piss off Jamila. Stephanie, Mike and Callum had all said they would save him, not realising that this would be at the expense of one of the others as Jamila had made it clear she would not put Claire up for the public vote. Daniel had, in a way, made his peace with Adrian, yet the guy had been such an arsehole in the first week, he was excited by the challenge of going up against him.

Claire had made it clear that she would save Adrian, although Adrian had said he could fight his own battles. Ironically, it looked like Daniel and Adrian might be the only ones who wouldn't change anything, although saying something and then actually doing it were very different things. Jamila had even indicated that she might *mix things up* should she be victorious in the challenge.

Zelda was looking groggy. Perhaps another late night for her, although it was now six in the evening. It was late in the day for a challenge, especially if they wanted it to go out that night, but who was Daniel to question editorial decisions.

Zelda introduced the challenge; it involved moving from one side of a room to the other without touching the lasers. Anyone touching the laser would be out and for those who made it across, the fastest time would win. If nobody completed the challenge, they would go again until someone did – this was not going to be over quickly.

"Jamila, as our current Complex Guvnor, you're up first," said Zelda, less bouncy than usual. Perhaps she had finally run out of fucks.

Jamila stepped forward and then proceeded to remove her clothes down to her underwear. She then started hissing like a cat and prowling towards the laser room. It was like one of those incredibly cringe-worthy moments on TV when it is so horrendous that you have to change channel until it's over – no such luck here.

She threw herself to the ground outside the room and start rubbing herself against the floor, wriggling and growling and then stretching into yoga positions. Everyone was dumb-founded, apart from her husband, Mike, who was doing all he could to stop from laughing. Unfortunately, others had noticed Mike's shoulders shaking which set them off as well. It didn't take long until everyone cracked up. Jamila just looked up at them and hissed – perhaps she had finally flipped.

Zelda asked her if she needed any help, Jamila just growled at her. Zelda went to move towards her, and then Jamila went into the room like a gymnast. Unfortunately, she was a gymnast who didn't keep her arse tucked in; less than a minute had passed when the buzzer went to say that she had hit one the lasers. She came running out of the room, hitting more lasers, making more buzzing sounds – she started ranting hysterically.

"This fucking piece of shitting crap. It's a fucking conspiracy. You're all a bunch of cunts. All against me because I'm strong and I'll beat all you fuckers. You wouldn't survive in the jungle, but I would. I am a lioness, hear me roar."

Then she started roaring and jumping around like she was a cat being electrocuted. She then picked up her clothes, hissed and walked over to the bench, sat down and started to get dressed, like nothing had happened.

"Erm... next up is Mike," Zelda said.

Mike walked up to the door of the laser room and stopped. He was about to do something and then clearly thought better of it. You could literally see the cogs whirring round. He just shook his head, smiled and went into the room. He did last slightly longer than Jamila, although he was not successful. His gigantic frame did him no favours. This was also the same for Callum when he went in and tried, although he got a little further.

Claire did very well. She was almost at the end when there was that familiar buzzer.

"Oh for fuck sake," she said from inside the room, causing much laughter.

The mood had lightened somewhat. Jamila was sat on the bench on her own. Everyone else was giving her a wide berth, which meant sitting on the cold floor. This didn't seem to bother anybody. Daniel had noticed Adrian look relieved when Claire had lost. He supposed he didn't want his fate to be up to anyone else either. It was Daniel's turn to be tense now as Stephanie gave it a try, but within ten seconds she was out of this round, muttering something about her arse.

Adrian went next and it was obvious that he wasn't really trying. He did enough to not be out straight away, but Daniel was sure when he hit the laser it was deliberate. Next up was Daniel. He had done something similar before at *The Crystal Maze* in London. There was a lot more to play for here, than a glass object masquerading as a crystal. This was about control, and Daniel wanted to be in control of his own destiny on this show for once.

Daniel took his time. He didn't have to be quick, as there wasn't a time to beat. He worked out that there were ten moves that would get him across the room and he would predominantly need to keep low, which he did. The whole thing seemed to take an age, but he was later told it was only four minutes. He felt such an amazing sense of accomplishment as he made it to the other side and pressed the button turning off all the lasers. He then walked out of the room to cheers and applause from everyone other than Jamila who seemed to be no longer channelling her inner cat goddess and was waiting to put forward a new name once Daniel saved himself.

"Congratulations, Daniel," said Zelda, walking forward. "You now have the opportunity to take yourself or Adrian off the block. If that happens then Jamila can choose someone else from the group to take their place. Are you ready?"

"Yes, I've thought a lot about this, in case I won this challenge and I really wanted to win this challenge for this reason. If I were to substitute myself then Jamila has four choices. Stephanie and Callum, I'd never want to take a risk on the two of you going home before me. I'm not sure my sanity would last without the two of you."

Callum and Stephanie both beamed at him.

"Mike, you've had a shit week, well a shit couple of weeks and although the possibility of going home might appeal because it gets you away from her," he said, pointing at Jamila, "if you're going to go, it should be on your terms and not hers."

Daniel watched Mike blink back a few tears. This made Stephanie flush, probably with lust.

"Claire," Daniel continued, "you've had a shit week as

well. Not many people could say what you said and then face everyone the way you did. I don't think we'll ever be bosom buddies, but I also don't believe in kicking someone when they're down. So that leaves me with only one option. I choose to make no substitution."

The next morning, Daniel was having a relaxed and quiet breakfast. One thing he was looking forward to when he got out of this place was some alone time. He didn't realise how much he missed his own company, until it was no longer possible to have it. There was always the risk of someone just walking in, you being called to the Confession Booth, or just the whir of a camera zooming in on you. He savoured these private moments – well, the façade of privacy anyway.

It was not to last as he saw Callum coming down the stairs from the apartment, making his way towards Daniel with one of those determined looks on his face. Callum had gone on one of his drinking binges again last night. It was his answer to any highly stressful situation, and a typical teenage response. It was at these times that the age gap between then seemed too wide.

"I need to talk to you," said Callum.

He stunk of booze. It took all of Daniel's willpower not to wince.

"If it's about last night then I don't want to talk about it. I made my decision."

"I thought we had something between us."

"I said we'd see what happens when we get out of this place."

"Well in two days' time you won't have to worry about that, will you?"

"Thanks for the vote of confidence."

"You'll have men all over you when you get out of here. Like…"

"Flies on shit?"

"I was going to say bees to a honeypot."

"Well let's go with that one then and thank you for the ego boost, but I seriously doubt your assessment of my pulling power."

"If I had the opportunity to make sure we could have some more time together then I would have taken it."

"And what if she'd put you on the block instead?"

"She would have put Mike up. That was obvious."

"The one thing Jamila isn't, is obvious. Just go back to bed, Callum. I don't want to argue with you and do bear in mind that I might actually beat Adrian in the public vote, but like I said thanks for the vote of confidence."

Callum stayed still just looking at Daniel. His brain slowly processing what had been said. Daniel sighed, jumped off the stool and made his way towards the gym. The last place he wanted to go, but the only place where he might get some privacy. The complex was starting to get to him. The slightest little thing seemed to set people off. It wasn't just the pressure of the game and all the tactics involved in that, it was the relationships. Who fancied each other, who was a real friend, who was using someone as part of their game plan; it was exhausting.

Callum was so inconsistent, although Daniel largely put that down to him being nineteen with the Irish temperament thrown in. Stephanie said he was a very emotional young man who wore his heart in his sleeve. That may be, but lately there had been a few instances of him simply behaving like a petulant child and it was a bit of a turn-off.

Stephanie was behaving like a love-sick puppy and all she could talk about was Mike. Do you think Mike is interested? What do you think people will think of me if I make a move?

He's still married so will this damage my career? I really like him, do you think he'll get back with his wife? If something happened in here, do you think she'll kick off? Do you think it's really over between them?

He missed Helen and her no-nonsense German bluntness. It had been the right time for her to go but Daniel really needed to speak to someone who wasn't so focussed on their own drama. The unspoken rule was if that you were facing execution then you got to be the drama queen. Even Mike just wanted to talk about how he shouldn't have stayed married to Jamila and what would people think of him for staying her with so long, or would him walking away make the public sympathise with her, so she could now win the whole thing – Daniel was at the end of his tether.

He went to the gym and pushed the door open. Adrian was in there working up his usual sweat, so Daniel turned around to walk back out.

"I'm not using any of the cardio machines. Go ahead and just help yourself."

"It's fine. I actually just came here for some peace and quiet. There doesn't seem to be any quiet corners today, and considering there are only seven of us left, that's a worry."

"I'll be done in five, so just wait around and then you can chill."

Daniel nodded and went and sat on the sofa. It was hard not to stare when Adrian doing one of his workouts. It was like the scene setting at the start of a porn film. You were just waiting for the other guy to come in, so things could progress after some pointless dialogue.

"You thinking about Saturday night?" Adrian asked.

Great, he wanted to talk.

"A bit, you just never know how these things will go."

"Well I'm sure you'll be fine. I was a complete prick for the first two weeks."

"Yes, but you have abs, and according to Claire, a big knob."

Adrian smiled. "In different circumstances, do you think we may have got on better?"

"I have no idea. I doubt our paths would ever have crossed to be honest."

"It's just we have a fair bit in common. Shame we got off on the wrong foot."

"Erm..."

"My foot, I know, but like I said. It's a shame."

What on earth did they have in common?

"How long has your mum been gone?" asked Adrian.

"Almost ten years, why do you ask?"

"Mine's been gone just over a year."

"I had no idea."

"It's not easy to talk about."

He was right. Even after all this time, it was hard to not experience a rush of emotion.

"Your dad not around?" asked Adrian.

"Never knew him. Mum said he wasn't interested."

"Same. See, more in common than you think."

How could Daniel not know this about Adrian? He had lived with this guy for over a month and had no idea they had such a major life experience in common. Losing his mother at such a young age had a lasting impact on him and had shaped the man he had become; Adrian can only have been a year older than Daniel when he lost his mother. He'd also said before that he had no siblings; in fact, he didn't really talk about any family. Had Adrian had anyone to support him? Daniel had his grandmother and he was not sure what he would have done without her. Daniel was suddenly hit by a wave of emotion and knew he had to change the subject.

"What's the first thing you'll do if you leave?" asked Daniel.

Adrian smiled, clearly realising what Daniel was doing. "Think I'll enjoy my own company for a while. Maybe even go away."

"I'd like to get away as well, but we have to stick around for the finale don't we?"

"That's four weeks away, plenty of time for some sunshine."

"True – that would be nice. All these outdoor tasks are not just getting on my tits, they're going to make then freeze and fall off."

"You'll have to wait for that beach holiday, though."

"Why?"

"You're not going anywhere. You'll get all the gay guys voting for you," said Adrian as he pulled up his vest to wipe the sweat off his forehead.

Knowing his fellow fickle gays, Daniel wasn't convinced that was a guaranteed outcome!

CHAPTER TWENTY

It was the day of the execution and Felix was anxious. He was never usually like this, but he needed Adrian gone so he could re-focus on the rest of the game. There was still a month to go and it was the first time Felix had felt that he wasn't in complete control of one of his programme narratives and he hated it. Reality TV was scripted manipulation, but this show was taking a life of its own, mainly because he seemed to have chosen a collection of characters that were not transparent and easily manipulated. Even though it made for fascinating TV and the best ratings he had ever had for any show in this late-night TV slot, he didn't like it.

The day following the substitution challenge, Felix wanted to be absolutely certain that Jamila was not crazy in any libellous way. She had stopped acting like a cat, yet Felix still had her checked over. There was already a kerfuffle on social media about Felix playing with people's mental health. The resurrection of Reality TV had brought with it new safe-guarding measures. Anyone with any known mental health problems in the last five years was out. This had made the fishing pool very shallow, but there were lots of crazies who didn't get treatment, although the psychologist they used for the audition process had to ask questions in the *right* way, so the favourites didn't rule themselves out with their own admissions. They had been close with Daniel. He'd had a major breakdown five years earlier and had only just made the cut-off. Felix had Daniel's medical records; although he could never use them, they were useful intelligence.

Felix remembered Daniel's conversation the other night with Stephanie and wondered if this mystery man could be connected to the breakdown. Had he caused it or was he part of the *healing process*? Felix gagged; the fact that the term *healing process* had even entered his consciousness was something that made him shudder. He just hoped he never said it out loud; he'd have to sack anyone who heard it.

Felix didn't recruit anyone with known mental-health problems; however, the guidelines said nothing about the mental state of the contestants when they left one of his shows. He was pleased to see Debbie was jumping to his defence, yet again. One thread title had particularly entertained him.

———

Felix Moldoon is a sociopath

Treehugger23: It is clear to anyone with half a brain that last night Jamila Edwards had a mental breakdown. Not only was she allowed to continue with her manic episode without medical intervention, but all her fellow neighbours were laughing at her. This is all about Felix Moldoon pushing his agenda. It is obvious this contest was rigged so Jamila wouldn't win and change her execution choices to get rid of her cheating husband.
DeliciousDebbie1985: This was not a mental break-

down. The woman was just looking for attention and if she wanted to execute her husband she should have put him on the block from the start. She's the one who pushed him away. He's a free man now to do what he wants. #DanielToWin

Treehugger23: The fact that you want Daniel to win when he is the most manipulative game player in there shows that you don't know anything. #JamilaToWin

DeliciousDebbie1985: You wanted Daniel to win the other day!

Treehugger23: That's before we saw what a manipulator he was. Look at that conversation with Adrian, who wanted to talk about his late mum, but Daniel changed the subject back on to his favourite topic – himself!

DeliciousDebbie1985: Daniel is one of the few genuine ones in there and it was clear that he found the conversation too emotional to talk about. I can't believe you want Jamila to win. She is a snake, who doesn't care who she steps on to get the money

Treehugger23: She is playing the game. She should win with the mental cruelty she has had to endure under that tyrant Felix Moldoon. Have you heard about poor Helen? She is completely alone with no follow up care. #ArrestFelix

DeliciousDebbie1985: Everyone knows what they are signing up for and Helen is hardly alone. She had friends and family before she went on the show and she still does. It's unfortunate that Meena's done a runner from both her families but can you blame her? One of them kidnapped her and lied to her for her entire life and the others have been looking for her for nearly twenty years and are suddenly not interested because she kissed another woman on TV.

Treehugger23: I don't think it's right to bring religion into this. I will have to report you to the moderators.
DeliciousDebbie1985: You were the first one to bring religion up!
Treehugger23: I'm reporting you to the moderators
DeliciousDebbie1985: For what? Because I won't jump on your little Jamila bandwagon
Treehugger23: Your comments about Jamila and Meena tell me that you're racist and that isn't tolerated on this forum.
DeliciousDebbie1985: So all I have done is made some assumptions about why Meena has disappeared, because her birth family rejected her and Jamila is the most unlikeable person in the world. Race has nothing to do with it.
Treehugger23: Reported!

——————

Debbie was on top form; as usual she saw the show for what it was. Some people were far too sensitive these days and claimed everything was bullying or abusive, just because they simply didn't like it. Felix was of the older generation who were more reasoned and logical about the fact that some people have a different point of view to you and there was no sinister or discriminatory motive to it. You simply can't agree with everyone. Not everything had to be an argument, but the generations after Felix seemed to be constantly offended. It was a wonder how they got anything done. However, these new youngsters coming into adulthood weren't so easily offended by everything, simply because they didn't really care about anyone but themselves.

An email arrived from the show's psychiatrist on his assessment of Jamila. She was fine and just acting that way to try to garner some sympathy from her fellow neighbours considering they had as good as ostracised her now. The psychiatrist had recommended that they introduce some tasks to reintegrate Jamila back into the group as if she continued to be ostracised she might then suffer from genuine mental-health issues. Typical doctor, covering his own arse; Felix would ignore it for now. If any further reports mentioned it again then he might have to do something, but for now he could ensure nobody else saw the report.

Desiree had been dragging her heels on the investigation into the mystery man from Daniel's past. He would ask her to explore the breakdown from Daniel's medical records and see if the two were linked; the timelines appeared to match.

At least when it came to the tasks for the show Desiree could still come up with a winner when it mattered – although the substitution challenge was not the most original idea, it had worked and earned her the bonus. They had to be very creative with the edit and remove every reference to *The Crystal Maze* which Daniel made. This meant they couldn't really show much of the follow-up discussion after the challenge because he wouldn't stop mentioning the bloody place!

The important thing to come out of this week was that Adrian would soon be out of the complex, Felix would have fulfilled his promise and that would be the end of it. It was a shame it had to come to this, as there was a part of Felix that considered for a moment that there might be an opportunity to form a relationship with his son.

Mrs P was back in the country for Adrian's execution. She was adamant that she wanted to be here for it. Felix just hoped that she didn't have any ideas about them building a relationship. The best outcome was for Adrian to get the opportunity to build his own future; Felix couldn't be part of it. He had worked too hard to bury his past and being Adrian's father was just the tip of the iceberg.

Luckily, Adrian had no desire to be famous. He could be very successful at modelling, which would only last so long and there were hundreds of guys with the same good looks and great bodies. He would be nothing unique in that world, just another pretty face. Thankfully, it would be easy to convince Adrian to put his fleeting moment of fame behind him.

A *quick* penetration of Lucinda on Friday night had confirmed that with over five million votes already cast there was an eighty per cent vote against Adrian. Felix knew that until he had those final vote numbers ready to pass over to Zelda he couldn't assume anything with this series, although he was now quietly confident that the public would deliver him the result he wanted.

What had been interesting to watch over the last couple of days, was Daniel's reaction to the impending execution. He clearly had no concept of how popular he was. He believed, due to Adrian's prior behaviour that he could win, yet this demonstrated that he only regarded his potential victory would be due to votes *against* Adrian, rather than *for* him.

He was very different to the last time he was up for execution, in that he seemed relaxed about it. This wasn't a defeatist attitude, he wanted to win and he wasn't going to give up easily. He was still plotting and scheming with Callum and Stephanie about the rest of the game, with Mike now becoming close to that group.

There was some tension between Stephanie and Mike, although nobody was doing anything. Just a little look here and there. Nothing to get moist about. It would be great TV if they could be pushed together, thus definitively ending his marriage to Jamila. However, if Felix left it to happen natu-

rally, people would turn off in their droves at the
action.

They just needed a little nudge and Felix had to be car
about how he gave that little nudge. The last thing he needed
was for all the women to be hated and him have an exclu-
sively white male final – the snowflake generation would have
a field day. He also didn't want Jamila to come across as a
victim. She was the best villain the show had ever had and he
was looking forward to using her on other shows. She was so
money hungry that she wouldn't give a shit about what
anyone else thought of her. Her story would never be about
redemption; it needed to be about revenge and Felix had to
take her attention off Daniel, so Daniel didn't get pushed too
far, explode and potentially ruin his chances of winning. It
was like a fragile and hormonal game of chess.

It was an hour before the execution and Felix was sitting in
his office when Mrs P arrived to talk to him.

"All on track?" she asked.

"Yes."

"Then, what?"

"How do you mean?"

"Are you going to spend some time with him?"

"I've got a show to run."

"You're not answering my question."

"I think it's best if he just has his money and disappears."

"Best for who?"

"Who do you think?"

"And what do we do with him before the final?"

"I'm sure he can look after himself."

"I'll keep an eye on him."

"Don't you need to get back to the island?"

"Yes, that's what I mean."

"Fine – anything else?"

"Yes," she said, sitting down. "Talk me through plan B."

"I don't make contingency plans. I don't need to and besides Adrian is leaving tonight. That is an absolute certainty."

"I don't doubt you there, Felix. You've made sure that Adrian is hated across the country."

He chose not to respond.

"What I mean, is, what if Daniel doesn't win."

"He will win."

"Are you so sure?"

In reality he wasn't, and she knew that. Historically, he would just assume that his storyline would prevail as mapped out, just like it had with the previous series; this series had him riddled with doubts.

Felix also hadn't fired anyone for five days; a new record. He was keen to not be in another situation which would cause someone else to go digging around his background, so he had been more lenient that usual, although he didn't want to arouse suspicion.

"I need to sack someone tonight."

"Here is a new pre-approved list," she said, passing it to him as she stood up. "I'll leave you to prepare for the show."

He glanced at the list, most names unfamiliar, not that it mattered. He waited for her to leave and then took out his cocaine. He then thought better of it as he wanted to be in complete control tonight. He would handle Adrian's debrief personally.

CHAPTER TWENTY-ONE

Daniel was nervous as he stepped into the execution tube for the second time; the last being a month ago, and what an eventful month it had been. Part of him wasn't worried about going home tonight. He had done what he had set out to do and had set up a platform to ensure people remembered what had happened nine years ago.

Stephanie had given him a huge hug before he got into the tube. Even though she said she wasn't worried, Daniel could tell she wasn't completely convinced it would go the way they hoped. Daniel reassured her that the worst outcome was that he wouldn't see her for a month. They were now friends for life and nothing was going to change that. Mike and Claire had been very grateful for what Daniel had done in the substitution challenge and it was good to see everyone else with a common purpose – to get Jamila out of the complex the following week. If she lost the Guvnorship then everyone else would nominate her for execution. It was then just about stopping her from winning the substitution and she was a gonner; then the best man or woman would win one million pounds.

Callum had not given Daniel a choice and kissed him in front of everyone before he got into the tube. This had caused everyone else to cheer, even Zelda. Daniel had shaken Adrian's hand and wished him luck. He'd genuinely meant it. The guy had been a fuckwit when he arrived although Daniel suspected that was all a front. He had experienced something difficult that Daniel could relate to and he knew that whichever Adrian was the true person, the experience in the complex would have had an impact in him; it was impossible for it not to. Daniel never saw the point in holding onto grudges; especially with something that in the grand scheme of things was not a big deal. Some people don't get along; deal with it.

No doubt, if it were Adrian to go tonight, his post-execution interview would talk about *his journey* and the *emotional rollercoaster* he had been on for the past few weeks. Daniel suspected his own interview would follow a similar theme. Did anyone not experience an emotional rollercoaster in this crazy place?

"Daniel and Adrian – it's time," shouted Zelda.

She was bouncing on the balls of her feet again.

"The public have voted and we have had over ten million votes..."

Could that be true?

"And I can now reveal that our fifth execution and tenth person to leave the complex is..."

Daniel looked at Zelda, looked at the others, looked at Adrian, looked at the floor, looked at the sky, looked at his nails, back to Zelda...

"By a vote of ninety per cent..."

Zelda pulled the lever and Daniel saw Adrian disappear from sight with a smile on his face.

The next few moments were a blur as the tube lifted up and Daniel's fellow neighbours, or friends as he now considered them, swamped him. Zelda thrust a microphone into his face and he mumbled *thank you* about a million times and some other gibberish that he barely remembered.

The one thing he did remember though was his embarrassment when Mike came up to him. Daniel held out his hand, yet Mike grabbed him into a bear hug, which inadvertently meant that Daniel grabbed Mike's crotch. This had made Mike laugh. As he was trying to breathe through Mike's hug, he spotted Jamila giving one of her, *I hate you,* looks. In that moment, Daniel decided that he might not be bothered about winning the entire thing, but he wanted to be there to end with his friends in the final. He looked back at Jamila and mouthed two words...

You're next!

"Right, let's break up this celebration," shouted Zelda over the noise. "I have an announcement to make. Can you all line up please?"

They all did as they were told with a few murmurings about what could be about to happen next. Hopefully it wouldn't be some ridiculous twist that would change the entire concept of the game.

"We have a twist that is going to turn the game on its head."

Zelda was screeching with excitement, forgetting she had a microphone, so the volume and pitch were horrendous, not to mention barbaric to any dogs living in the near vicinity.

"We are now going straight into a Guvnorship challenge... So, are we ready?"

There was an enthusiastic yes from everyone, still hyper from the execution result. Daniel had a fleeting moment of regret at his little *you're next* moment to Jamila and then saw that determined look on her face. In that moment, he knew he had to do everything he could to get her out of this complex so they could all enjoy the rest of their experience.

"Right, let's reveal the challenge," Zelda shouted dramatically.

Zelda pointed to the sky with her back to the door which was now sliding open. Realising her mistake, she did some bizarre dance to shuffle around and point in the direction of where the task was going to be. Unfortunately this caused her to lose her balance in her eight-inch heels and fly backwards, luckily into the burly arms of one of her security guards. She then proceeded to thank him, whilst stroking his arms and chest.

"Right, onwards... march."

Was she for real?

They arrived at a series of boards all with identical pictures and words on them. They were asked, or rather, ordered to stand by one each. There was a picture of each remaining neighbour including themselves, seven pictures of animals and seven words all symbolised a different colour. It was looking like another low-budget week.

"The task is simple. How well do you know your neighbours? Match the face to their favourite colour and animal. The first one to do it correctly wins. However, you only get one attempt; if you get it wrong, you are out of the contest. If nobody wins then you will all be up for execution, with the public deciding the final two throughout the week. Now, are you ready for this?"

They all shouted positively as it was the quickest way to move Zelda forward when she was *on*. Zelda blew a whistle, perhaps the claxon was in the shop, and the game began.

Daniel decided to pace himself and think about it. This wasn't a task to rush. He'd start with the colours. His favourite colour was red. He knew Stephanie's favourite colour was green and took a stab that pink belonged to Claire. Now he was into trickier territory – yellow, blue and purple remained, so he took a guess that Mike was blue, Jamila was yellow and Callum was purple.

Now to the animals – his was definitely a zebra, Stephanie loved elephants. They'd had some weird conversations at night; now they were paying off. He knew Mike loved cats as he had talked about having a pet one. Jamila had said she was allergic, until Mike had found out that was a lie, although he had never confronted her on it. Claire had banged on about her dog a fair few times so he made the assumption that this was for her and he was left with a snake and a monkey. Could Jamila really like snakes? That would be apt! One thing this task was bringing up was that Daniel didn't know Callum that well, or perhaps they didn't just talk about mundane crap such as favourite colours and animals – yeah, that was it.

Daniel heard the buzzer sounding, meaning someone had attempted to guess the correct answers; it was Jamila.

"That is incorrect, Jamila, you are out of the game."

Was it Daniel's imagination, or did Zelda seem pleased about that? He certainly was; it meant that no matter what happened in the rest of the contest, she would up for execution this week. The only downside was that it didn't necessarily mean she would stay on the chopping block until the public vote thanks to the substitution challenge. Then if she did face the public vote there was no guarantee she would go, although Daniel believed she had done too much for even Felix Moldoon to be able to manipulate the public into saving her.

Claire was next to run forward and she was eliminated, followed by Stephanie. It seemed just the men were taking their time. Callum was next and he was also wrong, shortly followed by Mike. It was all down to Daniel. He was going to go with his gut instinct and then paused for a second. Perhaps if he didn't get it right then having them all up for the chop might relieve some tension for the week and would certainly see the end of Jamila.

He quickly swapped his zebra with Stephanie's elephant and walked forward and pressed the button – he was out of the game as well.

"So, we don't have a Guvnor this week and you re all up for execution. The person with the least votes will be announced as safe on Monday, and the same each day until four of you are safe. The final two will then face off."

"Does the substitution challenge mean immunity for someone then?" Jamila asked, typically.

"There will be no substitution challenge this week," Zelda announced, bouncing away.

"What, but how are we supposed to save ourselves from execution. That's the purpose of the game – to win."

"You'll just have to appeal to the public, Jamila."

Boom!

Daniel was waiting for Zelda to do a mic drop, but it was not to be.

"Just so you know, Daniel, you were the closest. If you'd just put yours and Stephanie's animal choices the other way around then you'd have won the Guvnorship."

Daniel thanked Zelda for dropping him in the shit.

"You fucking did this deliberately," snapped Jamila. "Everyone knows that fat cunt loves elephants, because she looks like one."

"You're being well out of order, Jamila," said Mike, standing directly in front of her. "If you actually acted like a decent human being then you might actually have some friends in this place. Not to mention a husband. As soon as we get out of here, I want a divorce."

"Don't expect me to share the money with you then when I win. You all heard it, he asked me for a divorce before I won the money."

"Do you actually think you can win this show, with the way you've behaved?"

"It's a game. People respect someone who plays a good game."

"People also don't like bullies and that's what you are – a bully. Hopefully, after this week, I will never have to see you again."

And with that he walked away – well, towards the beer fridge in the kitchen. Zelda suddenly realised everyone was looking at her, so she turned back to the camera to wrap up the show and offer yet another apology for Jamila's language.

It was going to be another interesting week.

"Why did you do it?" Callum asked Daniel later.

"I think this is the best option."

"But you could have definitely put Jamila up if you'd won."

"And she may have saved herself with substitution."

"How did you know there wasn't going to be one?"

"It's what they did on the last series."

"Well, hopefully it will pan out."

"Do you think it won't?"

"Well you'll be okay, based on the nine million votes you just had against your competitor. The rest of us might not be so fortunate."

"It'll be fine."

"Just been nice of you to tell us what you were planning."

"It wasn't a plan. I just decided in the moment."

"Well, I suppose you know what you're doing. I'm going back downstairs anyway."

Callum left the apartment. He didn't slam the door – which, in a way, made it worse.

He was now sharing an apartment with Mike and Callum. Stephanie was in with Claire, and Jamila was on her own.

Three apartments had been closed off so there were limited options. Daniel wondered if another apartment could be closed after the next execution. As long as it was Jamila who left they'd be fine. He wasn't sure what Callum was so annoyed about.

The plan was going to work – how could it not?

CHAPTER TWENTY-TWO

Felix closed the hotel room door behind him. Adrian was sitting with a posture that demonstrated his overwhelming arrogance. This was the *real* Adrian.

"Where is my fucking money?" he snapped in his real, broad Lancashire accent.

"Do you have to always use that revolting language? It doesn't do you any favours you know."

"Look, I didn't agree to this meeting to get a pep talk. I've delivered my side of the bargain. Now pay up."

"The money will be in your account tomorrow. Now I want to discuss something with you."

"Money first, talk later. You can just log in to your bank on your phone and send me the money now. Then we'll talk."

"Listen, you stupid fucking prick. You can't just move a million pounds with an app on your phone."

"And you talk to me about language."

"Listen..."

"No, you listen. I agreed to go along with this charade at the detriment to myself because you promised me a payoff."

"And you'll get it..."

"Have you seen what people think of me after I played the character you created?"

"Look..."

"No you look. Sort the money and then come back and talk to me. I'm not going anywhere. Thanks to you I'm public enemy number two, after Jamila."

Adrian walked over to his bag, took out his passport and passed it to Felix, who took it without really thinking; he was fuming. He was giving this guy a million quid for nothing; well, as far as Adrian knew it was for nothing. The least he could do was speak to him.

"Now I can't go anywhere," he walked over and opened the hotel door. "I'll talk to you tomorrow, when I've got the money."

Felix simply nodded, in order to keep his temper under control and then left. The door shut quietly behind him. The money was always going to be paid. A million pound was nothing. However, he wanted to keep Mrs P sweet and out of his way; getting Adrian out of the UK for a bit whilst things calmed down would do that. However, the money was the only hold he had over him. He might be in a better mood in the morning, although Felix doubted it. He had that determined look on his face and he could also be dangerous if he started talking – he was definitely Felix's son.

Felix went to the hotel bar and called Mrs P, who was waiting at the airport. He told her to arrange for the money to be transferred immediately to the holding account they had set up for Adrian. It wasn't true what he'd said to Adrian. You could move as much money as you wanted in seconds if you had the right setup. She asked him when Adrian would be on his way. He just told her to confirm when it was done and cut off the call – he didn't want to tell her how their last conversation had gone. She was starting to get on Felix's nerves with her interfering.

Within half an hour Felix had polished off two drinks and received confirmation that the money was transferred. He downed his third double whisky and decided he would deal with Adrian straight away. Adrian would comply now that Felix had the literal carrot to dangle in front of him. There was a good chance Adrian wouldn't let him back in, so he got a key to the room from Reception. All the staff knew Felix. It was the hotel everyone stayed after being executed from the show. His staff also stayed here when they were working late. In fact, this hotel was only operating because of Felix's business, so when he requested the key of another guest's room he wasn't even questioned.

He arrived back at Adrian's room and let himself in. In the intervening time Adrian had somehow managed to get a girl into his bed and was going to town on her, at such frenzy that he hadn't even noticed Felix enter the room, until he slammed the door and turned the light on.

"What the fuck," shouted Adrian.

He attempted a graceful dismount and ended up falling off the bed. Unfortunately, he landed on a wine glass and screamed in pain as his arm was cut open. The woman seemed to have no decorum; she just stayed where she was, legs spread, assuming the last few seconds had been a minor interruption to her orgasm.

"You can leave," Felix said to her.

"I ain't going anywhere until I get paid."

Felix took out his wallet and handed her a wad of notes. She squealed with delight, gathered up her belongings and was out the door fully dressed in less than twenty seconds – now that was skill.

Felix walked over to Adrian who was still dazed on the floor. The cut was evidently quite deep as there was a lot of blood, so Felix decided to use this to his advantage. He stood on the wound and Adrian screamed in pain.

"I'd keep the noise down if I were you," said Felix.

"You're fucking crazy."

"Now, we are going to talk. I've got your money and you can have it before I leave tonight, but first you are going to listen to me."

"I don't have to do anything. I'll go to the press."

Adrian was lying on the floor, completely naked, condom still attached, which was something, especially as he was now screwing actual whores. His arm was bleeding badly and he was clearly in a lot of pain, yet he was still determined to argue back.

Felix changed tack, took his right foot off the wound and pushed his left down on Adrian's throat. Adrian tried to push Felix off, but he couldn't. Felix might be in his fifties but he was a strong man. Adrian was flapping around like a beached seal and it was rather ridiculous to look at.

"I could end your life right now and at any time I choose. Are you going to listen to what I've got to say, instead of being an idiot?"

Adrian nodded and Felix removed his foot, leaving Adrian gasping for breath. Felix walked over to the bathroom, grabbed a towel and told Adrian to wrap it around the wound and then cover himself up. Felix waited for a rebuttal once Adrian was on his feet, but he simply complied with Felix's request and sat down.

Felix stayed standing, to maintain an air of intimidation.

"Right, now just shut up and listen to what I've got to say and then you can ask your questions."

Felix took out his phone and pulled up the details of the

bank account for Adrian which was holding the one million pounds. He showed it to him.

"That is your money in an off-shore account in your name. If I transfer it to your UK bank account they will flag it to the taxman. Unless you can explain where it came from, and don't expect me to confirm anything, you'll lose at least half to him. The police may also be interested and think it is the proceeds of crime. This is the only way to get the money to you undetected."

"When do I get it?"

"I'm not finished yet. I will give you these bank details before I leave tonight with details of how you access the money without sending off any alerts. But first, I have something else which you may find helpful. Somewhere you can relax, until you've decided what to do."

"Where?"

"I have an island in the Caribbean."

"An entire island, to yourself?"

"Well, I have staff there. The place doesn't run itself. You can just chill out there and decide what you want to do. You'll need to come back for the finale to not arouse suspicion and then you are free to do what you want. Getting out of the UK will do you good. Like you said yourself, you're not popular with the public. Nobody will know you're there, so you won't be hassled by any press. It was always agreed that you'd go overseas anyway at the end of all this. Think of this as a taster of a life in the sun."

"I want to go somewhere they speak English though."

"They do speak English. This is just a stop-gap anyway."

"Okay, I'll think about it."

"You need to make a decision now."

"Why?"

"Because we're leaving tonight."

"We?"

"I will take you there."

"I can get on a plane myself, you know."

"Can you fly it, though?"

"You have your own plane that you can fly yourself?"

"Yes."

"Jesus Christ man, how fucking rich are you?"

"Very. Now let's go."

"What about my arm?"

"Mrs P will fix that up for you on the plane."

"Who is Mrs P?"

"She's an associate of mine and will look after you whilst you're on the island."

"So, she's your housekeeper?"

Felix smiled at the thought of Mrs P's reaction to that suggestion, although he decided not to confirm or deny Adrian's assumption.

"How remote is this place?"

"Very."

"So how do I get laid?"

Now was not the time to tackle Adrian's sex addiction.

"There are some live-in maids who will satisfy your needs."

"I ain't banging some old boiler."

"They're the same age as you."

"Excellent," he said standing up. "Let's go then."

"I'll leave you to collect your belongings and be waiting for you in the car outside. Give me your phone."

"Why?"

"Just give it to me. You can have it back when you come down."

"Not a very trusting person are you?" said Adrian, handing over the phone.

"No. You've got half an hour. Don't bother checking out. I'll sort it. Just don't leave anything behind."

Felix walked out and left Adrian by himself. He went down to Reception, explained what was happening so they didn't stop Adrian on his way out. He informed them there had been an accident and he would cover any damages on his account. He then went outside to get in the car. Adrian would be a while, so it gave Felix some time to think.

This next week was going to be challenging and the more he thought about it, the more he realised it was too big a risk for him to leave the UK. These instances where everyone was up for the vote were unpredictable. He had a good idea who the final two would be, but the order in which people were saved could often cause tensions to bubble over. He also wanted to ensure that the execution went the right way. The next person had already been earmarked for execution and Felix was not so sure he trusted Desiree to deliver that result. She had not been on top of things in the way she had in the past. She still hadn't located Daniel's mystery man and Felix wondered if he should task Mrs P with the challenge instead. She would probably have a result in a matter of hours; he then thought better of it as it would just encourage her to stick around and she needed to get Adrian out of the country. She was a calming influence and would encourage him to leave with her.

Felix made a call to his pilot and asked him to arrange for a co-pilot as he wouldn't be joining them. He'd not tell Adrian that until he was on the plane. It was probably best if they didn't spend too much time together. He wasn't sure it was the right move bringing this young man into his life, even if it would only be for a short time, but he didn't really have a choice. Until the finale, Felix would have to keep him under control and Adrian was a potential liability. Felix didn't want to imagine how much that liability would exacerbate once he had a million pounds to play with.

If Adrian was on the island with Mrs P it would keep her

distracted whilst Felix focussed on the game. He had neglected everything else in his empire these last few weeks as this show had completely consumed every waking thought; it was time to put an end to that. A few people had taken advantage of Felix taking a step back from the rest of his businesses empire and he couldn't have that.

The following morning with Adrian safely out of the country, Felix made call after call to set up meetings with the different managing directors of his various companies. He would give the studio a miss for the day. Now Adrian was out of the complex he knew the press would forget him and be focussed on the daily votes which would lead to a final two facing execution on Saturday night. Then he saw the latest article from Cecil Vonderbeet...

———

Felix Moldoon's Mole Executed
Cecil Vonderbeet

Last night, Adrian became the latest execution from Complex Neighbours, with over nine million votes against him − a new record. With such an unpopular neighbour leaving the competition, the viewing public must have been licking their lips in anticipation of the show's latest carcass to be flung their way. Alas, it was not to be when the post-execution 'bombshell' barely elicited a tremor.

Family infidelity, septuagenarian orgies, baby snatching and German lesbian fetish clubs were followed by... wait for it − a teenage caution for shoplifting! So what happened? Sources close to Felix Moldoon reveal that Adrian was this year's chosen victor, until the public turned against the model wannabe, following his relentless homophobia inside the complex. Once he was executed there was nothing to release to the press, as it was never intended for Adrian to lose a public vote.

With no family to speak of and no dark secrets, just why was Adrian selected to be on this show? For a man obsessed with his body and looks, why did he have no social-media footprint until six months ago? Where did he come from? What was his true purpose? Who is the real Adrian?

CHAPTER TWENTY-THREE

"The second person to be saved from execution this week is..."

"I wonder if there's time to go and have a dump?" Mike whispered to Daniel.

Daniel laughed, although stopped when he saw Stephanie scowl at him.

"Daniel."

Mike and Claire were the only ones who gave applause, which only lasted for a few awkward seconds. The tension in the complex was ready to bubble over. Daniel was now safe from execution, as was Mike who had been saved the night before.

Zelda bid them goodnight and said she would see them again tomorrow to announce the next person who was safe. She then did a bit to camera confirming that the phone lines had reopened and that all votes for the remaining neighbours would be carried forward to the next vote. Zelda was not looking her best; having to do a live show every night clearly did not suit her lifestyle.

Daniel's plan was starting to work. It was now Tuesday

and Mike and Daniel were safe. Mike had scored the least amount of votes on Monday, which Daniel was delighted about. The open confrontation with his wife could have backfired, but clearly the public loved him for it. The fact he was saved first was also a strong indicator that Jamila would finally be executed this week.

The latest vote announcement left Callum and the three women on the chopping block. There were still two people to save and Daniel was certain that would be Callum and Stephanie. However, his two closest friends in the complex did not have the same confidence and their constant whinging was starting to get on Daniel's nerves. They had to trust him; he knew what he was doing, it was all about control and patience. Patience was not something nineteen-year-olds had in abundance. As soon as Zelda had left, Callum had retreated from the group.

Jamila must have been furious when Daniel was saved. There was a consensus that she had been given a warning about her on-air outbursts, as she had been alarmingly quiet during the announcement; this was not something she had managed the night before when Mike had been the first to receive the good news.

"The first person to be safe from execution this week is..."

Daniel took the long silence as an opportunity to study his fellow neighbours. Stephanie was looking at Daniel with a smile, Callum was sulking, Claire was filing her nails, Mike was yawning and that fly was back under Jamila's nose; it had evidently had a curry the night before.

"Mike!"

Claire and Stephanie audibly gasped. Mike looked dumbstruck. Callum was looking at the floor. Daniel was delighted; Jamila not so much.

"Are you fucking kidding me? This lump of shit gets saved over me? He hasn't fucking done anything. It's because he's a white man, isn't it? It's fucking rigged. This is a game and he hasn't fucking played it. He's been sniffing around that fat slag and he gets rewarded for it. You know what I think of the public?"

Jamila stormed towards the camera and pushed Zelda out of the way. Zelda went to shout towards the security guards and then stopped; clearly there had been another instruction from the producers to let Jamila do what she wanted on live TV. Jamila faced down the camera, like a woman on a mission.

"This is a message for all you people watching at home. This is a game and not a popularity contest. I am not like these people behind me who seek a fleeting moment of fame, or hide their true intentions behind honourable motives, which are highly questionable."

She looked straight at Daniel after saying that; he didn't bite.

"I have never lied about my true motivations for being here which is to win the money. For all those who have voted against the others and supported the game I have played then I thank you. Those of you who voted for me to leave, over these woeful competitors, you can hide behind your morals and social-media profiles as much as you want, but at the end of the day it is clear to everyone what you truly are – spineless cunts!"

Callum had become even more distant from Daniel, who put it down to nerves about the vote. However, things got a little tense when he suggested that he would move apartments and share with Stephanie. She nodded her head in agreement with this arrangement.

"What's your problem?" Daniel asked.

"Isn't it obvious?"

"Well no, that's why I'm asking."

"We're supposed to be your friends and you put us on the block deliberately."

"I've explained why I did it."

"Perhaps we should have had a say in the matter, Daniel," added Stephanie. "We would never have put you up without talking to you about it first. Even if it was a tactical move, we should have been told."

"I didn't decide until that moment."

"You've never come across as the impulsive type before," added Callum.

"Are you calling me a liar?"

"I just said, you've never come across as the impulsive type before."

"It sounds like you're calling me a liar."

"That's not what I said."

"Well go on then, piss off to the other apartment."

"Daniel!" said Stephanie.

"Well, he needs to grow up. Did you not hear what Jamila called the public on live TV?"

"I was there wasn't I?"

"Nobody can come back from that. She'll be gone at the end of the week and we can enjoy the rest of our time here without her causing us to turn on each other."

"What makes you think this plan will work? The last time you tried to manipulate the game it backfired when Frank and Judy left instead."

"That was different. This is a certainty."

"You can't control everything, Daniel. You said yourself how much these shows are manipulated. If they want Jamila to stay, then she'll stay."

"Come back and talk to me when you can talk like an adult."

Callum stormed out, slamming the door.

"Daniel, that was bang out of order," said Stephanie.

"His immaturity is infuriating."

"And what were you like at nineteen?"

He gave her a look and the realisation dawned on her face. Daniel's mother died when he was nineteen; she had crossed a line, even if it was by accident.

"I'd like to be on my own, please."

Stephanie went to speak again and then decided against it. She left him to it and Daniel went into his bedroom. He wouldn't join the others for dinner tonight, he was too pissed off. This would delight Jamila, if she thought he was becoming isolated from the group, but he genuinely didn't care. He felt so overwhelmed with loneliness, that for the first time during the whole experience, he wanted to walk into the Confession Booth and ask to leave. It was a fleeting moment and something he would never do in this state of mind. He wouldn't be beaten by Jamila; he hated bullies with a passion and she was one of the worst he had ever encountered. He would see this through and at the end of the week, when she was gone, if his friends were still pushing against him, he'd walk away. With his mind racing, he thought he'd be up all night. He didn't join the group for dinner and before nine o'clock, he was fast asleep.

Wednesday night's vote saved Stephanie. Jamila made no reaction, although you could see her doing all she could to contain her rage, especially when the first person to congratulate her in a very tactile way was her soon to be ex-husband, Mike.

Callum had a face like thunder and stormed away from

the rest of the group. Daniel suspected that Callum behaving in this manner was not doing him any favours with the viewing public. Hopefully Claire's open expression of her sexuality would be enough to turn the female voters towards Callum, so the two women would face off for the final vote.

Originally Daniel had assumed it would be Mike and Callum who would be saved first. They were both good looking blokes and not fuckwits; typical winners for this type of show. However, recent years had meant that nobody could accurately predict anything anymore, especially something which involved the general public voting!

Daniel was back in the apartment getting changed. He certainly wasn't keeping away from the group tonight; last night was a one-off. Stephanie came bursting in, looking excited.

"Guess what?" she said.

"I thought we weren't speaking?"

"Oh we can forget all that now."

"Now you're safe, you mean."

"Oh stop being a moody bitch, it doesn't suit you."

"Excuse me?"

"Do you want to hear about the kiss I just had with Mike or not?"

Everything suddenly forgotten, he rushed over to her and they both sat down so she could tell him all the details. At that moment Callum burst in, looking royally pissed off.

"I see you're back up Daniel's arse again now you're safe."

"Honey, until last Saturday, the only one who wanted to be up Daniel's arse was you."

"Meow!" said Daniel.

"Look Callum, you'll be safe tomorrow, and this will all be

over," reassured Stephanie. "Now, do you want to hear some gossip?"

"Not really. And you don't know I'll be safe tomorrow. It's fine for both of you. You've got what you want."

"What are you talking about?" she asked.

"You want to be famous and you've got that now."

"Only if I win, honey."

"No, you had the singing contest and the profile this show gets. You'll get a deal somewhere."

"Not if Felix Moldoon doesn't sign me. I'm locked in for a year. I can't go anywhere else."

"He'd be an idiot not to sign you. Daniel's got his platform for his story. That's what you wanted. You beat Adrian and you're probably going to be the one who got rid of Jamila. You'll be popular and be able to remind people about what happened. You've both got what you wanted."

"And what do you want? I mean you said you needed the money for your family, but if you're this upset, what is it really all about?"

"Look, I don't want a sympathy vote. I want to win the money on merit, so I'm not saying any more, but next time you have a bright idea, perhaps ask your friends first if they mind being part of your little game."

Daniel was shocked to see Callum's eyes. It was obvious he was trying to stop himself breaking down.

"Callum, will you just talk to me..."

"I need to be by myself."

The next morning there was still a tense atmosphere; this was not helped by Jamila who had now resorted to trash talk to make Callum feel even worse about the impending vote reveal that evening. What had seemed like a good idea at the time, and would probably still get the right result, was going to have repercussions which Daniel hadn't realised. Nobody would be the same after this week; the place was like a pressure cooker. Daniel was never one to have temper tantrums. He was always in control of his emotions, although this week had demonstrated that when under pressure the natural instinct of fight or flight would kick in. However, in this place, flight was not really an option, so whether instinctively or not, fight was the only response to confrontation. Calm, logic and rational responses had been executed with the three brothers in the first week.

The only neighbour who seemed relaxed about things was Claire. Daniel had explained to her that he saw her up against Jamila, but he was certain Jamila's lack of remorse for her actions and her outburst on live TV would go against her and Claire had told him she wasn't concerned and that she trusted him; strange how things had turned out.

Once Jamila left there would be no common enemy to unite them all and then it would every man and woman for themselves. This point in the game was always going to come. At least the final three weeks would have less plotting and scheming. This would no doubt make boring TV, but bollocks to all that, Daniel had to live in this place.

Zelda arrived at the complex and told them to get into position ready for the live segment of the show. The three remaining execution contenders – Claire, Jamila and Callum, were lined up, ready to hear their fate.

"We are live, Live, LIVE! Are you ready for tonight's vote?"

There was a low murmur from the final three.

"The public have been voting all week for who they want to be executed on Saturday night and the neighbour with the least amount of votes has been saved each night. This is the final save. The remaining two neighbours will face off and one of them will leave on Saturday night and you can catch that momentous event here – LIVE."

Talk about an over-inflated sense of importance, thought Daniel.

"I can now reveal that fourth person safe from execution this week is..."

Daniel wondered if he had time to go and have a quick shower and make dinner.

"Callum." She waited a beat. "Claire and Jamila you will face execution this week. Do you have anything to say?"

"Bring it!" said Claire, basically giving the public what they wanted.

"Jamila?" asked Zelda.

"Cunt!"

Zelda's face was a picture.

"I'd just like to apologise to viewers for that. These votes are highly emotional for the neighbours and sometimes they say things they shouldn't. Let's go to a commercial break."

Zelda had confirmation that they were off the air and gave Jamila a death stare. She clearly wanted to say something, yet thought better of it. If Jamila was a likeable person the whole thing would have been hilarious. Instead, everyone was backing Zelda to the hilt. All except Callum, who only now did Daniel notice had disappeared in all the commotion. He went to go and find him when Stephanie grabbed his arm and said he should leave him alone for the time being. Perhaps she was right, he'd come around in his own time and maybe then he would understand why Daniel had done what he had.

CHAPTER TWENTY-FOUR

Felix breathed a sigh of relief – it had worked.

The vote had been close, too close. With ten million votes between the final two, there had been less than a hundred votes in it. Some carefully orchestrated press releases had ensured Claire's fate, although now there was nothing to release as her execution story. The situation had warranted Felix let other media outlets take credit for his work. They assumed they had gazumped the mighty Felix Moldoon and they were loving it, not realising they had been played by the master.

Claire had always wanted to be a big pop star. Her sister had wanted to be an Olympic athlete. Claire had a great singing voice; so did a lot of people. There was nothing *wow* about it, and she was also highly unlikeable. Her sister, however, was an all-round athlete and on track to be selected for Team GB in the Olympics, competing in the Heptathlon with strong medal contention. That was until Claire *accidentally* ran her sister over and permanently damaged her mobility. She could still walk, well after a lot of physical therapy, although running and jumping were out. Her sister had

ɔ depression and comfort eating, and was now
ɔse and living alone.

ion, Claire had bought her sister a cat as a peace
offering and the relationship between the sisters had thawed.
Unfortunately, one day the sister had sat down and crushed
her cat to death. The loss was immense, the depression
spiralled further, Claire was blamed and this ostracised her
further from her family. This had led to Claire seeking solace
in the arms of many a stranger and the product was the Claire
who auditioned for the show. The psychological assessment
had suggested that she was far too vulnerable to be on the
show. She had no medical history of mental-health problems;
it was just the psychological assessment which flagged up
some issues, so Felix had buried the report, and paid off the
psychologist. If he based his casting decisions on complete
psychological stability, he'd have a very boring show. He
worked within the guidelines but if someone had chosen not
to seek medical help for their problems they were fair game
as far as he was concerned.

Even though Claire's family didn't speak with her, they
had been respectful during her time in the complex and
refused all requests for press interviews. However, Claire's
sister had only been too happy to speak to the press with
some gentle persuasion from Felix – everyone had a price.
Felix wondered how many cakes half a million pounds could
buy these days.

Claire had been highly volatile on her exit, screaming the
studio down. She was gunning for Daniel, who she blamed for
her execution. As far as she was concerned, he had made a
gamble and cost her place in the complex. Fortunately, she
was too thick to realise that Daniel's strategy was a sound one
if it had been left up to fate. However, Felix had never been
keen on the unpredictability of fate. Jamila would never win,
although Felix wanted to rinse everything he could out of her

character, before throwing her to the vultures of the general public.

Jamila had been streaks ahead in the votes. At one time, it had looked like Callum could face off against Jamila in the final vote and there was no chance Jamila could have survived that. Research had indicated that Callum's sulking around and having a go at Daniel had turned the public off him a bit. Thankfully with Adrian out, Callum was now the best-looking bloke in the complex and the public were shallow.

As soon as Callum was safe, it was down to the two women and Felix had started to covertly pump out the press leaks; there was nothing in his newspaper. As soon as the story broke, Claire started to catch up in the votes.

The one thing this series had lacked so far was a big romance. At the beginning there was a lot of fucking; not something people rooted for long-term. The question was should Felix focus on the Mike and Stephanie thing bubbling away; or should it be Callum and Daniel, which had fizzled to a tiny ember. Desiree had suggested they follow both, as with only five people left, a Jamila victory in the next Guvnorship challenge was going to break one of the couples up. The public, however, were shipping only one of the romances in a big way.

———

Dallum Appreciation Thread

DeliciousDebbie1985: Starting this thread to discuss all things Dallum! Who is rooting for this romance? What does everyone think?

Sandra304: Love the idea of them together, just wish

Daniel would get over his hang ups and take a chance on Callum. He's such a lovely bloke and clearly smitten. I think Daniel is just playing hard to get!!!

DeliciousDebbie1985: Daniel is being respectful to his promise to his grandmother, which I think is really admirable, but I think they could still see how things go without jumping into bed

CNFanboy: Daniel is probably worried he won't be able to control himself kissing and cuddling a cute young thing like Callum. I know I couldn't!

Sandra304: This series is a bit crap when it comes to romances. We had three last series. All we have had this series is a couple of sex addicts putting the rabbits to shame!!!

DeliciousDebbie1985: Haha – you're right though. This series needs a big romance. There's no way anything is going to happen with Mike and Stephanie with Jamila still there, and if she leaves this week, I think Mike will still hold back until he leaves the complex.

Sandra304: I can't get into #Stike. Jamila might be a bitch, but they are still married. Daniel and Callum is just a slow burner!!!

CNFanboy: Slow burner? The show is over in three weeks. If they keep going this slow, we'll all die of old age! They are too focussed on getting rid of Jamila, but hopefully she'll be gone next and then I think something will happen!

Treehugger23: Jamila isn't going anywhere. Did you not just see the press onslaught against Claire to keep Jamila in the complex? That was all orchestrated by Felix Moldoon, who is the director of this glorified Hunger Games rip off. He wants Jamila there until the end and isn't interested in some romance for his ratings. If he was, he'd have probably forced them to have sex in some way. Give up, it's never going to happen as it isn't part of Moldoon's grand plan!

DeliciousDebbie1985: This is a Dallum appreciation thread, please post your conspiracy theory crap in the appropriate thread and only post here if it's on topic.

Treehugger23: Deluded!

———

Felix looked down at his island as he circled his helicopter. He had landed the jet on one of the neighbouring islands which had a runway and taken the last leg by himself. This place never ceased to amaze him. The custom-built imposing property was housed in the centre of the island. There was an eighteen-hole golf course leading to the white sandy beaches which circled the entire island. There was an Olympic-sized pool as well as another lagoon pool around a collection of six villas for guests, all with direct access into the water. Dozens of smaller buildings were scattered around the island for other leisure activities and staff quarters.

It had taken two years to get this place exactly as he wanted it. The island had been previously owned by some trashy American couple; the property was repellent and reeked of a lottery winner. They had lost everything and Felix had swooped in, getting the island at a steal. He had levelled the property and everything else on the island, literally rebuilding the place from scratch. Mrs P had questioned the purchase as she knew Felix was not the type who would ever retire and move to an isolated island for his final years; he'd get too bored. She believed he had really bought this island as a status symbol, so was surprised that for the past year since its completion it had been kept a secret. He hadn't even invited anyone to stay in the opulent guest villas; Adrian was the first person to see it besides Mrs P and the staff.

He landed the helicopter and jumped down; bending low, as the blades still hadn't stopped. As he approached the mansion, he saw Mrs P scurrying across the grounds towards him. She greeted him warmly and congratulated him on getting the right result in the latest execution. He was tired after the journey and being up most of the night before planning the week's schedule. He had left with the assumption that he would not be back until execution night. He wanted a whole week on the island – he needed it. He could still watch the complex from here as it had direct access to the studio; he just needed a break from the place. Desiree could run the show for a week; she had come up with another great Guvnorship challenge. It was simple yet would be full of drama and highly entertaining for the masses. Felix had an idea about who would win, but who would end up facing execution was a mystery. Usually Felix would be wound up about that lack of knowledge but only having landed a few moments ago, he already felt removed from the studio. Felix knew what the outcome of the story was going to be. The winner had been chosen, it was just the journey that was still up for grabs. However, there was an important part of the narrative that still had to be knitted together; he was hoping to find the solution whilst he was here.

"Where is he?" he asked Mrs P.

"He's in the gym, spends hours in the place and has the chef cooking him this caveman diet. Surprised he didn't ask for a pint of blood the other night. He has his steak so rare."

"Did you tell him I was coming?"

"No, you told me not to."

"Thanks – and thank you for dealing with Cecil Vonderbeet."

"He's quiet for now, but I doubt we've heard the last of him. A little rent-boy honey-trap isn't going to keep him down for long."

"Hopefully he'll keep his mouth shut until the end of the show. I see nobody else has picked up on the story."

"Aren't you going to go and see him?"

Felix stepped out of the shower, quickly dried off and then walked into his master suite. His case had already been brought up and the contents packed away; he'd only been in the shower ten minutes. He didn't need much luggage as he already had everything he wanted here. It was just his laptop and some papers which were on the dressing table, as well as a few personal items.

He had an office here but that was out of bounds to the staff. Felix cleaned it himself and even Mrs P wasn't admitted.

Today, though, Felix had no inclination to check in on the complex. That was the beauty of this place. The day-to-day drama suddenly became inconsequential.

Half an hour later, Felix walked into the gym and saw Adrian doing press-ups at a frantic rate. He was dripping in sweat, so god knows how long he'd been going. He saw Felix and stopped, stood up, picked up a towel and wiped himself down.

"I hear you've been spending a lot of time in here," said Felix.

Adrian just nodded.

"Sorry I couldn't come out with you straight away."

Adrian shrugged.

"Can we talk?"

"About what?"

"Call it a business proposition."

"Such as?"

"Perhaps you want to freshen up first?"

"Does this business proposition have anything to do with that complex?"

"Yes."

"Not interested."

"You could double your money."

"How?"

"Just get changed and then we can talk."

CHAPTER TWENTY-FIVE

Daniel woke up feeling like death – another post-execution hangover. Unfortunately, he had complete memory recall this time. After Jamila had growled at him, literally, he had to put up with Callum and Stephanie moaning about *wasted opportunities*. Daniel had started the evening drinking with Mike as he was the only one being reasonable about the whole thing. Daniel was being a tad manipulative, as he knew Stephanie would want to be in Mike's company. Daniel rationalised that he was tapping into his X chromosome for the sake of his own sanity, so could justify the tactic. He could tolerate Callum's teenage sulks as he was used to them now. They were his typical response when he didn't get his own way. Daniel suspected that a lot of what he said was a front. He was very similar to Adrian in his sense of entitlement. They were also both insecure; the only difference was that Callum would withdraw when he didn't get his own way.

Having Stephanie upset with him was what really got to Daniel. Her friendship in this crazy place was what had enabled him to hold it together. Now he had tightness in his chest, something he didn't experience much anymore, but he was emotionally intelligent enough to recognise what his body was telling him. He had to find a way to make amends and being a bit manipulative to ensure she spoke to him was the approach he adopted. He also knew he wasn't being very subtle and Stephanie quickly validated this summation.

"Don't think I don't know what you're up to, Daniel North."

"Can I get you a drink?"

She gave him a look, although quickly realised it would give her a few moments alone with Mike. She asked for a simple drink but he suggested a complicated cocktail; Mike had been the only one supportive of Daniel's decision so he was hoping in those few minutes Mike would have spoken to Stephanie. Daniel knew that Mike hated conflict, which is probably why his wife called him weak, but it wasn't a weakness; there was no shame in wanting people to get along and keep the peace. However, Daniel also knew he was manipulating Mike, but you had to do what you had to do.

Daniel returned with Stephanie's drink and a beer for Mike.

"Sit down," she snapped.

He did as requested.

"You know you're worse than a woman the way you've played us both. I can't believe you took advantage of Mike's good nature. He told me that if the producers wanted Jamila to stay, they would have done everything within their power to make that happen. I know that's come from you."

"It's true."

"He also said that at least it was Claire who had gone and not one of us and do you know what I think?"

He braced himself and looked down at the floor.

"He's right."

He snapped his head back up and saw that they were both laughing; they'd played him as well.

. . .

It was Sunday, a chilled day in the complex, hopefully! Daniel wanted to relax and have a day off from thinking about the game. He'd had a great evening with Stephanie and Mike. Callum was still sulking but he would come around; they were all united around one goal, which was to get Jamila out. If they succeeded, then came the tricky part of who exactly would make it into the final three. There were so many variables that the only thing Daniel was certain of was that if it was those four for the final challenge, he wouldn't be the one with blood on his hands and would throw the whole contest. He turned over in bed, his head banging, and started to drift back to sleep. He was then jolted awake when he heard the claxon sound for a mandatory task. He hoped he was still dreaming.

Jamila burst into the apartment. "Zelda is downstairs, it's a Guvnorship challenge – vengeance is sweet," she cackled and then left.

Daniel dragged his arse out of bed. There was a five-minute warning over the loudspeaker. He was having a shower first. There was no way he was going downstairs looking like crap when he knew it was definitely going to be on TV.

He showered, brushed his teeth, got dressed and made himself look vaguely presentable. The luxury of being a man was that this was all achievable in less than the five minutes available and he still had a few seconds to spare when he joined the others. Daniel was hoping that it would be a short task and the twenty-minute window of feeling amazing after showering when you have a hangover would not have abated before the challenge was over.

Stephanie had taken the *fuck-it* approach and had the dragged through a hedge backwards look going on. Callum had gone to bed early, so looked fresher faced than usual. Mike looked fine, which was annoying as he was the same age as Daniel and straight, not that straight made a difference, but it should! Jamila had also gone to bed early, after her growling and spitting routine, and was her usual focussed self. Zelda looked like she hadn't been to bed for a week. It was likely that this series had been the first time in years that she had known what a Sunday looked like.

"Welcome, neighbours," mumbled Zelda. "It is time for your penultimate Guvnorship challenge. Are you ready?"

"Yes, bring it. Woohoo. Let's fucking crush everyone."

At least Jamila was awake.

"How are the rest of you feeling?" asked Zelda.

There were mumbles of *fine*.

This had obviously not satisfied the producers as Zelda loomed towards them with her microphone.

"Stephanie, how are you feeling? Excited? Nervous?"

"Hungover and tired."

"Late one, was it?"

"No, I'm hungover and tired because I went to bed at nine with a glass of water!"

"Oh Steph, you are hilarious."

"My name is Stephanie."

"Er... that's what I said. So, Danny... How do you feel about last night's execution? I know you and Claire haven't always got along. Was it good to see her finally go?"

"No. I wanted Jamila to leave."

"And why's that?"

"I'd have thought that was obvious!"

Jamila hissed which startled Zelda, causing her to stumble backwards. She was caught by Mike; Stephanie had to muffle a laugh. Daniel looked at Callum who was smiling and then winked at him; perhaps things would be okay after all.

"Right, let's get on with the challenge shall we?" said

Zelda, recovering quickly. She was passed a megaphone by one her security guards. This caused most people to groan as it probably meant a physical challenge with noise.

"Challenge, reveal yourself."

The wall slid back and revealed a spinning wheel. Like the old-fashioned ones they had in the *Funhouse* at the local fairground in the last century, before health and safety laws went too far and declared fun was illegal. There was nothing to hold onto, other than your own friction. Everyone was instructed to remove their shoes and socks and get on the wheel with their backs to each other. Then the rules were explained – Daniel wanted to cry.

They all had to sit on the wheel and it would spin, until one person remained and they would go on to the next round. The remaining four would get back on and the winner of that game would go to the next round and so on until one person was eliminated. Potentially you would spin four times, and this would equal *one* round. Once again, this was blatantly rigged in Jamila's favour. It meant the producers wanted to keep her, but that she would be vulnerable on a public vote, so all Daniel had to do was find a way to ensure she faced one.

They all took their places on the wheel. Daniel wanted to be anywhere except sat next to Jamila. He wasn't sure if he'd be able to resist the urge to push her off and according to Zelda, that was against the rules.

The wheel started spinning for the first time, and they had barely picked up any speed before Callum was flying into the crash barriers which surrounded them. There was two metres of highly polished wooden flooring between the edge of the wheel and the barriers. The sort you'd get friction burns from if you had any exposed skin slide across it at speed. Thankfully, Daniel had worn long sleeves and kept his shoes on, so just the hands and face to protect.

The wheel was picking up speed and Daniel tried to

adjust himself but lost his footing and was off – not a great start. Mike soon followed, which meant the two women would fight it out for the first win. Unfortunately, any hopes of Jamila having to face the wheel again were soon dashed when Stephanie hurtled off at speed. Jamila had won the first game, so could now rest whilst the rest of them had to get back on.

Daniel wasn't feeling too bad at this point, but he knew the best strategy was to hold on and win an early game, so he could have a rest between spins, otherwise the feeling of being *okay* wouldn't last long. Within seconds that strategy was shot to shit when him and Callum came hurtling off and landed together in a heap, with Daniel's face in Callum's crotch – something which would no doubt become immortalised as a GIF. He apologised to Callum, who replied with a smile and another of his winks. Daniel didn't have time to think of a sarcastic rebuttal as Stephanie was hurtling towards them, which meant Mike had won the second game. Maybe he could beat Jamila!

The next game was similar, in that Callum was off first, closely followed by Daniel. This put Stephanie through to the next round and Daniel having to face the wheel for a fourth time. He couldn't come last, even though his stomach was starting to feel uneasy. He took up his place on the wheel. Zelda told them to *start spinning* with a grin on her face – bitch!

The wheel started and Daniel thought it would be best if he closed his eyes and just focussed on pushing his hands and feet into the wheel as hard as he could. The wheel had barely started to pick up pace before Callum was off. Daniel thought he'd found a strategy that worked, as although it was a strange sensation having his eyes closed, it had made his stomach churn less. However, he also wasn't stupid and as soon he heard Callum slide into the crash barriers, Daniel pushed himself off the wheel. This next round was going to be different; he could feel it.

Zelda would not let them have a breather; she wanted the second round to start immediately. Callum, having been eliminated, took his seat on the loser's bench. That wasn't Daniel being a bitch; there was a sign above the bench which said *Loser's Bench!*

The wheel started again, and Daniel's strategy was working. He was able to hold on a lot longer this time. He heard Stephanie go flying, closely followed by Mike. Could he win this game and get a rest? That would be amazing. The wheel started to pick up pace and he focussed all his effort into pushing his hands and feet flat to the ground. He felt movement beside him. Had she fallen off? He opened his eyes to check. That was the biggest mistake he could have made. First, Jamila was clearly going nowhere and just a few seconds of seeing the room spin at speed made Daniel's stomach lurch and he knew the twenty-minute window of feeling okay was definitely up. He thought he was going to be sick, so knew he had no choice but to push himself off, albeit discreetly. This put Jamila through to the next round, although Daniel now had a new strategy – to end his participation in this game as quickly as possible. Unfortunately, that didn't work out so well. Mike, as expected, won the next game. Daniel was expecting to then be eliminated, which would be the most wonderful thing ever for his stomach, but Stephanie lost her footing and slid off the wheel before Daniel could discreetly push himself off after a non-shameful period of time.

The third round started with another Jamila victory. On the second game, Daniel and Mike must have decided to do the same thing together and pushed themselves off the wheel. However, due to Mike's size, he hit the cushioned wall first, so he was out of the challenge. The final would be between Jamila and Daniel.

Daniel's brain told him to just give it up. He had been on the wheel nine times, to Jamila's three, and there had been no rest between games. However, his testosterone told him he couldn't, and besides if he won the final round then he would be Guvnor and Jamila could be going home.

"Right, back on the wheel Daniel and Jamila. It is time for the fourth and final round. This will be the best of three."

"Are you taking the piss?"

"No, Daniel. Can't make it too easy for you, can we?"

"Bring it," gurned Jamila.

Daniel got on the wheel and was prepared to be humiliated, not once, but twice. Then he could go back to bed. The wheel started spinning and Jamila decided to do a bit of showboating, banging the palms of her hands on the wheel and grunting. It sounded like the noise Mr Walrus probably makes when he is doing pleasurable fuck thrusts into Mrs Walrus. Unfortunately this strategy did not work well for her and she lost her grip on the wheel, hurtling off. There were whoops and cheers from the others. Daniel didn't wait for the wheel to stop; he just pushed himself off before he was sick. Ten times he had been on this thing now.

"Let's go again. I will fucking destroy you!" screamed Jamila in his face, so close he could smell the kale smoothie she'd had for breakfast.

Daniel dragged his arse back on the wheel. Jamila was silent this time and after what felt like an eternity Daniel was off and she did her slapping and grunting again. This time staying completely focussed with no chance of her coming off. The wheel finally came to a stop.

"Let's go again. Come on."

"I need a drink of water."

"That's against the rules."

"Is it?" he asked Zelda.

"Yes. Get on the wheel, Daniel," she replied.

Daniel felt dreadful. He had come out in a cold sweat and felt like he could vomit any minute. Every instinct in his body told him not to get on that wheel, but there was no way he was just going to hand victory to her on a plate.

Within seconds of the wheel starting, there was no controlling it and Daniel projectile vomited everywhere. The wheel was spinning so fast that it landed in his face, and based on Jamila's screaming she had been hit as well. In fact, it went so far that the last thing he heard before passing out was Zelda screaming at everyone to get out of the way.

He woke up with a light being shone in his eyes and a man he didn't recognise looking down on him; a very handsome man.

"Hello, and who are you?"

"He's fine," the guy smiled.

Daniel suddenly realised that he was on the floor next to the task area, with Mike, Callum and Stephanie all looking concerned. One of the complex medics had been checking him over and was now packing up his bag. Daniel sat up. He couldn't get over how handsome this man was. Daniel asked his name and the guy just smiled back and said nothing. He looked at Stephanie and she shook her head. Mike and Callum were laughing. The guy picked up this bag, told Daniel to drink lots of fluids and left.

"You might want to clean your face," said Stephanie.

"Why?"

"Because you were just flirting with your face covered in vomit."

Daniel managed to haul himself up and went to head upstairs to get a shower. Then he remembered the Guvnorship challenge.

"I'm guessing Jamila won, then?"

"Yep."

"When is she doing the deed?"

"She's done it."

"What? Whilst I was unconscious? That was nice of her."

"She wanted to wait, but Zelda insisted."

"So who am I up against?"

"You weren't put up."

"What?"

"It's me against Mike."

CHAPTER TWENTY-SIX

Felix spent the next few days enjoying some peace and quiet. Adrian had barely spoken to him since the first night and had rejected Felix's offer to double his money. The place was so vast that they didn't see each other often. Adrian always ate alone. Felix just had to give him time.

Desiree had been keeping Felix updated with how the show was going and he still approved the final broadcast each day – he wasn't making that mistake again. The substitution challenge would have to be carefully thought about. Jamila had discussed her strategy extensively in the Confession Booth. Felix had the recordings and they were fascinating to watch as she ran through all the possible scenarios. She spent an increasing amount of time in the Confession Booth as she had nobody else to talk to in the complex. The resident psychologist had again suggested they might want to intervene as Jamila appeared close to the edge. Felix had asked Desiree to silence or sack the psychologist, who, like the others, had been selected precisely because their history indicated that they weren't too precious about their professional ethics, especially if the price was right.

Felix watched back the recordings of Jamila rationalising the different scenarios. It was useful intelligence as it meant he didn't need to try to predict her next move.

"With the substitution challenge, there are five possible outcomes – well, five people who can win. There are numerous possibilities," said Jamila. "If Stephanie wins and saves herself Daniel will go up as Mike got less votes than him last week so that's the only chance I have to get rid of Daniel."

"What if Daniel wins?" asked Desiree, who was taking her turn in the Confession Booth.

"That is a difficult one, because he will want to save his friend, but that means putting his other friend slash not quite lover on the chopping block. Callum would definitely go over Mike based on the votes last week. I think he'll try to rig it so he can't win and then he doesn't have to make a difficult decision and prove he has a pair of balls. He's a sneaky fucker, that one."

"What if Mike wins?"

"Then I'll put Callum up so Daniel still loses someone close to him."

"What if you win?"

"I'll have to think about it, but I'm one step closer to the one million pounds. The way Mike has treated me will mean that no judge will give him a penny of it."

"What if Mike wins the money?"

"The judge will make sure I get my share."

"So you'll take half the money, but if you win, Mike gets nothing. Do you think that's fair?"

"Oh, I'll get more than half. Mike is a cheat and has treated me like shit. He deserves everything he gets. He leaves himself exposed to getting hurt by being far too nice and trusting. I told him this game would have some tough decisions to make, he said he was up for it, but in the end, Claire was right and he's just a pussy. I'd love to hit him where it hurts."

"In his wallet?"

"My husband doesn't give a shit about money, that's his problem. No, there are far better ways to hurt him."

Felix loved watching her; no feelings or emotion, she was completely obsessed with winning the money. In another life, she could have made a good partner, although he already had three ex-wives, which were quite enough. Not that they cost him anything. They had each received a fixed amount upon divorce and no maintenance. Two of his ex-wives were now dead, and he hadn't a clue where the last Mrs Moldoon was. She had simply disappeared with her settlement.

After reviewing the footage of Jamila again, Felix had an idea. It could also be an opportunity to get Adrian to talk to him, so Felix could clarify something he knew, but wanted to be certain about. He put a call in to Desiree.

"Desiree, it's me. Are we all ready for the substitution challenge?"

"Yes, all ready for tonight and the show is going live just like you asked."

"Could Jamila win this?"

"Possibly, but it wasn't set up for a particular person. You said any outcome would result in drama."

"I know, but I want Jamila to win now."

"Felix, we go live in a few hours. Remember you are five hours behind us."

"Just do something simple that plays to her strengths."

"But what if she puts Daniel up?"

"She won't, as we're going to dangle the biggest carrot

under her nose that she won't be able to help herself. Now listen, this is what I want you to do…"

After a hectic few hours of back and forth with the studio, everything was in place for what would be a phenomenal live show. That was if Jamila willingly played along as she was shrewd enough to know when she was being played. Felix walked into his dining room where Adrian was just finishing his mid-afternoon meal; he ate six times a day. Felix was usually too busy to even eat three meals. Adrian briefly looked up when Felix entered and then went back to his food.

"Do you want to watch the substitution challenge with me?" said Felix.

"I want nothing more to do with that place."

"It's going to be a good one. It's going out live."

"What poor bastard are you throwing under the bus this time?"

"Why don't you come and find out? Besides, I'm heading back to the UK earlier than planned. I'll be leaving in the morning, so you'll have the place to yourself until the finale. Come and watch the show with me and have a drink."

Adrian's curiosity clearly got the better of him; he shrugged, put down his cutlery, downed his glass of protein shake and followed Felix into another part of the mansion. They walked in silence, Felix choosing not to say anything as he wanted to be certain that Adrian would watch the show with him. If all went to plan, this was going to be event TV.

They walked into Felix's snug, which Adrian hadn't seen before as it was usually closed off. He was trying to look relaxed, although was clearly impressed. The purpose built one-hundred-inch screen took centre stage. Felix went behind the bar and made himself a whisky on the rocks and opened a beer for Adrian. There were comfortable sofas all around the room, which was double the size of most people's entire ground floor. Adrian remained standing, watching the screen, so Felix joined him and gave Adrian his drink.

"Cheers!"

"Who's up for the vote this week?" asked Adrian.

"Stephanie and Mike."

"Jamila's doing?"

"Who else?"

"That woman is a psycho. Absolutely obsessed with money."

"Is it a bad thing to want wealth?"

"No, but not at any cost. She's lost her marriage because of this show."

"Stephanie had a lot to do with that though, didn't she?" said Felix, hoping Adrian wouldn't realise he was feigning ignorance about his own show.

"Not at all. If Jamila hadn't treated Mike like shit, he wouldn't have even considered looking elsewhere. Nothing will happen between them in that place, even if Jamila leaves. He wouldn't do that to humiliate her, he's not that sort of bloke."

"So no big romance then?"

"When they leave maybe, but it won't happen in there."

"Like Daniel and Callum."

"Daniel just won't do anything to embarrass his grand-mother. She's the only family he has. I can understand that."

"That's just a line to not get stuck in a TV romance though, surely?"

"Not at all, there's definitely something there. You can feel the tension between the two of them, but it won't happen in there, not whilst his grandmother is at home watching him on TV."

Felix shrugged to imply he didn't care, although he did care. The public wanted this romance to progress from a PG rating and there was only one way that was going to happen. Felix had already carried out some independent research, the kind Mrs P wouldn't approve of, and she had a very high tolerance threshold. He would need to make some calls later to get things in motion, but he'd wait to see how this substitution challenge panned out first.

"Neighbours, it is time for your substitution challenge and we are live, Live, LIVE!"

Zelda explained the substitution challenge. There was an oversized jigsaw made up of ten pieces on one side of the challenge area. They had to assemble the puzzle on the other side by transferring all the pieces, one by one. The neighbour who assembled the puzzle first would win and would have the power to change who faced execution this week. The puzzle itself was easy; it would be speed which won it – this played to Jamila's strengths, although Felix had learnt with this series that nothing was ever certain.

The claxon sounded for the start of the challenge and Jamila took the lead, although she was closely followed by Mike and Callum. Daniel and Stephanie didn't appear to be making any effort.

"Daniel's already given up," said Felix.

"Speed isn't his thing."

"He's good at puzzles though."

"That puzzle is piss easy. It's blatantly rigged for Jamila to win."

"The other two are giving her a run for her money."

"That woman has endurance. Do you know how many marathons she's competed in?"

Felix did know. Jamila was a competitive woman and it had been that side of her which had won her a place in the complex. Her husband was just an unfortunate bolt-on.

"Callum is falling behind now," said Felix.

"You don't even make it subtle anymore about who you want to win these contests."

"Think you know how this show runs, do you?"

"I've got a pretty good idea."

"Want a job?"

"Back on that, are we?"

"Doesn't even have to be in the UK. You know I have programmes all over the world."

"Look, I'll think about it."

That was progress from the outright 'no' when Felix had first arrived. They continued watching the rest of substitution challenge in silence as Mike finally fell too far behind his wife to catch up. Jamila had all her puzzle pieces transferred and was in the process of assembling it together. Mike still had two to transfer, Callum had three, and Daniel and Stephanie had moved four pieces each and were walking back and forth having a chat.

In less than five minutes since the challenge had started, Jamila had won. There was a resigned sigh from the group as they all moved forward, ready for Jamila's decision on whether she was going to change her original choices.

"Jamila, you have won this week's substitution challenge and you now have a decision to make. You can change one of your choices for execution and we will open the public vote and someone will leave on Saturday, or you can leave them as they are and you can decide who between Mike and Stephanie will leave the complex... now!"

There were gasps from the remaining neighbours. Stephanie burst into tears and Mike shot a look of contempt at his wife. Jamila looked like she might orgasm in her pants any moment.

"Nice twist," said Adrian, smiling.

"You think?"

"As a viewer, definitely. If I was still in there, I'd think you were a complete arsehole."

Felix laughed. "What do you think she'll do?"

"Bite your hand off."

Adrian was right, as Jamila barely spent any time thinking about it before confirming her decision.

"I'd like to let my original decision stand, Zelda."

"Right, so Mike and Stephanie, you have one minute to say your goodbyes and then it's time to get into the tubes."

Zelda corralled them towards the other side of the communal area where the execution tubes were being revealed. Daniel and Callum were trying their best to comfort a distraught Stephanie, who was clearly convinced she was going to leave. Mike had nobody to comfort him, although he seemed more concerned about Stephanie than his own potential fate.

The online reaction snowballed. Forums crashed, social media was in meltdown and they were the number-one trend in the world; all in a matter of seconds. The show had now reached unprecedented heights of popularity and it still had more than two weeks to go. Ratings could only keep pushing higher.

"Tell you what," said Felix to Adrian. "I'll make a bet with you. If you get it right, I'll give you that extra million, no strings attached."

"No strings, with you – really?"

"I mean it."

"And what if you're right?"

"If you want that extra million you'll need to earn it, by working for me."

"Deal, although that's not a promise to come and work for you."

"Understood. So who do you think she'll execute?"

They watched on the screen as Mike and Stephanie

walked towards the tubes. Mike suddenly grabbed Stephanie and kissed her passionately and Felix then knew which way this would go, but would Adrian do what he expected him to do?

"Well, after that Stephanie's a gonner."

"You think so?"

"Yeah. You see Jamila will want to get rid of the competition and she will have won by being the last woman standing. She likes to win and deep down she must know she can't win the whole thing. Nobody is that deluded. This will give her time to worm her way back into Mike's affections and he's popular with the public. She'll play it tactically."

"Okay, so your vote's for Stephanie. Shake on it."

They shook hands and turned back to the screen. Stephanie was a blubbering mess in the tube. Daniel was in tears. Callum was trying to hold it together whilst comforting Daniel. Mike just had eyes on Stephanie who was now trying to smooth out her clothes, realising she was not going to be leaving in the dress she had specially chosen and had spoken about for weeks. It was also her first time in the execution tube – would it be her last?

Zelda passed Jamila an electronic tablet and explained that she would need to use that to make her selection and that would activate the lever so she could pull it. The camera moved away from behind Jamila so nobody could see the decision she made.

"Have you made your selection, Jamila?"

"Yes, I have, Zelda," she said, passing the tablet back to her.

Felix received an alert on his phone confirming Jamila's decision.

"Is there anything you'd like to say before you pull the lever?"

"Oh, yes there is. Mike, that little display you did just

then to piss me off and save your little, or should I say fat, bimbo was pointless. When my mind is made up, nothing is going to change it. Clearly you don't know me at all."

She pulled the lever and the executed neighbour disappeared from sight...

CHAPTER TWENTY-SEVEN

Daniel was in shock – Jamila had just executed her own husband.

Zelda had left fairly quickly, especially when she asked Jamila for an interview and had been told to go and fuck herself. Stephanie was a blubbering mess. Callum was comforting her. Jamila walked towards Daniel.

"So we're the final four. Wanna hug it out?" she asked, opening her arms.

"Why?"

"He was the stronger competition."

"Bullshit, it was that kiss. It pissed you right off. You did what he wanted you to do. He played you."

"I did what *I* wanted to do. Mike was always my first choice. He's popular with the public. You'll be gone next. I'll beat those two without even trying."

"You're a psychopath."

"I'm actually a sociopath. Get it right, Danny Boy!"

She skipped off towards the kitchen humming a tune – the woman was crazy. Daniel went over to Stephanie who had stopped crying and was sitting on one of the sofas. Callum walked towards him.

"What did she say?" asked Callum.

"That Mike was always her first choice."

"Bullshit."

"I actually think she's telling the truth."

"So why put Stephanie through that?"

"Because she's a sociopath."

"Well we know that, but why?"

"No, she just told me that she's a sociopath."

"Brilliant, we'll all be murdered in our beds!"

Stephanie came out of the bathroom with her hair wrapped up and towel around her. The swelling around her eyes had gone down and she was looking better,

"Feel better?" asked Daniel.

"A bit. How long was I in there?"

"About half an hour."

"Must have lost track of time."

"You wanna talk about it?" asked Daniel.

"Yeah, but I don't wanna start crying again."

"At most, you'll see him in two weeks."

"I can't believe he did that – kissing me like that. That was what saved me."

Daniel decided not to fill her on his little chat with Jamila. There was no point anyway. Mike had obviously kissed Stephanie in the hope that it would incense Jamila so much that she would execute him. Whether that was what made up her mind or not was irrelevant, Daniel wasn't about to ruin the only positive thing about that moment for Stephanie.

The night before the execution Daniel had chatted with Mike. He wanted to check that Stephanie wasn't just some rebound to piss off Jamila, as Stephanie was falling for Mike in a big way and Daniel didn't want to see her hurt. However, he was also not going to be the one to come in the way of whatever it was they had going. Daniel had nothing to worry about though, as Mike had reassured him that his feelings for Stephanie were genuine. He just wanted to wait until they were both out of the complex before asking her on a date.

Later that night, Callum and Daniel were in the apartment they were sharing with Stephanie. She was in the shower again. They were on the sofa. Callum was laying down with his feet in Daniel's lap. He wanted to talk about what their next move in the game would be. Daniel wanted a night off tactics, although it seemed like there was never anything else anybody wanted to talk about.

"So how are we going to get rid of Jamila this week, then?" asked Callum.

"We don't."

"Why the hell not? She doesn't deserve to be in the final. It should be us three. That would be perfect."

"Yes, one gay man, one sexually fluid and a fag hag who are all very close friends – gripping TV."

"You think the Guvnorship challenge will be rigged in her favour?"

"Haven't most of them been that way so far? Besides, the last Guvnorship challenge is always a series of tasks with elimination rounds."

"Maybe we'll win, but then who goes up against her?"

"I will," said Daniel.

"I can't pick you."

"Could you pick Stephanie?"

"Well not after this week, no."

"So that leaves me."

"Oh shit yeah, so who are you going to put up if you win?"

"You!"

"Oh, cheers."

"I don't want to risk Stephanie becoming depressed and turning the public off."

"You mean like I did?"

"Well I didn't want to say," Daniel smiled.

"Well we don't know that's what happened. It's just your assumption."

"You're a nice guy and you're hot. I think you'll be fine."

Callum blushed and there was an awkward silence which just hung there. Thankfully, broken by Stephanie coming out of the bathroom ready for bed.

"What you two talking about?"

"Tactics."

"Let's do tactics tomorrow. Get the wine out of the fridge. I will say one thing though, one of you two will have to go up against Jamila. Men beat women all the time in these things. It's too big a risk putting me up against her. They may go for her drama over my fabulous personality."

They all looked at each other for a second and then started laughing – it was much needed.

Daniel, Stephanie and Callum were now sharing an apartment whilst Jamila was on her own. They had closed off four of the apartments now, although thankfully they hadn't gone any further than that. In the last week it was usual for the final three to live in the same apartment. The thought of living with Jamila for a week in such close quarters made Daniel shudder. He would need to put something behind the door in case she tried to smother him in his sleep; he still hadn't forgotten her sociopath comment. He'd taken it as the threat it was no doubt intended – how these people got through the background checks was highly questionable.

The day after Mike's execution had been challenging. Jamila was barely visible and although that may seem like a blessing, it made Daniel feel uncomfortable. There was nothing pleasurable about seeing someone so excluded, even if it was a situation of her own making. However, it was Friday and they had been told the final Guvnorship challenge was to begin that day, therefore any compassion towards Jamila would no doubt soon evaporate.

They'd tried to work out who Jamila was going to put on the chopping block, but there were so many variables. Daniel knew he was a certainty, but which of the other two was the unknown. They decided that they may as well just all throw themselves into the challenges and forget the tactics this time. She knew she was gone as soon as she was up, so she would fight to the bitter end.

The final challenge was usually an amalgamation of previous challenges. Not literally, there was no austerity on the final challenge; they just took on a similar theme. There was usually an endurance challenge, a mental task, and a physical task, but there had been a few changes this series so anything could happen.

The claxon sounded; it was time for them to get on with it. By the end of the day they could be sipping sweet victory, well wine – the vodka was out. Daniel was going to have to do a detox when he left, and have a liver function test; there was little else to do between the tasks and the plotting.

Zelda was waiting for them in the main task area. Jamila was already there bouncing on the balls of her feet dressed like she was attending an aerobics class. This was evidently meant to look intimidating, although she didn't quite pull the look off thanks to the unfortunate camel toe. Daniel saw a look flash over Stephanie's face which implied conflict over sisterhood and having something to laugh about later. She chose the latter with a sly grin on her face.

"You lot are going down!" said Jamila.

Daniel started looking around, putting his hand above his eyes to give the impression he was looking off into the distance.

"What are you looking at?" Jamila asked.

"The time portal to nineteen eighty-five that we appear to have walked through."

"Fuck off!"

"Do you actually want us to be able to broadcast this challenge?" snapped Zelda.

"Are we going live then?" Callum asked.

"No, the first two challenges will be today, which will then be broadcast tonight and the final challenge will be live-streamed tomorrow."

Daniel groaned.

"What?" asked Stephanie.

"Probably means the final challenge will be an endurance one."

"Yeah, bring it," gurned Jamila.

"Right – focus people," snapped Zelda. "Can you all get into position and then I can set up the task. I'd like to do the intro in one take."

They did as they were told. Partly to get the thing over with, and because it was absolutely freezing. It had been snowing and it was so cold that some of it was still settled on the ground. Why the task had to be outdoors was as yet unknown.

"Welcome neighbours, to your final Guvnorship challenge. There will be three tasks in total with one of you being eliminated from the competition in each round. By the end of today there will be two of you left who will face off in the final challenge tomorrow. The winner will choose who will face the final execution before the grand finale and only the substitution challenge will be able to alter that. The execution will be solely decided by the public this week. There will be no additional power to the Guvnor, other than guaranteeing themselves a place in the final. Are we clear?"

"Yes," they all shouted in unison.

The wall slid back and revealed an obstacle course.

Daniel remembered that Jamila had messed up the last time on the obstacle course, although this one looked far more complex.

"This is a combination of physical and mental challenges. You will each work through the course in turn and complete all the challenges. If you fail any of the challenges, you will have to start again. It is about who completes all the challenges with no mistakes in the fastest time. The slowest time is eliminated. Jamila, you look raring to go, so we'll start with you. After she makes her first attempt, Stephanie will follow, then Callum, with Daniel bringing up the rear."

This caused a lot of laughter; even Jamila slipped out of her serious mode for a few seconds. Daniel expected that they'd have to redo that part, but Zelda had confirmation in her earpiece that they were leaving it in. Daniel looked over the obstacle course and groaned. If this was the first challenge then what the hell were the rest going to be? The difficulty level usually intensified as things went on.

Zelda asked Jamila to stand by the start line which she dutifully did. Zelda was still giggling about her faux pas, or perhaps she was still buzzing from the night before. It was only nine o'clock in the morning so the latter was highly probable. Zelda blew her whistle to start the game and Jamila was off like a whippet which had been rogered by a cattle prod.

It was easy to follow what she was doing on the physical challenges, but the mental challenges were hidden from view.

When Daniel eventually entered the game, he didn't rush on the first obstacle – monkey bars, which Stephanie had flunked on her first attempt. Suspecting the obstacles would get harder as the game progressed, he knew he had to pace himself and not burn out. He got through the monkey bars on the first attempt this time and it was hard to not do any showboating; he had to remain calm so as not to let excitement screw anything up on the rest of the course.

The second challenge was the first mental one and was fairly logical. You needed to wire a circuit so the light came on. You only had one go at it, which was slightly frustrating, so he took his time. This was in spite of Jamila's motivational diatribe.

"Will you hurry the fuck up!"

Jamila had flunked on the fifth obstacle, the balance beam, and was waiting to start again. Her being left at the start line would in no way impact her time, so Daniel refused to be rushed. He completed the circuit, or what he felt was complete, pushed the button, which confirmed his success and he moved onto the next challenge. This involved climbing a wall in one go with just a rope to support you. Daniel psyched himself up and then went for it, managing to clear the wall first time. The next challenge was easy and just involved throwing some rings over a cone, although Callum had screwed this one up on his go. You had to get three out of five to pass the station and Daniel got three with his first throws.

Next was the balance beam – Jamila's nemesis. He walked over this straight away. He was now in the lead. Nobody had got to this part of the challenge without flunking and this was his first go. He didn't want to get too excited as there were still two obstacles left. One thing was for certain. This challenge had been set up for Stephanie to fail. There was no way she was going to master that wall.

The next mental challenge was numerical, one of Daniel's strong points, but he still took his time despite Jamila turning the air blue. Callum and Stephanie were huddled together in their coats cheering him on when he wasn't concentrating on a specific task, whereas Jamila was still in her leotard doing warm-up stretches. Daniel inputted an answer and it was correct. He now moved on to the final physical challenge, which looked like it belonged on *American Ninja Warrior* and not a Reality TV show which housed contestants who'd had nothing else to do but eat, drink and sleep for the past seven weeks.

He had to leap across some stepping stones which would start sinking the moment he stepped on them, dropping him in mud, which would no doubt be freezing cold. If he went down, he would be sent back to the start.

Daniel deduced that to get across you had to do it in one fluid motion, switching from foot to foot and striding like a gazelle. There were five blocks between him and victory and the noise from Jamila was now beginning to grate. What wasn't helping was Stephanie and Callum chanting over her. Although well intentioned, the din was making it difficult to concentrate. He could tell them all to shut the fuck up, but all that would do was let Jamila know she was getting to him, causing her to intensify her onslaught. It would also piss off the other two, so he kept his mouth shut and tried to block them out. He just had to go for it. This task was clearly set up to not be passed on a first attempt. Could Daniel prove them wrong?

Daniel steadied himself and then simply went for it without thinking about it and not looking at the floor – bounce, bounce, bounce, bounce, bounce, bounce. He looked down, he'd done it. Callum and Stephanie were screaming with delight. Jamila was stamping her feet, actually stamping her feet, and then he heard Callum.

"Push the button."

Daniel came to his senses and pushed the button registering his time.

"Congratulations, Daniel," shouted Zelda. "You are through to the next round."

"What? No, that's not how it works. What if we beat his time?" screamed Jamila, clearly not impressed by this development.

"Let me explain the rules again for you."

Daniel normally hated anyone using such a patronising tone, yet on Jamila it was perfect.

"It is about the quickest time per round. Daniel was the only one to complete the course on the first attempt so he goes through to the next round. If all four of you had completed it on the first round then the slowest time would have been eliminated. Am I clear?"

"So what happens if I complete it on the next round and those two flunk?" asked Jamila.

Confident as always.

"You go through to the next round..."

"And those two get eliminated?"

"No, only one gets eliminated each round."

"But we'll be here all fucking day with that fat bitch."

"Do you want us to just eliminate you from the contest, Jamila, for your disgusting behaviour?"

"Like you'd even try. Now can we get on with it? I ain't got all day."

Zelda looked like she wanted to throttle the woman.

Jamila went off again, far too quickly, missed the monkey bars completely and fell flat on her face. It was a beautiful moment and one which would be etched in Daniel's memory for eternity. He admired Zelda's professionalism as she didn't falter in her demeanour and simply pressed on with the challenge.

Stephanie was next and she managed the monkey bars this time, but the climbing wall was a no go, as Daniel suspected. Jamila was delighted to see she was back in the game. Her panic was back ten minutes later when Callum successfully completed the course on his third attempt. It was now down to the two women and there was only one way this could go.

After Jamila completed the course on her fifth attempt and Stephanie flunked again, Zelda announced that they would move on to the second part of the challenge straight away, which resulted in a loud groan from everyone. The pleasing part was that the challenge would be inside. It was another *how well do you know your neighbours?* challenge. This played against Jamila, given she was an anti-social bitch who hadn't made an effort to get to know anybody else.

However, there was a twist. This wasn't about how well you knew people from inside the complex; there was a list of scandalous stories and you had to guess which former neighbour was associated to the scandal. It was clear to Daniel that these were the execution stories.

They had a screen in front of them with the former neighbours on one side and a series of questions about the scandals on the other. They had to drag the names across, and they had just five minutes to do it. The first three executions, which were all groups, were clustered together, so that made it a little easier.

The first question asked who was in a swingers' club, so Daniel opted for Frank and Judy. He had no idea why; it was more that none of the other scenarios seemed to fit. There was a question asking who had injured their sister causing the end of their athletic career. Daniel knew it couldn't be any of the groups. He knew Adrian was an only child like him. It wouldn't be Mike or Helen, so it could only be Claire. At least now he knew why the public had chosen her to leave over Jamila. There was no doubt in Daniel's mind that the story would have been leaked in advance to guarantee Claire's fate.

The next question asked who was born due to infidelity, which could be anyone, so he moved on. There was a question asking who had been caught shoplifting, which seemed a minor indiscretion for a show like this. The next asked who had cheated on their partner with a model. Daniel knew that was Mike, as he had told him when they had been chatting one night. It had been a minor thing, but Mike had suspected it would be his execution story. There was a question asking who had been kidnapped at birth. The fact that it seemed like something out of a soap opera and given the dramatic way the sisters were executed before they split into singles, Daniel knew it had to be them. The final question asked who had a secret fetish for leather and bondage. By process of elimination, Daniel thought that could be Helen. That left infidelity and shoplifting. Given the three brothers were executed first, they wouldn't have had a minor story. Felix Moldoon wouldn't have allowed that. It meant that Adrian was the shoplifting story. Surely a guy like that would have had something darker in his past. Daniel couldn't think about that now, as Zelda had given them a thirty-second warning. He dragged his final answers into place and gave them one last look. He was happy with his choices and just hoped it was enough to get through to the final round.

Zelda announced that Daniel had won and was through to the final challenge. She didn't say how many he had got right, so they weren't going to reveal the answers. They probably thought that it would cause debate between the remaining neighbours, and frankly Daniel didn't give a shit who had done what, so long as Jamila lost.

Callum and Jamila were tied, so Zelda announced the tie-break question. They needed to list the order in which people entered the complex. This should have been easy for Daniel to answer, as he was the first in, although even he struggled to recall. It was Daniel, Stephanie and Adrian, then he drew a blank, probably because it was at that point he had realised Adrian was a complete wanker.

Zelda asked them each to use the screens to put the neighbours in their chosen order. They only had two minutes and it was silence whilst the two concentrated. Callum looked stressed, which did not fill Daniel with optimism. Once the time was up, Zelda gave the horrendous, yet expected, news that Jamila had won the tie-breaker. The final round would be between Daniel and Jamila.

"I'll fucking destroy you," she snarled at Daniel.

"And on that note," chirped Zelda, interrupting quickly. "I will see you both tomorrow for the final challenge."

The rest of the day passed without further drama. Shortly after Zelda had left the complex, Jamila had departed to the gym. A quick look through the door saw her in full meditation mode; hopefully she'd stay there for the rest of the day.

Stephanie and Callum were excited at the prospect of Daniel being the final Guvnor. It was agreed Jamila would go up against Callum as that was the best chance she had of being executed, although Callum couldn't spend the week sulking. The public vote would be for longer as the substitution challenge would be on Monday, leaving five days for the public to vote. A lot could happen in that time.

"What if she wins substitution?" asked Stephanie.

"You're up against Callum, there's no other choice," replied Daniel.

"And if any of us win, we leave it as it is," added Callum.

"I haven't won the thing yet. We're getting a bit ahead of ourselves. She could be Guvnor."

"Who do you think she'll put up?" asked Stephanie.

"I honestly have no idea."

After dinner, Daniel opted for an early night and was getting ready for bed when he was called to the Confession Booth. They did pick their timing. Daniel noticed the voice was a woman he hadn't heard very often and guessed she was someone senior who only worked the Confession Booth when a challenge was coming up. She probably wanted to discuss his tactics for the final challenge, so they could edit them into the nightly show.

He walked downstairs back into the main complex. No sign of Jamila. Stephanie and Callum were chatting on the sofa. He just shrugged at them as he had no idea why he'd been called. He walked into corridor for the Confession Booth and was surprised to see Zelda was waiting for him. She had a strange look on her face and asked Daniel to follow her through a different door to the one for the Confession Booth. He followed Zelda down a corridor. It led to a room which appeared to be in the main studio. There was a woman sitting at the table who looked vaguely familiar. She greeted Daniel with a warm smile and asked him to sit down. He wondered if he had done something wrong and was about to get a warning or something.

"Daniel, my name is Desiree. I'm the senior producer. We met a couple of times during your audition process."

That's why she was familiar.

"I'm afraid I have some bad news."

Daniel felt his stomach lurch.

"Your grandmother died last night."

It felt like his heart had been punched out of his chest.

Sensing he needed some time to process it, she said nothing. Zelda was sitting next to him and gently took his hand. It was comforting. He didn't know what to say, except...

"How?"

"They believe it was a heart attack."

"Erm... so what do I do now?"

"Well, if you want to go and be with your family we can arrange that."

"I don't have any family. She was the only one I had left."

"I'm so sorry."

"If I leave, does that mean the others all get through to the final?"

"That's a very noble thing to say, Daniel, but no, it will just mean we only have two people in the final week."

"And if I leave now, Jamila will be Complex Guvnor?"

"Yes, but you shouldn't think about that. You also don't have to make a decision now. You just take as long as you need. You can stay here by yourself and then go back and join the others when you're ready. You can come back to the Confession Booth and ask to leave at any time you want."

He genuinely didn't know what to do.

"I really need to think about this," he said.

"Of course, but like I said, you don't need to make a decision now. Do you want some time on your own?"

He nodded. Desiree stood up, as did Zelda. They both went to leave and Zelda gave Daniel's shoulder a slight squeeze. That almost made him break down, but he didn't. The tears wouldn't come just yet, or at least, he wouldn't let them.

"Just knock on the door when you're ready to go back, if that's what you want to do."

And with that they left him alone, so incredibly alone.

· · ·

Daniel woke up. It was dark and he wasn't sure what time it was. Stephanie and Callum had been brilliant and even Jamila had shown she could be a human being by suggesting Callum and Stephanie stay at her apartment if Daniel wanted to be by himself. He wasn't sure what he wanted, and whether he should stay or go. Nobody was pushing him to make a decision, but it was all he could think about. Nothing would happen without him being there anyway as there was nobody else who could take care of the arrangements, other than his grandmother's friends. The show was only another two weeks at most and he knew his grandmother would want him to stay and see it out.

He had made his mind up, but the thing holding him back from saying it out loud was what other people would say or think of him. Why should that matter? Because it always mattered. Humans always care what other people think of them, despite what they might say.

Daniel looked up, as Callum walked in.

"Do you want some company?"

Daniel nodded and Callum sat down next to him and took his hand.

"You decided what you're going to do yet?"

"I'm back and forth."

"Well, you know you have mine and Stephanie's support no matter what. And don't be worried about us. One of us being left with Jamila on our own for a week is nothing compared to what you're going through."

Daniel wasn't sure why, but in that moment he leant forward and kissed Callum gently on the lips. They looked at each for a second and then the kiss became more passionate and within seconds they were pulling each other's clothes off.

CHAPTER TWENTY-EIGHT

Dallum Appreciation Thread

Sandra304: I can't believe our boys have finally got it together. I'm so happy!!!

DeliciousDebbie1985: Amazing isn't it! I'm sooooo happy that Daniel has someone to be there for him at this difficult time #RIPDanielsGran

CNFanboy: Delighted about this, such a shame it's under such difficult circumstances

Treehugger23: Difficult circumstances?! What is wrong with you people? What is so amazing about the fact that Daniel's grandmother has died in suspicious circumstances and the first thing Daniel does is screw a teenager on TV!

DeliciousDebbie1985: P**s off troll!

———

"So, what do you make of it all, Desiree?" asked Felix.

Desiree said nothing, but he could tell there was something on her mind.

"Out with it," he snapped.

"I still think we should have been honest with him about the circumstances of his grandmother's death."

"We were, she had a heart attack."

"Because she disturbed some burglars."

"I don't see the point in distressing the boy any further and besides, he seems to be over it, based on last night's activity. The public now have their romance and everybody's happy. Debbie is delighted!"

"A grief-stricken screw, which will be guilt-ridden today, is hardly front-page news, whereas his grandmother's murder already is."

"Who said she was murdered, it was a heart attack."

"But if those guys weren't in her house, she would probably be okay."

"I don't think it would be right to speculate on the outcome of a police investigation. Besides, she clearly had a weak heart, so it could have been anything that finished her off. Now are you ready for the Guvnorship challenge tomorrow? We can't push it back another day as we need to live stream it."

"Yes, but this has put a black cloud over everything. Do you still want to do an endurance challenge?"

"It's tradition, we have to."

"But it will play in Jamila's favour."

"What is your point?"

"Well, then Daniel will be up for the chop, although she may develop some humanity and put the other two up."

"It doesn't matter. Look at the poll ratings, the trends, the forum discussions, video views and the betting odds. Everything is pointing to a Daniel victory in the finale next week.

Then he can bury his grandmother and start preparing for *Celebrity Tone Death*."

"Do you have *any* feelings?"

"I think we all know the answer to that one. Now piss off and leave me in peace. Your little rat dog whimpering is starting to get on my tits."

She went to say something and then thought better of it and left. He sat back in his office chair and stretched, before taking out some cocaine, chopping up a nice fat line. He snorted it in one and sat back again, gently closing his eyes.

It's all falling into place.

Felix realised he had spoken too soon when the final challenge for the Guvnorship turned into an unmitigated disaster. It had been decided to rerun the log challenge, although this time the log would keep turning very slowly, adding an extra level of difficulty.

To make the log task even more gripping, they would have different weather belting down on them – the weather machine had cost a fortune. It would be highly dramatic and for that reason Felix had taken all programming off the air on one of his cable channels so he could live stream it all day. He planned to switch the broadcast to his mainstream channel in the evening. They would then throw in some of the more extreme weather elements, which would mean the winner would be announced on live TV – it would be sensational for ratings with these two big contenders battling it out against each other. It had been dubbed online as *good versus evil* and Felix was more than happy to sponsor that interpretation.

However, less than five minutes into the challenge, Daniel stepped off the log, walked over to Jamila and shook her hand, congratulating her.

It was being live streamed so there was nothing they

could do. Jamila even protested that it wasn't a fair fight as Daniel's head wasn't in the game and she didn't want to win something so easily, because someone was grieving. It was probably the least self-centred thing the woman had ever said, although that fleeting moment of humanity was somewhat broken when as soon as Zelda confirmed Jamila's victory she chose Daniel and Callum for execution, causing both men and Stephanie to cry in a group hug.

Following the debacle of the Guvnorship challenge, Felix was keen to get the public vote going as quickly as possible so he could ensure the execution went the right way. Felix had to think of the best angle to play for the week. Based on all opinion polls and their own research, if nothing changed with the substitution challenge, Callum would be going home on Saturday night. They would push that story angle; something around the fact that the two who had now finally found each other and would be torn apart before the finale would make a good headline. #*Dallum* was the top trend on social media and despite Felix's own feelings around Daniel North, the viewers wanted this romance and he was going to give it to them.

They had been unable to show much of their first night together as they'd had sex for the cameras – literally. This had to have been Daniel's doing, he was the manipulative one. Normally, on these shows, people would have a fumble under the blankets so you could show the rhythmic pumping without breaking any broadcasting regulations. The boys had used no blanket, in fact when Callum had reached for a blanket, Daniel had pulled it away. They couldn't even release the footage online, because it was basically pornography. Felix had considered leaking it, although given he was already being vilified for not informing Daniel of the full circumstances of his grandmother's death, he decided to save it for a rainy day. You never knew when something like that could come in handy.

Felix was in the office early for a Monday morning – well, any morning; they were going ahead with an early substitution challenge. Felix had decided to fix it so Daniel would win; meaning Stephanie would go on the block and most likely go home against Callum. Although this would not be an easy choice for Daniel, Felix believed that Daniel would want the victory in his grandmother's name and to definitively beat Jamila in the end.

This outcome would be much better for the show as it would leave the boys alone to continue their romance in front of the cameras and completely ostracise Jamila. When it came to the finale and she was executed in third place, it could finally push her over the edge and give Felix the ten million viewers he had promised his advertising clients. To be safe, they would have security on standby in case Jamila's sociopathic side turned violent. He looked up as Desiree entered his office.

"Felix, can I have a word?" asked Desiree.

"Make it quick," he snapped, as she shut the office door and sat down.

"It's about these press releases."

"Which ones?"

"The execution ones."

"Daniel or Callum?"

"I'm not talking about this week, I mean the historic ones."

"What about them?"

"Well we had the three brothers and the family infidelity,

then Frank and Judy with their swingers club, the sisters with their kidnapping..."

"Your point?"

"I'm getting to it. Helen was next and her story was about her secret life in the German fetish scene. With Claire, we had the story about her ruining her sister's athletic career, and although we released that early, we still capitalised on it. Then we had the kiss and tell from that model for Mike, which will no doubt screw him over in his divorce and I doubt Stephanie will come back to him."

"And?"

"Well in the middle of that we had Adrian..."

"Yes?"

"Well, it was just a minor offence for shoplifting."

"I didn't see you as a champion of Cecil Vonderbeet."

"I'm not. It's just there's no record of the caution."

"Did I ask you to look into it?"

"No."

"You clearly have a point, Desiree, so out with it."

"Well, why did we go soft on Adrian? It's not your style."

"That's all there was."

"Then why was he cast?"

"For the eye candy."

"But we have a plethora of models apply every series, who don't get through because they haven't got a dark past."

"Well his views were extreme so I knew that would generate interest."

"Even they were all over the place. It was like he was an actor playing a part, because he literally changed character overnight, on more than one occasion."

"What are you implying?"

"I think he may have been a mole."

"You're fangirling over Cecil again. You think I put a mole in there?"

"I didn't say you put him in. I think there could be more to this, so I've started digging around into his background. You know there's nothing on him from more than five years ago. It's like his background has been completely made up."

"Stop."

"What?"

"I put Adrian in the show."

"Why?"

"I owed his mother a favour."

"Is that why the original plan was for him to win?"

"Yes, but he didn't really do himself any favours, so when he left I paid him off. I don't want to discuss it any further. He's overseas now and won't be back until the finale."

"But he's not overseas."

"What do you mean?"

She passed over a competitor's newspaper, which was open at their showbiz page. It had a photo of Adrian looking wasted and another locked in a deep clinch with Claire. Her legs wrapped around him in some trendy bar.

"When was this taken?"

"Last night."

"Leave it with me – and Desiree, not a word about this to anyone else. I'm trusting your confidence. Can you do me a favour and respond to the regulator about why we didn't hold a public vote the week Mike was executed. There's been a complaint that we have broken our own rules. I can only guess who the complaint came from."

She nodded and left.

Felix called for his driver – he knew were Adrian would be.

. . .

Felix knocked on the hotel door and heard the soft padding of feet across the expensive carpet. The door opened and there was Adrian, towel draped around his waist.

"Do you always answer the door dressed like that?"

"Well, if you've got it..."

"And without asking who it is?"

"I looked through the spy hole."

"Course you did. Now, are you going to let me in or not?"

Adrian stood aside for Felix to come in. Felix took in the room and its opulence. He saw the empty bottles of top-quality spirits and champagne as well as cocaine debris. He looked in the bedroom and saw bags of clothes from designer shops and used condoms scattered around the floor.

"Have you been using whores?"

"I don't need whores. Have you seen me?"

"Yes, Adrian, but whores are discreet. You are technically a celebrity now."

"I know – and fuck me, the women are hot for it."

"You've been splashing the cash as well, I see."

"Well, like I said, if you've got it..."

Felix clenched his fists so his nails dug into the palms of his hands. He had to control his temper. This stupid kid was going to ruin everything.

"I thought we agreed that you would stay on the island until the finale."

"I was bored shitless."

"Where's Mrs P?"

"She flew back with me."

"Well, you can go back until the finale."

"I don't think so."

"If you want that job and the chance to double your money, you'll do as you're told."

"I've got all I need, although it may be in your best interest to give me that extra money. Then I can go away and you don't have to worry about me talking about our little deal."

"You can say all you want, you'll never prove anything. Do you think I'm some sort of amateur? All you'll do is let people know you have all that money so you'll lose half to the taxman."

"Nice try, but I don't think there are any laws about accepting a gift from your father."

CHAPTER TWENTY-NINE

Daniel woke up from another afternoon nap – he could get used to these. He'd been napping a lot since he had been in the complex, as most days there wasn't a lot to do. Once the food task was out of the way, that was it. There would be no more Guvnorship challenges and there was only one substitution challenge left. The hours you would normally waste looking at funny cat videos, hot guys on Instagram or getting stuck in a Wikipedia loop were not an option here; you were cut off. It was nice to just sit and think, doze off and relax with your own thoughts; it was doubtful that it made for gripping TV.

He wondered what people would think of him staying in the complex after his grandmother's death. He suspected some people would get it and others wouldn't; either way, everyone would have an opinion. That was the way the world was nowadays; everyone had an opinion on everything and felt a compulsion to share it. His grandmother had spoken of a time before modern technology when people minded their own business; it sounded wonderful. Now people could put their opinion out there for the endorsement of likes and shares; it was a saturated world.

Daniel thought about the substitution challenge, which was to broadcast live that evening. Despite knowing his head was still not fully in the game, he was determined to win. He wanted to ensure the only person who controlled his position in the game was himself, aside from millions of viewers of course. He also didn't want Jamila to win the final challenge; it would only be a small victory to beat her as she was already in the final. However, it was all that was on offer, so he'd take it.

Callum and Stephanie were also determined to beat Jamila. Daniel had a feeling that if Callum won he would take himself off the block, which would put Daniel up against Stephanie. They both believed that whoever went up against Daniel was going home, but neither of them seemed fazed by it. The last week had brought everything into perspective. Jamila was still being a bitch, but she was now more of a passive-aggressive bitch. This was her attempt to try to be a civilised human being; it was clear that this wasn't something she could do naturally. Daniel preferred it when she was just outright aggressive; it was easier to deal with. With the substitution challenge looming, Daniel suspected that the Jamila they all knew and disliked would be making an appearance later on.

"Welcome, neighbours, to your final LIVE substitution challenge."

Daniel was sitting at a table. It was one of four tables in a grid; each of the remaining neighbours had their own table. The tables were shaped in an octagon so you could look straight ahead and see the other three. There were low partitions, so you could still see each other but not see what was on their tables. You would have to stand up to see what the others were doing, which Daniel suspected would be against the rules.

The task was indoors, thankfully. A blizzard had descended on them overnight and the snow was fairly deep in the outside area of the complex. Daniel was unsure what they'd have to do, although given they were sat down, assumed it would some be form of mental challenge. This played to his strength of being the only person left in the complex who had any degree of patience and very much against the most impatient person Daniel had ever met in his entire life – Jamila.

"There are three parts to this challenge," Zelda began.

Her choice of dress had resulted in a double eyebrow raise from Stephanie, who had whispered that it looked like Zelda had popped in to do the show before a night out – at a strip club. Her outfit was incredibly revealing and Daniel wondered if that was the real reason they were indoors, so Zelda could wear this dress. It was a bright fuchsia pink all-in-one dress, which if it didn't cover her midriff could be mistaken for a mini skirt and a Wonderbra. Daniel suspected she would want to step it up for the finale and wondered if she would wear any clothes at all.

"The first part of this challenge is a jigsaw of one hundred pieces. You will see the box has no image on it, so you will have to work it out yourselves."

This was good; Daniel had spent much of his youth completing jigsaws with his grandmother.

"Once you have completed the jigsaw, and it must be fully completed, it will give you a maths problem. You then need to solve that, as it will provide you with a four-digit code. You must enter that four-digit code into the box under your table. This will open the box, but be careful as you only get three attempts to get the code right or you are out of the challenge."

Excellent – Daniel had gotten the top grade in his maths A-level.

"Inside the box, there is a riddle. Solve the riddle and shout out the answer, but be certain as you only get one chance. If you're wrong, you are out."

Daniel was also good at riddles. Thankfully he had never vocalised any of these skills in front of Jamila, or she would claim that it was rigged, even though Daniel was convinced that the majority of the challenges throughout the entire series had been orchestrated for Jamila to win – no doubt her antics brought in the viewers. Had the producers designed this challenge in Daniel's favour? He looked to his left at Callum, who smiled at him and gave him a wink – yes, that's exactly what the producers wanted.

Daniel suspected that Jamila knew her potential limitations with this challenge, even though she would never vocalise them. She clearly hoped that they would all flunk so nobody would take control of the game. She was going to be disappointed.

"The first person to win the challenge will seize power over who will be up for the final execution and potentially miss out on a place in the grand finale. You are not allowed to look at each other's work and repeat offenders will be disqualified. Is everybody clear?"

There were mumbles to confirm they understood.

"I SAID: IS EVERYBODY CLEAR?"

"Yes," they shouted in unison.

"Let the task begin."

Jamila was her typical impatient self and tipped out all the pieces of her jigsaw immediately. It looked like she was attempting to put them together without really thinking of the end game. She was, no doubt, one of those people who assembled flat-pack furniture without reading any of the instructions.

Daniel took his time. He turned over all the pieces and it was a plain white background, with numbers on it. He separated the pieces into three groups – edges, plan white central pieces and those with the maths problem on it. He remembered Zelda's instruction that the entire puzzle had to be completed so decided to leave the numbers until the end. It would be too distracting to have the maths problem in front of you, when you still had the more challenging pieces of the jigsaw to complete.

He pushed all the pieces with numbers to one side and quickly got working on the edges. He didn't glance up to see what the others were doing, although based on the noises still coming from Jamila; she wasn't off to a great start. Daniel's strategy paid off and his puzzle was complete in around five minutes.

"Congratulations, Daniel. You are on to the second part of the challenge."

"What the fuck!" shouted Jamila. She stood up to get a look at Daniel's table.

"Sit down, Jamila. Consider this your first warning."

Jamila sat down looking mutinous and went back to her puzzle, muttering obscenities under her breath.

Daniel looked up briefly at Callum and Stephanie. The all exchanged a smile before returning to the challenge. He looked at the maths problem; it was long division. There was no paper and pen, so he had to think carefully. It didn't appear that anyone was close to completing their jigsaw. There was an overwhelming urge to look at what the others were doing, although Daniel resisted as he didn't want to risk a warning.

He returned to the maths problem and simply had to work it out in his head, using his fingers as needed. He calculated it and was sure the answer was zero, although Zelda had said it was a four-digit code. He calculated it again and the answer was still zero. He must be missing something; perhaps having not studied maths for ten years had finally caught up with him. After a third attempt gave the same answer again, he was reaching the end of his tether. The small grunts of pleasure from Jamila implied she was catching up.

Daniel removed the box from under the table and pressed zero on the key code – nothing. The box buzzed to indicate he was wrong.

"Bollocks!"

Jamila sniggered.

He looked back at the puzzle and calculated it again; still zero. Daniel pressed zero again, only this time he did it four times. If he was wrong, he still had one more attempt. He wasn't wrong though, as the green light came on and he opened the box, taking out a folded piece of paper with the riddle on it...

I can be cracked.
I can be made.
I can be told.
I can be played.

"Congratulations Daniel, you are on to the third and final part of the challenge."

Daniel watched Jamila lift her box out from under the table. This was going to be close.

"You need to complete your puzzle first, Jamila," replied Zelda.

"I have completed my puzzle. I know the answer."

"You need to put all the pieces together, not just the maths problem."

"Why? What a load of shit." She stood up again.

"Sit down, Jamila."

Daniel saw Zelda press her earpiece, someone was talking to her.

"Jamila, you were warned. You are disqualified from this contest."

"What? You can't do this."

"There's no need to do that, Zelda," said Daniel, holding up the riddle. "The answer is – a joke!"

"Daniel, you are the winner of the final substitution challenge."

"Are you fucking kidding me?"

Jamila started ranting and raving about the contest being fixed and how it was all a conspiracy. She then called Zelda a cunt, which meant they had to switch to a commercial break. Zelda called security, who had to cajole Jamila into leaving. She was apoplectic when Zelda informed her that she wouldn't be staying for Daniel's decision. As there was only one other possible person to be up for execution, her presence was not necessary.

Daniel took a moment in the chaos of the drama to talk to Callum and Stephanie who were both delighted he had won, although he sensed a slight tinge of jealousy from Callum; it was natural as he wanted to win the money and he believed that this result would mean he was going home. Daniel told them both what his decision was and knew from their reactions that they understood why it had to be this way; there was only one way this was ever going to go.

"Daniel, congratulations on winning the final substitution challenge. You have three options. You can save yourself, meaning Stephanie will face Callum in this week's execution. You can save Callum, meaning you will face Stephanie, or you can make no substitutions and you will face Callum in the public vote this week. Have you made your decision, Daniel?"

"I have, Zelda."

"Please give us your decision and your reason for that decision."

"As you know, Zelda, the last few days have been some of the most difficult of my life, and the support from these two is something I will be forever grateful for."

He gestured to Callum and Stephanie, who both smiled at him.

"I have thought about leaving, given what's happened, but my grandmother didn't raise me to be a quitter. However, I think the final battle should be between these two, as I know the public will do the right thing and make sure Jamila is the first one executed in the final."

"Daniel, we need your decision."

He nodded and then looked directly into the camera.

"I ask the public to please send me home, so I choose to make no substitutions!"

CHAPTER THIRTY

Dallum Appreciation Thread

DeliciousDebbie1985: Who else was in tears when Daniel asked to be sent home? My heart broke for him. #SaveDaniel

Sandra304: I don't know what to do as I really want Daniel to win the whole thing and it's only another week!!!

DeliciousDebbie1985: If we send him home, we'd give him what he wants and he'd be well happy with Stephanie or Callum winning

CNFanboy: It was emotional, but there is no way I can vote for Daniel to be executed. He has to win!

DeliciousDebbie1985: Sometimes you just have to do the right thing

Sandra304: The right thing is for Daniel to win!!!

CNFanboy: Agreed! He was just emotional at the time. Imagine how he will feel when he wins! #DanielToWin

Sandra304: Exactly!!!

Treehugger23: #JamilaToWin

Sandra304: Troll!!!

Felix was in his office dealing with the fallout of the substitution challenge. Felix had thought it was possible that Daniel might not save himself from execution; he just wasn't expecting him to make a direct plea for the public to vote him off.

The show was live so there was nothing they could do about it. Thankfully, it hadn't done too much damage. All the research indicated that Callum would still be leaving at the weekend and a week later Daniel would be crowned the winner. In spite of Daniel's plea, it was clear that the public didn't think any of the others were a worthy winner. Callum had only won one challenge and that was when Daniel was hungover and Zelda had made a monumental fuck-up. Jamila had won almost everything but she was about as popular as a venereal disease. Stephanie, albeit a nice girl, had not won any challenges and that was something people remembered. Comments online suggested that the public felt she had flown under the radar to the end due to her friendship with Daniel.

At the beginning of the series, Felix had been adamant that Daniel was going to be a mid-series execution and disappear back into obscurity, but now he wanted him to win. There had already been a number of lucrative offers for Daniel once the show was over – Felix was going to make a fortune. Once he'd made the fortune he'd drop Daniel, who would find it virtually impossible to go back to a normal life. That was the drawback of instant celebrity and despite all the warnings from Reality TV stars of the past, they all still truly believed that they'd be the one to break through – they were deluded.

Mrs P was still ignoring calls. Felix's staff on the island said she had left with Adrian on Saturday morning. She had instructed the staff not to tell Felix – what was she up to? The conversation with Adrian had not ended well. He was clear to Felix that he didn't want a relationship with him; he just wanted what he was due. He then had the audacity to ask Felix for ten million. Felix had lost his temper and told Adrian to disappear or he wouldn't even get to keep the million he already had. What Felix couldn't understand and what really shook him, which was not something that happened often, was the betrayal from Mrs P. She had been clear that Adrian could never know Felix was his father, so why had she suddenly changed her mind and told him?

"What is it, Desiree?" asked Felix.

He wanted some peace and quiet and she was hovering around his desk. Thankfully she didn't have that yappy thing with her.

"I was going to suggest you speak to Lucinda to get an update on the voting figures."

"Why? You said we had nothing to worry about."

"It never hurts to know what's going on."

"Lucinda's away."

"For how long?"

"Until next week."

"Is there any way you can contact her?"

"No. She's with a group of hairy women in some forest in Finland."

"What's the address? I can get hold of her."

"What are you worried about, Desiree? I thought you said this was a sure thing."

"It is. I'm just being cautious and covering all bases."

"Have you learnt nothing these past few years? You know what you need to do to get the result you want, don't you?"

She looked nervous but nodded.

"You can leave now."

She hesitated for a second and then walked towards the door.

Felix wasn't worried, though it didn't hurt to keep Desiree on her toes. She had become a bit sloppy this series and Felix had needed to intervene more than he would have liked. He was hoping he could have stepped away from the day-to-day running and focus on some new shows he had in development. That was not to be. This show had taken on a life of its own and he would still need to be hands-on for the summer series. The audition process would be underway shortly and he would need to up the ante, especially after this series, in order to keep the viewers engaged and the money flowing.

Desiree had also had no luck finding the mystery man from Daniel's past; in fact, he had told her to give up on it. Nothing had come out in the press so far and with the death of Daniel's grandmother any kiss and tell now would appear to be incredibly bad taste. That should keep the other media outlets from running it if the guy appeared and went to one of Felix's competitors. There was no way he was giving Mrs P the job of tracking this guy down after what she'd done; Felix wasn't sure if he'd ever be able to trust her again.

Felix's phone buzzed with a message, he glanced at it; it was Mrs P demanding he come to his house near the studio immediately. He called her back; she didn't answer. If she was going to play stupid games, then she could wait.

With nothing other than daily tasks until the execution in two days, there were only a few staff members present to keep the studio ticking over. Felix entered and there was an element of panic.

"Relax. It's a quiet day. Where's Desiree?"

"Lunch," replied one of the producers.

"Did she do the Confession Booth chats?"

"Yes, we're just editing them."

"I'll take them as they are." He held out his hand.

"They're a bit rough."

"I didn't ask for a commentary."

"Yes, sir."

He copied the footage on to a flash drive and handed it to Felix, who took it back to his office to review. He wanted anything to keep busy, so he wasn't tempted to cave in to Mrs P's demands.

The producer had been right, the footage needed a lot of editing, although it was useful to know what each of the remaining neighbours were thinking. He watched Callum first, who had always been a bit of drip when he was on his own, and not as confident as he came across in the complex. He would be apart from Daniel for a week, although the way he was going on, it was like he would never see him again. The footage would be useful in showing him as a needy teenager, which would turn off anyone who was going to vote in his favour for this week's execution.

Daniel's footage was next.

"Daniel, how do you feel about the impending execution?" asked Desiree.

"I just want the weekend to hurry up and get here now, so I can get home and start making arrangements."

"What if you don't leave on Saturday?"

Daniel shrugged. "It's only another week, isn't it?"

"Will you miss Callum if he is executed?"

"Of course, but like I said, it's only a week."

It went on like this for twenty minutes – a load of unusable crap!

Next he turned to Stephanie's chat in the Confession

Booth, where at least she was being honest. She was clear that if she had to choose for herself she would prefer Daniel to stay. Although she was close to Callum, Daniel was her bestie. However, she was supportive of Daniel's decision to leave and hoped that the public would do the right thing.

What was this bullshit – how could this snooze fest be even considered for broadcast?

Finally, he turned to Jamila, who still believed she was going to win the show. She argued that people would respect the way she had played the game and reward her for it. She had won the most challenges and made the most difficult decisions about who to put up for execution. There was a particular extract that Felix liked...

"I executed my own husband. It had to be done. He was cheating on me. I'm the victim here and I think I've empowered women all over the world to not let their men fuck them over. It was not like I enjoyed it. This was just game play. You have to do what you can to win. It's a competition for a million pounds. It's that simple."

"Do you think Mike could have won?" asked Desiree.

"Definitely, he was a contender. It's why I wanted to do the show with him. He's a likeable bloke and always popular, he's just such a pussy."

"Do you think Stephanie could win?"

"Jesus, no, she hasn't got a chance in hell."

"What about Callum?"

"He'll get all the moist teenage girls and boys voting for him, but that's not enough. He's only won one challenge. He's typical of that generation, just expects a million pound to be handed to him without doing anything. He's piss weak. At least Daniel's played the game."

"Do you think Daniel could win?"

"Hopefully Daniel will go home this week. Don't get me wrong, he's the strongest competitor left and I want this win to be a challenge, but if he wants to go then hopefully he will get what he wants and the public will do the right thing."

Even Jamila was becoming a bit soft.

Felix dropped the footage of Jamila into a video editing tool and spent a few minutes cutting it and putting it back together, so it seemed like a seamless conversation. Technology was such a great thing; it enabled you to take what people had said and with a few tweaks here and there you could completely alter the narrative of what they were saying. It didn't take long until he had it how he wanted. He played it back...

"I executed my own husband. I enjoyed it."

"Do you think Mike could have won?"

"Jesus, no!"

"Do you think Daniel could win?"

"He's piss weak. The public will do the right thing."

Much better!

Felix returned to his office after sharing the new footage with Desiree. She didn't question it – good girl. She still seemed distracted and was flapping about some food task. He'd told her to delegate it to the others and focus solely on the execution narrative. Callum would be leaving on Saturday night and she needed to make sure that they rinsed everything possible from the Callum and Daniel romance whilst they could.

When Felix walked into his office, he saw Mrs P sitting at his desk.

"Why are you ignoring me, Felix?"

"You've been ignoring me for days."

"Close the door. I wanted to talk to you somewhere private, which is why I asked you to come to your house. You left me no choice but to come here."

Felix closed the door, giving him a few seconds to calm down. He locked the door, engaging the soundproof system.

"Why did you bring Adrian back here?"

"That's not what I wanted to talk to you about."

"Why did you tell him I was his father? That wasn't for you to tell him."

"Don't be ridiculous. He already knew."

"How?"

"His mother told him."

"When?"

"No idea."

"And you didn't think to ask him?"

"Look, Felix. I had to come back here. Adrian wanted to come with me. I said he would have to wait until the finale. He said if I didn't let him come, he would tell the press that you were his father. I was too preoccupied to argue with the boy and then when we got to the airport, he just took off."

"And what was so pressing that you had to come back?"

"To sort out this mess you've created."

"What mess?"

"The murder of Daniel North's grandmother!"

CHAPTER THIRTY-ONE

It was execution day.

Daniel had found the last couple of days more bearable, but in spite of that he still hoped this would be his last day in the complex. It had been a tumultuous experience, but one he wouldn't change. There had been times during the past week when he wished he hadn't come into this place; he had missed the final days with his grandmother. However, she had always said that you had to just grab opportunities when they were presented. He knew that when he left the complex he would have his platform to remind people of what had happened on that night nine years ago.

He would have never recovered from that experience if it wasn't for his grandmother; she had been there in the immediate aftermath. He wished she would be able to see what he would do next, although he wasn't completely sure what that would be now; he couldn't really focus beyond getting out and giving his grandmother the send-off she deserved.

Callum wasn't sulking about being nominated this time. If he thought the vote could go against him, he hadn't vocalised that. It was nice to have someone to cuddle up to. However,

Callum was nineteen, so if Callum was playing the part of big spoon, as he was taller, then it wouldn't be unusual for Daniel to suddenly feel something pressing into his back.

Nothing had happened between them since that night, other than a few kisses and cuddles. Daniel wasn't sure what had come over him, he had heard of grief making you horny before, although he believed that was a myth – apparently not. It had been Daniel's idea to not cover up their modesty, as he knew that if it was too explicit it couldn't be broadcast. It was only the next day that Stephanie suggested that a duvet moving up and down might be less embarrassing than when the raw footage was *accidentally* leaked online. Oh well, there was nothing he could do about it now, although if he'd known people might be watching it one day, he would have sucked in his stomach and manscaped.

Daniel walked into the kitchen to find Stephanie baking.

"What you making?"

"Chocolate fudge brownies!"

"You spoil me."

"Who said you were getting any?"

"Well, it would cheer me up you know."

"Piss off. You know that won't work with me."

He smiled. "Need any help?"

"Nah, all done. Just got to put them in the oven."

"Where are the others?"

"They're both in the gym."

"Together?"

"Yeah, they went in together as well."

"What's she playing at?"

"It was Callum's idea."

"Suppose you have to live with her for another week."

"It's going to be weird without you here."

"It's only a week and you never know. I might have to stay."

Stephanie finished putting her brownie mix into the tray and then into the oven. She gestured for Daniel to sit down at the dining table and poured them both a glass of wine, carrying them over to join him.

"Bit early, isn't it?"

"It's three o'clock."

"Only seven hours left. This day is dragging."

She took his hand and gave it a gentle squeeze. He felt a rush of emotion and then quickly buried it; he had to hold it together. Tonight was going to be difficult enough, no matter what the outcome.

Stephanie had been Daniel's main source of support. Jamila had tried to be pleasant, although whenever she said something nice, she looked like she was trying to hold in a fart. Daniel appreciated the effort, although nothing she said would reverse two months of being an absolute bitch. However, it was a refreshing change to not have her sniping and her inner cat goddess had been temporarily subdued.

Callum clearly wanted to demonstrate his support, although was never sure what to say. There were these awkward moments when he would go to say something, not know what to say, so he would just give Daniel a hug. He wasn't complaining; at least the hugs standing up didn't result in any excitement below the legs from Callum – not yet, anyway.

It was early evening and Daniel was feeling groggy after the bottle of wine he had shared with Stephanie and the nap which followed. Jamila had suggested they all have dinner together and had offered to cook. Daniel questioned whether she was going to poison him to be sure that he would be leaving that night, and then he stopped thinking like a drama queen.

Jamila was famous for her high carb meals and the last thing Daniel wanted to do was look bloated in his post-execution interview. He knew he'd put weight on whilst he was here as for the first time in his life he had a little bit of a belly and having always worn a medium, his t-shirts were now a little tight. If she made another large vat of pasta, which he would not be able to resist, he could be executed looking like a melon in a condom. Thankfully she had opted for roast chicken with salad and homemade bread, which smelt incredible; it tasted delicious as well.

Stephanie looked conflicted as she was the baker in the complex and was clearly wondering if this bitch was going to try to steal her crown in the last week; she also couldn't deny that the bread tasted great. The conversation was a bit stilted as nobody wanted to talk about the impending execution in case it moved on to the topic of Daniel's grandmother. After a five-minute chat about nonsensical crap, Daniel told them to stop pussyfooting around.

"Who do you think is going to go then, Stephanie?" asked Jamila.

"Daniel wants to go, so hopefully he will get his wish."

"Yeah, but who do you *think* will go?"

"I'm not answering that," she snapped, glaring at Jamila.

It was a couple of hours before the execution and Daniel was in the shower; he'd been in there for about twenty minutes, but he was enjoying the solitude. There had been an awkward moment when Callum had asked Daniel if he wanted him to join him. Daniel had jokingly told him to piss off, not realising that he was deadly serious; he'd looked a little hurt. Even if they were away from the cameras, Daniel would have given the same response. A shower is one of the few times you can be completely alone with your thoughts and your mind can wander to all sorts of places without it placing you in imminent danger; as long as you kept your balance.

Callum didn't seem perturbed once Daniel was out of the shower and was his usually chatty self when he was getting ready. Daniel had to think carefully about what he was going to wear as he didn't want to be called a teenage chemistry student ever again. Callum could throw on any old rag and look amazing; it was very irritating.

The time was dragging. The last time he had been up for execution hadn't felt like this, but then that was very different; he had wanted to stay that time. Now, he just wanted out. In a week's time he could be winning one million pounds, but he didn't care. The thought of staying here for another week filled him with dread. The one thing that had got him through this week was the fact that he would be leaving tonight. He had made out to the others that it was only another week and he could handle it if he did have to stay, but in reality he wasn't sure that he could. He suspected if he survived tonight Jamila would be back to her old self as she did all she could to win the grand prize.

It was time...

Daniel had opted to wear a suit. He wasn't sure why, but everyone had complimented him and he could tell it was genuine, especially Stephanie; she looked shocked. Cheeky bitch! He'd only brought a suit into the complex in case they had to dress up for a task. His grandmother had told him to take a suit, saying that a man should always have a suit in case he needs it. Callum was wearing the same suit jacket and tight long-sleeved top underneath he had worn when he was last up for execution, seven weeks ago. This was Daniel's third time in the tube – would he get the result he wanted?

Stephanie was wearing a beautiful black dress, although

she had a jacket over her shoulders given the execution tubes were still outside. Jamila was immaculate as she always was for an execution, with the exception of the two shock mid-week executions when she was wearing her heat-seeking stretch pants for the associated challenge.

Callum passed Daniel a drink, although he could only sip it; the butterflies in his stomach seemed to be having a fight, or an orgy. The final hour had dragged the most. He just wanted it over with now; the not knowing was getting to him.

"Nervous?" asked Stephanie.

"I just want to know the result."

"Shouldn't be too much longer now. It's past half ten, so she'll have to come in soon and announce it. How are you doing, Callum?" she asked.

"Like Daniel, just want to know."

"Here we go," said Jamila.

Zelda had appeared through the door and waved at them. It always took a few minutes for her to set up, so Daniel took that time to say his goodbyes.

He took Callum to one side and took his hands. He wasn't sure what to say to this young man who had entered his life two months ago. Of all the things Daniel had expected on this programme, this was not one of them. He hadn't felt anything like this about anyone for a long time. This man had encouraged Daniel to lower his guard and he couldn't wait to see what happened when they were both away from the cameras.

"Enjoy the last week, Callum. Don't let Jamila get to you and look after Stephanie. I'll see you in a week and you can take me for that dinner with your winnings."

"*If* I win."

"If not, then Stephanie can buy us dinner."

Daniel kissed him gently on the lips.

"My turn," said Callum.

"What do you mean?"

"Well, nothing is ever certain, so in case the result doesn't go the way you want, I have a few things to say."

"Okay."

"Thank you for just being you. This incredibly brave and wonderful man. I'm sorry for being a stroppy bastard at times, it's only because I didn't want to leave you or for you to leave me, but now I'm okay with whatever happens and that's because of you. So that's all I wanted to say – thank you."

Daniel breathed; he didn't want to cry. He gently stroked Callum's cheek and smiled. It was time to say goodbye to Stephanie.

"You look gorgeous," she said.

Always could boost your confidence this one.

"You all set?" she asked.

"I just hope it goes my way."

"Well if it doesn't, you've got to see the positive in that. It means the public love you as much as I do and they want you to win, because you deserve to win."

"But..."

"Let me finish. I understand why you have to go and I just want you to be happy, whatever happens in the next few minutes. And remember, we've only got ten months to plan our joint thirtieth birthday party."

"You'll be on your world tour by then."

Stephanie laughed. "I'm already booked that night if the BBC requires my talents for the New Year's Eve Extravaganza."

"Stephanie Chapman."

"Daniel North."

"Cheeky fucker!"

Daniel saw her eyes water, so he pulled her into a tight hug.

"It's time, guys. Can you all take your positions," said Zelda.

They did as they were instructed and walked over to the execution zone. Jamila walked over to Daniel and proffered her hand.

"Good game, Daniel."

He looked at her hand and opted to give her a brief hug instead.

"Ladies and gentlemen, welcome to our final execution before the grand finale. It's Callum versus Daniel. Gentlemen, take your places in the execution tubes."

Daniel had already said his goodbyes, so he kissed Stephanie on the cheek once more and walked towards the tubes hand in hand with Callum. As they came to the moment when they needed to go their separate ways, Daniel to the left and Callum to the right, Daniel lifted Callum's hand and gently kissed it before letting go and walking towards his execution tube.

Once he was on the platform, the glass went up around him.

Zelda ran through her usual spiel, Daniel just zoned out whilst she prattled on. For some reason, this time the dramatic pause seemed quite small. Zelda reached for the lever and pulled. Daniel's whole body felt a huge weight lift as the floor opened up beneath him.

He was free!

CHAPTER THIRTY-TWO

Felix was in disbelief at such a catastrophic fuck-up.

He hadn't seen the moment. As soon as he knew what was going to happen, he couldn't watch it. His plans had failed. Daniel North had no contractual obligations to honour. Unless he wanted to pursue fame in the next ten months, which was highly unlikely, Felix couldn't touch him.

When he had arrived at the studio a few hours before the execution, he had sensed something was wrong.

"Did you get a voting update from anyone?" Felix asked Desiree.

"You said Lucinda was away."

"She's my source, don't you have your own?"

"Well yes, but I didn't think it was necessary. All the online polls point to a large majority voting Callum out. The bookies have even stopped taking bets on it as it's a hundred to one on for Callum to go – it's a certainty."

"Nothing is a certainty. Well, it's on you if it doesn't run to script."

"Stop worrying and relax."

Felix wasn't sure he liked this chilled version of Desiree. He preferred her like a coiled spring and full of tension. You know where you stand with people like that.

"So what's been happening today?"

"Stephanie baked brownies and chatted with Daniel, Callum and Jamila did a yoga session, they all had dinner together which Jamila cooked. Now they're getting ready for tonight. Pretty chilled day."

"Gripping stuff!"

"It can get like this at the end when the big characters have gone."

"But she is still in there, and so is Daniel."

"And they barely talk to Jamila apart from at meals. That yoga session was mostly silence, even though it was Callum's suggestion."

"Well let's make them talk to each other. Close all the apartments, bar one as of tonight. In fact, get Zelda to tell Jamila to pack up her stuff straight after the execution and move in with the others immediately."

"Okay, I'll sort it."

Just before the time of the execution, Felix went into the main studio hub to watch it on the big screen. They were about to go live and Zelda had just finished her link before the commercial break and was now making her way into the complex. The last execution before the finale was always a good one for viewing figures. They would open the phone lines for the winner straight after the execution and have a full week of campaigning.

The final week of the show was always a challenge to keep the viewers interested. They wanted to see who would win, but the more competitive elements of the game were over.

No matter what tasks they threw into the mix, it didn't have the same lure as the previous weeks. In the past these shows had done mid-week executions and fucked around with the prize money, but Felix didn't do any of that and besides those shows had about ninety people left in the finale so they had to kick people out early. This show just had a final three and he intended to keep it that way.

Felix had noticed a commotion coming from the corner and heard a high-pitch scream from Desiree. He went over and she was in tears; unusual for her. She could be over-dramatic at times, but she wasn't one to openly show emotion; it was one of her more redeeming qualities. She passed him a piece of paper. He looked at it and said nothing. There was nothing he could say. He simply nodded and passed it to the runner. The entire studio was silent, waiting for him to react. He wouldn't give them the satisfaction of exploding. His silence would terrify them more. Once the show was over he would sack the lot of them, but the blame for this fuck-up lay with Desiree and she would pay for it; there would be no comeback for her from this.

He turned and left the studio, walking back to his office, as the events unfolded on the screens behind him.

Felix called Mrs P and told her what had happened. She said all the right things and told him to stay away from other people until she got there. She was still in the UK and was on her way over. The reason it had all fallen apart was because he had allowed his focus to be split and put his trust in others – he would never make that mistake again.

The door to his office opened. It was Desiree. The last person he wanted to see.

"Probably best you keep away from me for a while, Desiree."

"I just came to give you this," she said, holding up an envelope which she put down on his desk.

Felix walked over to the doors and slammed them shut.

"You seriously think resigning is going to fix this complete fucking disaster?"

"No, but what else can I do? What's done is done."

Felix noticed she didn't seem overly bothered by what had happened.

"Of course, I am happy to stay on another week and see the series through to its conclusion. It would be difficult for you to get anyone else now."

"Are you fucking serious? Get out!"

"I don't think so, Felix. We need to talk about my severance."

"You resigned. You get fuck all."

"I don't think so. Not after all the shit I have put up with from you for the past three years. I knew this day would come and I've been preparing for it."

"You mean you fucked up on purpose."

"No, I just knew there would be a day when something might happen that made it so I couldn't carry on working here. I am actually surprised to have lasted this long."

He walked right over to her, almost nose to nose.

"You get nothing."

"Fine we'll do this the hard way, then. I just want what I'm due."

"Going to sue me are you? Forgetting your confidentiality agreement? If you sue me, you'll never work in television again."

"Oh I'm not going to sue you, Felix. That takes up far too much time."

"Then what..."

"I'm going to blackmail you."

Felix laughed.

"You see, I know Adrian spent time on your private island. I know he's back in the UK and spending a lot of money, which he can only have gotten through you."

"Is that it?"

"Well, no. You see I was questioning why you would be going out of your way to give Adrian money."

"That's my business."

"Yes, and I made it my business. You see, you taught me well, Felix."

Felix wondered just how much she actually knew.

"Adrian is your son."

He didn't react.

"This could ruin you, Felix, so I think ten million should do it."

What was it about everyone wanting ten million? "Are you taking the piss? I'm not giving you fuck all. Adrian's gone, you can't prove anything."

"I know where Adrian is."

"Where?"

"We'll get to that later."

Felix was raging. Was Adrian in cahoots with this bitch? How long had that been going on? Was she just bluffing? Felix couldn't be sure, so he had to play for time.

"Having a secret son isn't going to ruin me, is it? So, I'll have to drop this show. I have others. Do you want to put all of your colleagues out of a job?"

"Adrian is just the tip of the iceberg though, isn't he?"

"Go on then Desiree, thrill me with what else you think you've found out."

"Adrian isn't your only son, is he? You see, I always questioned why you were so obsessed with Daniel North. Suppressing his story, wanting him to have a mid-series execution so he'd be forgotten and then when Adrian was on his way out you changed and wanted him to win the show. Why was that?"

"It was the singing contest. I could make money out of him. It's just good business, You know that, you stupid bitch."

She wiped her face where he had accidentally spat on her.

"Can you get out of my space?"

He stepped back slightly.

"Interesting how Daniel and Adrian ended up hating each other, isn't it? I never imagined that the two of them could be so intrinsically linked."

Felix grabbed her by the throat with one hand. Her little rat dog started barking, but he didn't stop squeezing. She looked terrified. She was clawing at him, trying to get him to stop. He then used two hands and lifted her off the ground, slamming her against the wall. He just kept squeezing and squeezing, whilst her dog kept barking. It was like he had no control over what he was doing. It was complete survival instinct. He only stopped once she was no longer fighting back. When he finally let go, her body slid against the wall into a heap on the ground. Her dog, now out of the oversized handbag, was yapping so much that Felix wanted to stamp on its head. It was barking at Desiree and yelping as it knew something was terribly wrong.

Felix, still in survival mode, started to take slow deep breaths to bring his heart rate back down, so he could think clearly. The first thing was to lock the office door so he wouldn't be disturbed and then he had to shut the dog up. He walked towards the doors just as they opened. It was Mrs P. She scanned the room taking in the whole situation and quickly closed the door behind her, locking it.

"Take the dog into the basement. There's some food in the kitchen down there, it'll shut him up for a bit."

"What are you going to do?" he asked.

"Tidy up your mess again Felix, like I always have."

Felix went to pick up the dog, but he was having none of it. In the end Felix had to scoop him up with Desiree's bag and muffle him whilst taking him downstairs. He went into the kitchen off his secret meeting room and found some food for the dog, but he wasn't interested, he just wanted to get back to Desiree. In the end Felix locked him in the kitchen, and even though he was going ballistic, by the time Felix had closed the door to the basement and returned to his office, the dog couldn't be heard.

Mrs P was crouched over Desiree when he walked in.

"Is she?"

"Yes, Felix, she's dead."

"Shit!"

"You need to get out of here."

"She said she knew where Adrian was."

"Is that why you killed her?"

"No, she knew about Daniel. How could she know?"

"Well she's not going to be telling anyone now, so go and find Adrian."

"He won't even speak to me."

"Find him and then I'll speak to him."

"What about her?"

"Leave that to me."

"And what about the show?"

"Leave that to fate. Does it matter now?"

"Not really."

"Then go, I'll talk to the staff once all this is sorted. Just get away from here."

Felix went to leave.

"Felix, don't forget your glasses. It's not worth the risk."

Felix picked up his dark glasses and put them on.

"I don't know what I'd do without you here."

"Felix, I'm your mother, where else would I be?"

. . .

When Daniel North had auditioned for the show, Felix knew he had to have him. If he hadn't then Daniel would have taken his story to another show and Felix would have had no control over how that story was told. Felix had never anticipated Daniel's popularity being what it was. However, once the story broke, Felix ensured it was buried as quickly as possible with his dramatic execution stories. Then something changed; Daniel showed that he had talent, real talent, and Felix knew he could rinse Daniel for all he was worth. Once he had made Daniel completely dependent on fame, he would have ensured the bubble burst, making the fall back to reality all the more devastating. Now that plan was shot to shit as well. Daniel North had left the complex on his terms – he had won!

CHAPTER THIRTY-THREE

One month later

Daniel was happy.

He was surrounded by his new group of friends. Callum was now one million pounds richer. It had been close between him and Stephanie, with just a couple of per cent in it on the final vote. Jamila had received about three votes so was eliminated first. That wasn't an exaggeration. Out of eight million votes, only three were for Jamila. It didn't even register as a percentage of the final tally.

Online conspiracy theorists surmised that three people had simply dialled the wrong number. Jamila's execution story dredged up a series of infidelities which had put the ball back in Mike's court when it came to the divorce; especially as he only had the one infidelity exposed in the newspapers. Stephanie wasn't fussed about the kiss and tell. She was content with Mike and they were in that early relationship honeymoon period of constantly holding hands whenever they were together, which was always.

Helen also had a new relationship. The thing with Meena hadn't worked out. She had fled from the family who had raised her, and her birth family had rejected her. Nobody knew where she was. Her sisters were keeping a low profile. Helen was dating the New York music mogul, Brenda Krotz. They were one of those couples who felt the need to show the world that they were lesbians and constantly kiss and grope each other. They would glare at people, daring at them to question it, and claim it was discrimination. Thankfully Ms Krotz was not present today as she was busy preparing for Felix Moldoon's other reality TV hit, *Tone Death*, on which she was a judge.

Stephanie was fulfilling her dream by entering the upcoming celebrity version of the show. She was in a category of former *Complex Neighbours* contestants, alongside Claire and Jamila, which Daniel did not envy. Although Claire had started to redeem herself before her execution, she had not kept a low profile since leaving the complex. She placed the blame for her execution with Daniel, seemingly ignoring the extensive press campaign about how she had ruined her sister's life and career.

Daniel had not mentioned that he was offered a place on the show at the expense of Claire and it was only because he had politely declined that she was on the show. Daniel was sure that although the show was about singing talent, even a pair of arseholes with great singing voices would not succeed over someone as fabulous as Stephanie, who also had an amazing voice – that would be lunacy.

Daniel had not stopped in the month since his execution. The relief he had felt when that floor opened beneath him was indescribable. Once through the post-execution rigma-role, he discovered his execution story was about the time he had worked as a male prostitute. It was a story he had antici-pated and had prepared his grandmother for, although that no longer mattered. It had also meant that his late-night chat with Stephanie had not been broadcast, which he was grateful for. He wasn't bothered that people knew he had done a job like that, but he had also spoken of someone from his past; a very special someone. That was all history, but it had been his only real relationship and it wouldn't have been fair to the guy for the press to suddenly be trying to find out who he was. Daniel was now with Callum and they would see how things panned out. For now, he was just enjoying his company and appreciated not having to worry about TV cameras.

One thing Daniel had not been prepared for was finding out the true circumstances of his grandmother's death. He was furious that the producers had dared to keep that from him. She must have died feeling absolutely terrified. Daniel had demanded to see Felix Moldoon. This was denied and when Daniel refused to leave until they spoke, he was informed that Felix was not even in the studio. He had then asked to speak with Desiree, the woman who had lied to his face about his grandmother's death – she was also unavailable.

Daniel eventually gave up and was taken to a local hotel were contestants stayed after their execution, yet once his chaperone had left, he departed the hotel and returned to his grandmother's house, refusing any press interviews. He thought there might be an issue about him breaching his contract, but the producers had let him be. He only went to the finale to support Callum and Stephanie and that was with a pre-agreement that he would not be interviewed. There had been a second when Zelda had loomed towards him with her microphone; however, a producer had called her over, whispered something in her ear and she never came near him again.

What Daniel couldn't understand was why Felix Moldoon had not attended the finale or the wrap party. They were told he was out of the country, which made no sense given this was his hit TV show. Desiree hadn't made an appearance either and when he again asked where she was, nobody seemed to know or even care. The fact that Daniel had not been allowed to speak to the people who had deliberately withheld the circumstances of his grandmother's death had forced him to give his one and only press interview. There could only be one choice and that was the one person who might get a reaction from Felix and force him to talk to Daniel.

"I'm talking to Daniel North today, giving his one and only interview after leaving the complex."

"Thanks, Cecil."

Daniel was nervous. This was a new experience for him. Luckily, it was pre-recorded so if he screwed up, or something came out the wrong way, they could reshoot it – that had been the deal.

The money he had been offered for interviews was ridiculous. This interview alone had netted him a hundred grand. He had thought of doing the interview for free, to make a point, yet Stephanie had told him to take the money and use it in a positive way.

"So how do you feel to be out of that place, Daniel?"

"Relieved, although I wouldn't change it as I met some lifelong friends in there."

"And a lifelong partner?"

Daniel smiled. He had agreed as part of the interview that he would talk a bit about life in the complex, provided the main part of the interview was focussed on his story. Cecil had suggested they get the complex part out of the way first to pull the viewers in and then he could talk about his story and future plans. The interview was to be uploaded online and Cecil would complement it with an article.

"Things are going well, Cecil, but it has only been three weeks."

"True, and what a remarkable young man Callum is. Giving so much of his money to pay for his grandparent's residential care."

"Yes, well he didn't want them to be split up and his grandfather needs a lot of support."

"Very commendable – and he kept that secret whilst in the complex?"

"He didn't want to win on a sympathy vote."

"I see, so what plans do the two of you have as the most famous gay couple in the country?"

"I think there are a few of our established celebrities who might take issue with that reference, Cecil."

Cecil laughed.

"Well we hope to get away for a few days after my grand-mother's funeral."

"I'm sure it'll be good to get away for some time alone. So, have you managed to speak to Felix Moldoon since the show ended?"

Daniel didn't really want to talk about his grandmother's death but knew it would be an inevitable part of the interview.

"No, I haven't Cecil. He still refuses to see me."

"Is there anything you'd like to say to him now?"

"I just want him to explain why he choose not to tell me the real circumstances of my grandmother's death."

"And he won't?"

"No, and his senior producer won't speak to me either."

"Desiree?"

"Yes."

"I believe she doesn't work for Moldoon's empire anymore. She resigned on the night of your execution, although the rumour is that she was dismissed with a large settlement."

That was news to Daniel, and he knew Cecil had dropped that on him to get a reaction. He wasn't sure how to respond, so he just shrugged. It didn't matter that she no longer worked for him, she would no doubt be subject to a non-disclosure agreement so there was no way she would talk, even if he did manage to track her down.

"Will we be seeing you on any other TV shows in the near future, Daniel?"

"There has been a bit of interest, so just seeing if anything feels right."

That wasn't strictly true. Daniel had been inundated with offers of work and for some astronomical sums of money, but he wasn't interested in pursuing a TV career. However, Daniel was well aware that Cecil hated Felix Moldoon as well and had set up the question deliberately.

"If I do anything, then it'll be for the other broadcasters of course," Daniel smiled.

Cecil seemed pleased with the response, and Daniel hoped they could move on to the real reason why he was here. He had no intention of pursuing anything which would result in a commission for Felix Moldoon, so his options were limited for the time being. He was fine with that.

"Daniel, tell everyone about your exciting plans you have away from the TV cameras."

"I'm setting up a charity. This charity will be in memory of those killed in the bombing nine years ago and will be to support LGBTQ+ victims of violence. The money I have received for this interview will be used to help with the initial set-up. We're looking for donations so we can start helping people straight away. Five percent of all donations will go into a fund, which in time will be used to create a permanent memorial to not only those who died that night, but those who survived."

"Wow, so you're not going back to your old job then?"

"They were very good at keeping my job open for me, but they understand that this is something I need to do. However, there are other ways for me to support them, without being there every day."

"It's interesting that the memorial will also be for the survivors as well. I've never heard about that before."

"Well, we are all Henry Parker's victims, Cecil. We have all coped with it differently. Some people have never fully recovered, whether that be from physical or mental injuries. Some have managed to move on and don't want to be involved and that's fine as well."

"How about you?"

"For me it's the guilt."

"That you survived and your friends didn't?"

"In a big way, but I also wonder if I could have done something."

"How do you mean?"

"I saw him."

"The bomber?"

"Yes, well I didn't know that's what he was. He just seemed a bit out of place and was muttering to himself. I had to walk past him to get back onto the dance floor where my friends were. I looked him in the eyes for a split second, and they made my blood run cold. I'll never forget those eyes. Something didn't feel right, so I headed back to the bar to talk to the manager. Perhaps if I had gone to my friends instead, they could have moved off the dance floor and not been under the upstairs bar when it came down on top of them."

"Or perhaps you'd be dead as well?"

"Maybe, but we'll never know."

. . .

The majority of the elderly mourners had left. Daniel had hired the function room of a local pub his grandmother was fond of. It also provided an exit strategy should he have not wanted to stay late, yet he found he had no desire to be alone. He had been drinking all day, although didn't feel drunk.

His grandmother's friends had started helping with the funeral arrangements before his execution. They were so warm and welcoming, but he had needed somebody his own age to sound off at in those first few days out of the complex. His wish was granted when Mike and Helen showed up two days after his execution. They had been a huge support in that first week, in spite of their own dramas. Now, here they were, at the funeral of a woman they had never met. The woman who had been at the centre of Daniel's world for his entire life; what would he do without her? He had assumed this day was years away as she was only in her seventies. However, looking around he knew he was not alone; he had friends for life.

"Is anyone hungry?" he asked.

"There's still some buffet food left," said Mike.

"I mean real food, hot food."

"What like?"

"A curry."

"I know a place. Let's go," said Mike, draining his pint in one.

They all piled out to find a cab, leaving Daniel to thank the landlady for the food and looking after them all day. It had been a long day, yet even though his grandmother's killers were still at large he felt some sense of closure.

Daniel went outside and saw them all getting into a black cab, with Mike providing instructions on where this infamous curry house was. It was obviously in some secluded place as

Mike had to give an accurate address and London cab drivers knew everywhere in the city.

"How do you know about this place then, Mike? You don't live in London," asked Daniel.

"I've been a few times."

"With Jamila?"

"I didn't say that."

Everyone laughed.

"Look, the curry is good. Jamila has family down here and we went a few times."

"Well let's hope they aren't all there tonight," remarked Stephanie.

"Fuck 'em if they are. I'm hungry!" replied Daniel.

This resulted in more laughter – perhaps he was drunk.

"Your speech today was very beautiful, Daniel," said Helen.

"You already told me that Helen, but thank you. I forgot to ask, are you going to be staying in London now?"

"Brenda wants to spend the summer in New York, as her business is there, but we are here for now, yes."

"New York in the summer, isn't that horrendously hot?"

"She has air conditioning and a pool."

"Perfect then, let me know if she has a spare room."

"Well, I can check."

"I was just joking, Helen."

"No, but Brenda will be working a lot during the summer and she has a place in the Hamptons as well, perhaps we could all have a holiday?"

"Are you serious?"

"Well, she said to invite my friends over. She's in Los Angeles a lot, so I'll check her diary. It'll be good if she can join us for some of the time and you can all meet her properly."

Everyone was delighted by the prospect of a holiday. It

was the end of March and although spring was here, there was still a distinct chill in the air. Callum and Daniel had planned their short holiday away from it all now the funeral was over. They thought that Gran Canaria would be a safe bet for weather at this time of year, but Stephanie had pointed out that as they were now *allegedly* the most famous gay couple in Britain, going to the Gay Mecca of Europe probably wouldn't give them the relaxing time they were looking for. They had booked to go to Fuerteventura instead, which was a quieter island and mainly full of older holidaymakers who would either not know them, or not create a fuss.

Callum had wanted to splurge and go to the Caribbean first class and five star all the way, but they could only spare a few days, so were sticking closer to home. Daniel didn't feel completely comfortable with Callum paying for everything so they had come to an agreement that Daniel would sort out the flights and Callum would pay for the accommodation. Therefore, they were flying *EasyJet* with extra legroom and staying in a private villa with its own pool, yet within a complex, which meant they didn't have to cook. How ironic that they would be in a complex again.

"We've got some news as well," said Stephanie as she threw her arms around Mike. "Mike's moving down to London."

"That's brilliant," said Daniel.

"He's moving into my place."

"That's amazing."

"I know it's sudden, but, it just feels right, you know what I mean?" she said, looking expectantly at Daniel and Callum.

Daniel and Callum both gave each other a look which said they were happy to not compete with this one. Yes, they hoped it could be for the long-term, but again it had been less than a month since they had both been away from the cameras.

"Mike's company has an office in London and he's already spoken to them about a transfer."

"That's brilliant!" mustered Daniel.

Stephanie scowled at him.

"No, it is. I just didn't know you were going back to the day job, Mike."

"Well, I only did the show because Jamila wanted to win the money. I only took a sabbatical and they've been very good about it. My boss said he was pleased we were no longer together, in fact a lot of people have said that to me. Shame they never told me when we actually together."

"People don't. They just slag you off behind your back. It's the British way!"

Everyone laughed.

Daniel had laughed a few times today; it was what his grandmother would have wanted. If he ever got any answers from Felix Moldoon it wouldn't change what had happened, so Daniel wasn't sure if there was any benefit in wasting any more energy in trying to speak to him. Daniel's decision to audition for *Complex Neighbours* had been to fulfil his purpose; to share his story. He had achieved that, and it had been on his terms. The fact that he hadn't won didn't matter, because he had won the best prize of all. Lifelong friends and no contractual obligation to Felix Moldoon! Daniel was a free agent to do what he wanted. Other than his charity, he wasn't sure what the future would hold, and the uncertainty excited him more than it scared him. The only thing he was certain of, was that he never wanted to set foot on another Reality TV show for the rest of his life.

FREE BOOK!

JOIN MY READERS' CLUB AND GET YOUR FREE BOOK!

www.nicklennonbarrett.com/freebook

NOTE FROM THE AUTHOR

Thank you for reading my book – I hope you enjoyed it!

Daniel North walked into my head many years ago, demanding his story be told. At the time, I was busy writing the DCI Fenton Murder Trilogy, but as soon as that was done, I could give him the attention he craved. If it wasn't for all your support with my previous books, I wouldn't have been able to push through the procrastination and self-doubt to bring Daniel's story to life. I just wanted to say thank you for your continued support.

If you enjoyed this book, then please consider leaving a review on the online bookstore you purchased it, or anywhere else that readers visit. The most important part of how well a book sells is how many positive reviews it has, so if you leave me one then you are directly helping me to continue this journey to one day becoming a full time writer. Even a line or two would be incredibly helpful. Thank you in advance to anyone who does.

If you would like to find out about my other books, and read my short stories then please visit my website – www. nicklennonbarrett.com.

ALSO BY NICK LENNON-BARRETT

Reality Bites Trilogy

Reality Bites

Reality Bites Back

Reality Bites Back Again

DCI Fenton Murder Trilogy

Murder for Political Correctness

Murder for Health and Fitness

Murder for Social Media

Printed in Great Britain
by Amazon

82384909R00192